W9-AWI-883

The Other Morgans

By Carter Taylor Seaton

ISBN 978-1-64663-170-4

Published by

◄ köehlerbooks™

3705 Shore Drive
Virginia Beach, VA 23455
800–435–4811
www.koehlerbooks.com

~THE~
OTHER
MORGANS

CARTER TAYLOR SEATON

VIRGINIA BEACH
CAPE CHARLES

Other Books by Carter Taylor Seaton

Father's Troubles
amo, amas, amat....an unconventional love story
Hippie Homesteaders: Art, Music, and Living on the Land in West Virginia
The Rebel in the Red Jeep: Ken Hechler's Life in West Virginia
Me and MaryAnn
We Were Legends in Our Own Minds: A Memoir of the Rock Era

"There's no place like home. There's no place like home."
L. Frank Baum, The Wizard of Oz

⌣ PROLOGUE ⌢

At the edge of the pasture stood a young woman in jeans so tight her mother often questioned how she got them on. A single black braid split her back like an exclamation mark. In her left hand, she held an envelope from the Fayette County sheriff's office. Her heart sank as she stared at it. She knew what was inside—the farm's annual tax bill. Each year she dreaded its arrival. Opening it, she realized the amount was even more than last year's.

How the hell is that possible? This farm ain't worth a penny more than it was when Daddy died. And I sure as shit didn't vote for no tax increase.

Tears sprang, but she blinked them away. Unless her garden crop was spectacular, or she was able to sell one of the cows, she knew she'd once again be pinching from her monthly mine-widow's pension to accumulate enough to pay the full amount before the October deadline. Things like a new insulated coat to replace the one she'd ripped on the barn door, porch roof paint, and a new high tunnel for the garden would have to wait. The fear of losing the family farm for delinquent taxes was an albatross that had hung around her neck since her husband Jeff's death in a mining accident four years earlier. Since then she'd become her own Robin Hood, taking from one envelope of cash to fill the empty one meant for taxes. So far, she'd managed, but each year her anxiety returned with the mail. She replaced the sheriff's greeting in its envelope and put it in her back pocket.

She sighed again, then opened a cream-colored envelope addressed to Mrs. Audrey Jane Porter. The envelope's paper felt rich and thick, unlike most of the mail she received. She turned it over. On the back was an embossed gold crest and a red wax seal.

What the hell is that? Looks like a puddle of candle drippings. I ain't never seen such on a letter.

She had to open it just to see who would send such a thing. Inside was a sheet of official-looking letterhead. At the top, a gold crest matching the one on the envelope wrinkled the stiff velum page. She ran her sweaty fingertip over it, causing a smudge; instantly regretting the blemish, she wiped her hand on her jeans. As she read, the letter ruffled in the breeze that was blowing a dust devil across the parched earth. August was heating up to be a scorcher, and the swirl of dust reminded her how much the gardens needed rain.

She skimmed the letter quickly. It made no sense. Reminded her of the Publisher's Clearing House notices her mom received that she always pitched, knowing they were bogus. She would have tossed this one, too, but was intrigued by that crest.

I don't know if your father or grandfather ever told you, but your grandfather, James Ramsey Morgan, had a step-brother, Jackson Parkhurst Morgan, who lived here in Dillard County, Virginia. He would have been your great-uncle.

AJ, as she had been called since childhood, stared into the distance as if searching for the place the letter spoke of.

I don't know a damn soul in Dillard County, Virginia, let alone the rest of the state. I never even heard of no relatives anywhere but here on Turkey Knob.

As she lowered the sheet, the horse dancing at the end of the oval riding ring caught her attention. Leaning on the fence, her elbows rested in the cradles Gunner had chewed into its top rails. Now some of those boards looked scalloped. Wondering why he did that, she stared again toward the tree-covered mountains.

The work-thinned young woman often stood in that spot in the late afternoon after her chores were done. It felt like a sanctuary to her. It was her way of winding down. There she could savor the ancient maples, oaks, and poplars that blanketed the hills protecting her. Spring's tender new green gave her hope, renewed her faith in the soil. In the fall, the glorious riot of color made her heart swell. But she feared this year the drought would stifle that familiar rise of gold, crimson, and orange. Even the stark winter view always invigorated her. Black branches etching charcoal designs on the snow-covered hillsides. These were her mountains, her place. Home. Yet sometimes she felt like chucking it all. Running the farm was a constant battle against Mother Nature, broken-down machinery, and an aging pickup. Some years she came out a few dollars ahead, but most of the time she lost. And every day she felt as if she were behind the eight ball. Her dad had been a successful farmer, but her husband, Jeff, hadn't known a plow from a harvester. Since her father died, she'd been the farmer, and she was worn out.

She picked up the letter again.

On April 24, 2015, Jack Morgan died at ninety-four. His will left his entire estate to his stepbrother, James, your grandfather. Mr. Morgan never married and had no other siblings. Since your grandfather is deceased, and we have recently learned that your father, Don Ray Morgan, is also deceased, you as his only child are the heir to your great-uncle's substantial estate, which includes a home here in Dillard County.

It still seemed unreal, like winning the lottery, which she played by habit with no expectation of ever winning the big jackpot. Her heart raced momentarily at the possibility of such luck; then she looked up again and saw Gunner trotting slowly in circles as if bidden by an unseen master, and reality returned.

It's gotta be some scam or hoax. I ain't no damn heiress. No way.

Gunner's tail kept up a beat like a metronome. It needs blued, she realized, suddenly chagrined she'd let it go. This current faded yellow tint was unbecoming of her statuesque dapple-gray gelding. She made several mental notes. *Get out the bluing, and creosote that fence before he eats it clean in half.* She smiled as Gunner nickered to her as if he knew her thoughts. Then she read the letter once more. This time, she re-read the deeply indented words, trying to take them in.

. . . you are the heiress to your great-uncle's substantial estate . . . I am writing, therefore, as the administrator of the estate. I knew your great-uncle Jack his whole life; we even went to grade school together. I also knew about your grandfather, James, but he left Virginia when he and Jack were young adults and Jack never told me where his brother had gone. I suspect he never knew. It has taken me some time and effort to find you, so I was very relieved to finally get your address.

I realize all this may come as a shock to you, so take a few days to get used to the idea, and then call me at 555-123-9876 so I can talk to you about what you need to do about the matter.

The rest told her how to contact the lawyer, a Mr. Morton Mulgrew, but she couldn't focus on that right now.

Holy shit! Maybe I really am a rich heiress, after all.

This needed to sink in. She'd been born and raised on her Fayette County mountain in West "by God" Virginia, and in all her thirty-three years had never stepped foot outside the state's borders. Her family and that mountain had overshadowed her entire unremarkable life. It wasn't that she didn't love both, or, for that matter, every inch of her farm in Gimlet Hollow. She did, deeply. But as she stood, letter in hand, she allowed herself to dream. It wasn't the first time she'd done that, either. She'd always wanted more, although she didn't know what *more* was. Once, college had been her *more*—that is, until she had been forced to drop out after only one semester. But now that she held the actual possibility of *more* in her hand, she wondered if another life were even possible.

As the breeze returned, Gunner ambled to the fence, nuzzled AJ's free arm, and then reached for an apple from an overhanging branch. "Reality check, buddy?" she asked the horse. "Don't worry, I probly ain't going nowhere."

She jumped as the screen door squealed and then slapped shut. "Mama, Granny says it's suppertime. We're having fried pork chops," yelled AJ's daughter, Annie. AJ folded the letter, returned it to its fancy envelope, and slid it into her jeans' hip pocket along with the tax bill. Excited but wary, she knew she needed to tell her mother, but this wasn't the time. She needed to know more first.

"Coming," she yelled back across the yellowing yard.

⌐ CHAPTER ONE ⌐

Following her call the next morning to the attorney, AJ realized this *was* real. She had inherited an estate in Virginia, but he'd said it came with conditions. He said he'd explain them, but she needed to come see the estate as soon as possible. AJ had told her mother, Alice, who immediately responded, "Goodness! Go! Then sell the place. We can sure use the money."

AJ had also told her boyfriend, Dewey Bennett. His attitude was decidedly less enthusiastic. It had taken lots of talking on her part to make him understand that she *wanted* to go see what this inheritance meant. But eight-year-old Annie had been inconsolable until AJ promised she'd be in charge of Gunner while she was gone.

So, by daylight the following Friday, AJ had washed the truck, topped off the oil and gas, and was heading down Gimlet Hollow Road. The night before, she marked an old map with a highlighter to show her the way to Hadleigh, Virginia. Since she didn't know the route, she was afraid to rely on her phone's GPS system, even if Dew thought it flawless. He'd stopped complaining about her making the trip after she learned the estate would cover her travel expenses, even though her financial situation wasn't his business. He even agreed to man her produce booth at Saturday's farmer's market in Fayetteville. In exchange, she promised to be gone only two days.

Annie had cried when AJ threw her suitcase in the truck, but she stopped when Alice promised to let her read that morning instead of feeding the chickens. Alice stood waving, her glasses on the end of her nose and her smile broad under her tower of teased hair, which AJ would have described as more salt than pepper. Although badly out of fashion, except at her church, The Church of Turkey Knob Holiness, she'd worn it that way as long as AJ could recall.

As AJ drove, she replayed the conversation with Mr. Mulgrew in her head. He'd said the estate was "quite substantial."

What's that mean? More than just a house? Maybe the furniture, too? I sure could use a new couch. Well, maybe a bed for Annie, too. What's this shit about "conditions with which I'll have to comply" before the estate's mine? He'd never said, saying that was best explained in person. *Does that mean I got to prove my relationship to this mysterious great-uncle? That should have been Mulgrew's job, and he said he done it.*

Soon after Gimlet Hollow Road became Turkey Knob Road, it opened onto Rt. 19, and the truck ride smoothed considerably. In town, AJ was able to pick up a radio station and caught the early weather report—hot and humid, but no rain. She'd hoped it might rain some while she was gone; her garden needed it badly. Still, her drive would be easier if it didn't. Because she'd packed a snack and a thermos of coffee, she didn't plan to stop until she arrived. According to MapQuest it was only a four-hour drive. That is, if she didn't gawk at the scenery like a kid at Disney World.

They used to be one state. It can't look that *different.*

In West Virginia, the mountains hugged one side of Rt. 60's twisted path through Hico, Rainelle, and Lewisburg. Treacherous chasms dubbed by the Department of Highways as "scenic overlooks" fell away on the other side. As she reached the first Virginia rest stop, the peaks seemed to have moved into the distance, and to shrink somewhat, leaving broader valleys. The mountains felt less protective, and her anxiety mounted.

Virginia is different, lots different.

Despite her desire for something different, something more, as she drove, she found herself hoping that where she was headed might be very much like home. Once she entered Hadleigh, it *did* remind her of Fayetteville, and she felt comfortable again. Both downtown areas consisted of only a few short blocks with red brick and limestone storefronts from an earlier century on each side of the main street. The county courthouses, with their similar clocktowers, dominated one prominent corner in each, while the banks stood across the street, where they probably had been since the towns were founded. She believed she could find her way around this town as easily as her own.

⌒

Mr. Mulgrew's office was in the same block as the turreted courthouse, but she didn't spot it at once. After passing a train station that could have been a Civil War movie set, AJ made two trips around the next block before she found a place to park. Out of the truck, she smoothed her Sunday-go-to-meeting dress, a navy-blue linen she rarely wore, and climbed the steps to the old house.

Mulgrew's secretary greeted her with a fawning "hello" after AJ gave her name, but AJ thought it sounded phony. Before she could cross to the roomy leather chair on the waiting room wall, an interior door opened and a portly man approached. His broad smile, yellowed teeth, and walrus moustache reminded AJ of Teddy Roosevelt. She was generally fond of moustaches, but Mulgrew's was the color of Gunner's dull tail and looked unkempt. Her smile faded as Mulgrew extended his liver-spotted hand in greeting.

"Mrs. Porter, I'm so happy we've finally met after all these months searching for you. Come in, come in," he said without actually introducing himself. Surprised, AJ simply nodded. Mulgrew grasped her hand and shook it with more vigor than she expected. He turned and walked into his inner office. AJ followed.

"I hope you had an easy drive," he said. "Did you have lunch?" She shrugged and started to explain. Mulgrew seemed to take her gesture as an affirmative answer and, without much pause, continued. "Fine. We'll talk a bit and then I'll take you to Langford Hall. I want you to see what you've inherited."

While he arranged himself in his desk chair, leaned back, and lit his cigar, AJ found her voice, albeit one her mother would have called "putting on airs." In her best proper English, she finally said, "It's nice to meet you, too, Mr. Mulgrew. But what's Langford Hall? I thought you said he left me a house. That sounds like a hotel or a castle."

Mulgrew guffawed, again showing his stained teeth. He began coughing, nearly choking on the drag he'd taken of his cigar. His feet hit the floor as he worked to clear his throat.

"No, no, dear. That's the name of the estate Jack left you. The current home is on a substantial tract of land, and was named after the gentleman, your ancestor, Langford P. Morgan, who first owned a tiny log home on it back in the early 1700s. It's changed considerably, but Langford Hall has been around in one configuration or another for quite a long time. Now it's quite an impressive structure."

AJ's jaw dropped open. "You mean like that creepy old mansion in *Jane Eyre*?"

Mulgrew chuckled again, this time without the cigar in his mouth. "Trust me; it isn't at all creepy. If you'll give me a moment, I'll explain everything, including the terms of the will. Just relax and listen."

AJ perched on the edge of the leather-covered side chair like a tardy student in the principal's office, listening intently.

"As I told you, your uncle, actually your great-uncle, Jackson Parkhurst Morgan, had no relatives other than his estranged brother. He loved this home and wanted it to remain in the family in perpetuity." He saw her frown. "Into the future," he said, tapping the ash from his cigar into a large crystal ashtray. "So, he sent me on a search for his brother, James. When we found him, or rather records about him, Jack was devastated to learn he had long since died. Then Jack died before I learned about your father, Donald, and before I found you, so his will was written in a bit of a vacuum."

Mulgrew picked up a stack of papers, straightened them by tapping the bottoms on the desk, then replaced them to his left. "Without concrete information as to the existence of any heirs," he continued, "he put the estate in a trust, which included certain caveats, or stipulations to which one—should one be found—would have to adhere before the property could pass to that heir. One is that he or she—that is, *you*—would have to live here for an extended period to decide whether or not to accept ownership, or to allow the trust to sell the assets instead. And the second is you must learn how to manage the estate before making that decision."

He paused, took several short puffs, and gave AJ another toothy smile. "He didn't want it to fall into incompetent hands, you see. I'm sure you can understand that." A large plume of blue smoke floated around his face. "There's currently a farm manager who can teach you all you need to know, but it will take some time. Jack and I discussed a period of nine months to a year."

AJ stared at Mulgrew for a moment. Then she exploded out of the chair. She towered over his desk, waving her hand to clear the thick smoke. "You've got to be freakin' kidding me. He musta been crazy. Who'd want to leave their home and come to a place where they never been? Live for a whole year in some dreary old house and manage his affairs? No way, Jose! No freakin' way."

The irony of her words struck her. *Who indeed? Me! I just been dreaming of a life like that.* But faced with this abrupt upheaval of her life, she found herself inexplicably rebelling against the very thing she'd long dreamed of.

She returned to her chair and took a deep breath, trying to regain her composure. "I got my own life, mister, and my own place to manage, thank you very much."

Seemingly unruffled by her outburst, the lawyer continued with nonchalance, as if people reacted this way every day.

"I understand, but you might change your mind after seeing it. Trust me, it's far from dreary. But if you don't, you can always sell it, after the *settlement period*, as we called it, and go back to West Virginia." He shrugged as if it mattered not a whit to him. "In fact, there's a developer who had been begging Jack to sell. He wants to put up hundreds of spec houses knowing this land is prime property. Of course, Jack wouldn't give him the time of day. After you learn about the history of the estate and your family's long connection to Virginia, I think you'll agree with your great-uncle. Nevertheless, I urge you not to make a rash decision, Mrs. Porter. Langford Hall is an important part of Dillard County's history. It would be a shame to destroy all your family built."

Her tone mellowed, as did her objections. "But I can't afford to move here. Keeping up a place like that would cost a small fortune. And how am I supposed to pay my bills back home if I ain't there to tend my farm? It's nuts." She started to rise again, but Mulgrew tapped his cigar, then raised his hand like a traffic cop.

"Wait. Please. Hear me out. All the bills for Langford Hall will continue to be paid by the estate, and you'll get a substantial allowance while you are gone from home that should cover your ongoing expenses both here and there."

For the first time, she leaned back. "Well, do tell. That puts a different slant on things, don't it? There's still my daughter and mother, though. I don't think they'd take too kindly to me being gone for a whole school year if that's what you're talking about."

"Mrs. Porter, you don't have to make a decision right now. Why don't we go see your new home? Mr. Morgan's secretary, Isabelle Collins, is there waiting to give you the fifty-cent tour. She was with Jack for many, many years and knows both the home and your family's history. She's a fascinating woman who served as a docent at Monticello for years before she came to work at Langford Hall. She loves telling visitors about the house and all those who lived there over the last two hundred years. It's like she knew them personally. I think you'll like her."

"What's a docent?" AJ asked. "Some fancy name for a housekeeper?"

"No, dear," he said. "I'm sorry. That's a guide, usually at a museum, who knows all about the place and its artifacts. They give the tours and talk about what the visitors are seeing."

"Oh," AJ said softly, ashamed that she had asked. Not sure what to say next, she waited while Mulgrew puffed on his cigar.

"Would you like to go to Langford Hall now?" he finally asked.

"Let me get this straight. I inherited this mansion with a name, right? And you want me to move here and take care of it and its farm, right? And you're planning to pay all my expenses here and back home, right? How do you even know how much they are? What about the taxes? You going to pay them, too? What if there ain't enough money? What happens then?"

"Mrs. Porter," Mulgrew said softly and with the smile he might use on a confused schoolgirl. "Aside from the value of the house, your great-uncle had over twelve million dollars in investments at his death. And the farm operation continues to earn a substantial income. The land encompasses over four thousand acres of working farmland producing soybeans, wheat, other crops, and cattle. I don't think your expenses will be a problem."

AJ's eyes widened and her jaw dropped. She swallowed hard, then erupted like a volcano. "HO-LY SHIT! Twelve million freakin' dollars? Where'd he get that kind of money?"

Mulgrew grinned at this outburst. "The old-fashioned way; he inherited it." He laughed. "Come on, I'll tell you all about him as we drive." He rose, tamped out his cigar and walked around his desk.

He extended his hand to AJ once again. Mortified by her language, she joined him but ignored his hand, and followed without another word like a chastened child.

⟋ Chapter Two ⟍

Mulgrew talked incessantly as he navigated Ridge Road out of Hadleigh, leaving AJ to scan the feed stores, used car lots, and an anachronistic full-service gas station along the way. Her mind, however, was on neither the attorney's patter nor the scenery. She heard him tell her that her great-uncle Jack had inherited the estate from his father, Reeves. A traditionalist who believed in the English rules of primogeniture, Reeves hadn't thought it necessary to provide for anyone but his first son, Jack. Since James—whom Reeves had neither expected nor wanted—was born of a second wife, he had been given the short end of the inheritance stick. Mulgrew believed James had felt cheated because he got only the offer of a college education. He thought this was why he had left home.

But AJ couldn't get over what he'd said back in his office. *Twelve million? And I didn't even buy a lottery ticket!* He discussed at length the farm's businesses: beef cattle, soybeans, wheat, and in the early days, timbering. He spoke proudly—as if he had some hand in it—of his friend's position on the town council, as a justice of the peace, and of his nearly successful run for a local judgeship. All these years later, Mulgrew still groused that crooked vote-buying by Jack's opponent was to blame for his defeat. AJ barely heard him say Jack had a law degree but had never practiced; she was still trying to wrap her head around the impact of $12 million. *Lord, wait until Dew hears this! He's gonna shit his britches. And Alice will never believe it.*

"Here we are," Mulgrew announced as he turned toward the ornate wrought iron gate between two whitewashed-brick entrance walls. Each bore a deeply carved inscription: *Morgan 1722* on one side and *Langford Hall* on the other. At Mulgrew's touch on the remote clipped to his visor, the gates swung open. AJ's eyes widened as they crept up the winding, gravel drive, which was shaded by a canopy of towering magnolia trees. As they approached the house, the magnolias were set farther apart, and she could see the sun glistening on the slate roof. The whitewash on the bricks had faded over time, giving the house the look of a late summer rose. Nevertheless, Langford Hall sat impressively surrounded by a precisely trimmed privet hedge. Enormous boxwoods shaped like balls flanked each end of the shrubbery fence. *It's a dadgum mansion, and it's near as big as the Greenbrier! My God! I've never seen a house this big except on HGTV.* "Good Lord, Mr. Mulgrew. Did one person—did Jack—live here all by himself? It's as big as a hotel."

Mulgrew laughed and tapped on the horn. "For the most part he did, but he did have some rooms cordoned off as a museum. And of course, there are many guest rooms. And in the old days, servants lived on the third floor. It's storage now. Come on, let's go. I want you to meet Ms. Collins."

The ponderous hunter-green front door adorned with a pineapple-shaped doorknocker opened, and a petite, older woman wearing a wide-brimmed sunhat stepped onto the broad expanse of the wraparound porch. At the sight of Mulgrew and AJ, she threw her arms open wide. Mulgrew climbed the steps and moved smoothly into her embrace. "How are you, Morton? It's always good to have you visit," Ms. Collins said between pats on Mulgrew's back and air kisses. "And this must be Audrey. Welcome, my dear. We are so glad you've come."

Ms. Collins stepped forward to hug AJ as well, but AJ extended her hand instead. The older woman graciously stopped in her tracks and took it.

"Thank you, ma'am. Nice to meet you too. This house is something else. I never . . . it looks like some movie star's house."

"Would you like to see inside?" Ms. Collins said as she headed toward the door. "And please, call me Isabelle."

"And I'm AJ, not Audrey," AJ replied with a nod and a smile. As the door closed behind them, its brass doorknocker sounded a solid thud. AJ flinched, tucking a loose strand of hair behind her ear.

The room felt cool and vaguely damp, as if the doors and windows were never opened. To AJ, it smelled like Witcher's Funeral Parlor back home. Her nose wrinkled involuntarily. On the floor of the two-story entrance hall, a burgundy-and-green Persian rug softened their footsteps. AJ felt as if she should lower her voice to match. Directly in front of the trio, a wide, serpentine staircase bordered by dark banisters wound its way to the second-floor landing. Its treads were carpeted in a complementary burgundy runner. AJ craned her head back to see the top landing.

"We'll see the upstairs later," Isabelle said. "Morton, you don't need to go with us. You know every inch of the place. Why don't you go into the library and we'll join you shortly for tea or something stronger?" She chuckled. "Come with me, AJ."

As they walked through the rooms, each more amazing to AJ than the last, Isabelle gave a running commentary on the artifacts in each room. Open floor-to-ceiling windows announced to AJ that she was in the South. She'd seen this kind of architecture—wraparound columned porches, tall windows made for ventilation, and winding staircases—in movies like *Cat on a Hot Tin Roof*, or her favorite, *Gone with the Wind*. Isabelle pointed out Dolley Madison's silk shoes on a living room side table, positioned casually as if she'd just removed them after dancing. The room looked as long as a basketball court. Ornate tapestries and oil paintings of pastoral settings covered the walls, as if this were a museum.

As Isabelle waved toward Thomas Jefferson's fiddle atop a dining room highboy, she dramatically asked AJ to imagine him retrieving it after dinner to accompany the dancing. AJ could see it; the living room was as large as any ballroom she'd ever read about, although she'd never actually been in one. Dances she'd attended were strictly of the high school gymnasium or community-center square dance variety.

As they rounded the dining room table that could seat eighteen, Isabelle spouted off the names of the imposing Confederate officers in the oil portraits, which she said were painted on the Civil War battlefield, but AJ didn't catch them. She was overwhelmed.

In the back of the house lay another large room, but in comparison to the others, it was more like a closet. Isabelle paid particular attention to a tall grandfather clock with a pendulum as big as a cymbal, saying it had been brought over in the 1700s from England. The desk, she said, had belonged to James Madison, who gave it to his friend and neighbor, AJ's great-something-grandfather. On and on they went through each room on the first floor: the gentlemen's drinking room with its well-stocked bar and cut-glass crystal of all shapes and sizes; the butler's pantry; another small, informal dining room; a room dominated by an enormous gun cabinet filled with what looked to AJ like ancient muskets and rifles; a black-and-white tile-floored sunroom filled with ferns taller than both of them.

AJ snickered at a plant that resembled the man-eating one in *Little Shop of Horrors*. Isabelle avoided the kitchen, saying Clara wouldn't tolerate interruption. Slightly put off by the unfriendliness of whoever this Clara was, AJ said nothing. By the time they reached the large paneled and book-stuffed library where Mr. Mulgrew sat on a long leather sofa, his feet propped on the low table in front of him, AJ wanted something stronger than tea. It was too much. *All this could be—is—mine. All I have to do is tell him I want it.*

"Well," began Mulgrew. "How you do like your new home?" He chuckled and patted the sofa as an invitation for AJ to join him.

"I'm sort of in shock, Mr. Mulgrew," she said as she chose the opposite end from the attorney. "I mean—it's a museum. Stuff in here is centuries old. It don't feel like a place you actually live in."

Isabelle took the opportunity to excuse herself for a moment.

"I understand, dear," Mulgrew replied. "Jack liked having all these historical things around him. They were his ties to his past, his heritage. But they could be packed away, put on the third floor. It's your decision, assuming you decide—"

"Of course she'll decide to keep it and to live here," interrupted Isabelle as she returned pushing a teacart. "It's her heritage, too. Would you like some ham biscuits, dear, or a lemon tart? Sweet tea?"

"Thank you," AJ said, reaching for a tart and one of the tiny square biscuits. "Did you make these? They look delicious."

"No, dear. Cook did. Langford Hall has had Clara for years and she's divine. After Jack died, she stayed on. She'll continue to, if you want her, of course."

AJ looked past Isabelle toward the direction she supposed was the kitchen.

Clara? So that's who didn't want to be interrupted. What does she mean, "If I want her?" It sounds like she's property, too. Is she like Scarlett's Mammy? One of Mr. Jack's old servants? I'd feel bad if she was. Still, I'd have a cook instead of me or Alice doing it! Can't imagine. Bet she wears a starched apron. Reckon she's got one of them fancy stoves, and a hanging rack with fine steel pots and pans like on HGTV? Bet they ain't near as good as my old iron skillet and banged-up pressure cooker with the blown gasket. But, damn, I'd never have to wash dishes again. Sure wouldn't care to be on this side of that swinging door just for once.

"I'm sorry, Isabelle. What did you say?"

"I said would you like to walk the grounds a bit? See the cemetery where your ancestors are buried?"

"I would, but first don't you want to know more about me, Mr. Mulgrew? You got no idea who you're fixing to turn all this over to," she laughed.

"Of course we would," Isabelle answered even though the question wasn't directed at her. As she nestled into the club chair across from the sofa, AJ wondered if Isabelle ever took off that hat. In AJ's world, hats were for church. She thought it downright weird to wear one at home.

"Well, like you know, I run our family's farm back home. I have since my daddy died. Well, that is, me and my husband, Jeff, did until he was killed in the mines."

She continued with the facts of her life that would have appeared on a resume if she'd had one—or in her obituary if someone cared to write it when the time came. But what her words didn't convey, and what she'd never told anyone, was how the responsibilities wrapped up in those facts weighed as heavily on her as the slate that had fallen on Jeff's chest. Who could she tell? Not her widowed mother, for she was part of that lodestone. And, not being the church-going type, AJ had no pastor to whom she could unburden herself. She'd never shared her worries with Dew, either, for fear he'd think she was looking for a man to support her. She was sure he'd run for the hills like a scalded cat if he thought that.

At Jeff's funeral, friends who helped her up from where she lay weeping on the raw dirt had said, "Let us know if we can help." But even then, AJ knew there was nothing any of them could do, really. She knew their comments for funeral platitudes. She'd even said them herself at other funerals. At twenty-five she was husbandless, fatherless, pregnant, and suddenly responsible for keeping the family farm going, and her mother and soon-to-be-baby from starving.

AJ's husband had been the opposite of her daddy, D. Ray. Jeff was a sweet man without a mean bone in his body, the type who would watch over his family like a mama bear. Hungry for the love D. Ray didn't, or couldn't, show, she'd married Jeff within a year of D. Ray's death. It grieved her still to realize he hadn't known she was pregnant before he died.

She'd held off telling him until she was sure she wouldn't lose this one like she had the other two. But Annie was a healthy baby, carried to term, and born six months to the day of Jeff's death. Now she regretted her decision each time she saw her husband in Annie's crooked smile.

Remembering that Annie had found a dead frog in their creek, AJ said in an obvious non-sequitur, "They's mountaintop removal mining in our area. You know what that is?" They nodded as she continued. "Well, it's getting closer and it's poisoning our creek. So is drilling for gas. I'm not sure if we can hold out from those companies. The land on Turkey Knob is stinking rich with gas and oil, and I expect they'll be looking at ours next. Me and my neighbors have been protesting, but sometimes it feels like I'm banging my head against a stone wall.

"Couple of years ago, I went to a protest where women were shaving their heads in a sort of a joining with the mountains what had their tops blown off. I didn't do it but lots of people did. They reminded me of Mother Jones, that old lady who tried to organize unions, you know? One old woman had a sign that said, 'Hair grows back. Mountaintops don't.'" She wiggled her fingers to form air quotes. "Now it's the fracking people. They's drilling all over. If it ain't one thing, it's another." After a sigh, she took a drink of her tea, which gave Isabelle a chance to jump on the move-here-and-forget-your-troubles bandwagon.

"Just think, all those problems would disappear if you came to Langford Hall. We don't have any of those issues over here. You'd live like a queen. As would Annie, and your mom. Come with me. I want to tell you more about your other family, your Virginia family, while we walk the grounds."

Isabelle stood as if she'd taken charge from Mulgrew, and he let her. He lit a cigar and put his feet on the table. "Sounds like a good idea, Isabelle. I'll be right here when you return." He picked up a copy of the *Charlottesville Daily Progress*, and, looking like he owned the place, dismissively turned to the financial pages.

⟶ CHAPTER THREE ⟵

The two women passed through the sunroom and onto the back portico with AJ trailing behind her guide. Before them a tree-dotted lawn stretched as far as AJ could see. About twenty yards away, she spotted a narrow aisle that split a stand of boxwoods. Isabelle pointed at it.

"That path leads to the cemetery where your ancestors are buried. Come on. I'll introduce you."

As they stepped off the porch and into the sunlight, Isabelle hesitated and AJ accidentally brushed against her. As she did so, AJ noticed the scent of the lavender dusting powder her granny used to wear. Wondering what Granny would think if she could see her now, AJ smiled. She also noticed a straw-like quality to Isabelle's hair, and her smile broadened. *She's wearing a wig! I bet she don't take off that hat because she's afraid her hair'll go with it.* Now, AJ couldn't take her eyes off the blond waves. They reminded her of Marlo Thomas's collar-length brunette flip in *That Girl*. But Marlo's hair bounced; Isabelle's didn't.

"I know your family's stories so well from giving tours I sometimes think of them as my own," Isabelle confessed as they reached the bottom of the steps. "But this is the first time I've ever told them to an honest-to-goodness Morgan family member."

Approaching the low brick wall that set the cemetery apart from the rest of the lawn, she took a set of keys from her pocket and unlocked the rust-dappled iron gate. She motioned for AJ to step through, then closed it behind them. It creaked as if it hadn't been opened for ages.

"Guess we need to oil that," the older woman muttered. "It must have rusted this spring."

Back in tour-guide mode, she began pointing and talking. "The earliest grave here dates back to 1740. It belongs to Langford Pierce Morgan, who built the original house here. He was a surveyor sent over by King James II and was given this land as payment for his work. Originally it included about twelve thousand acres, but over the years one or another of his descendants sold parts of it. Now it's only about four thousand acres." AJ laughed at the idea that *four thousand* acres could be referred to as *only*. Her farm was a bit over ten, fifteen if you counted the woodlands.

"Langford isn't the oldest Morgan we have on record, though. His grandfather four generations back was the Reverend Rowley Morgan, a Presbyterian minister in England. Remarkable man. He sided with those who wanted to break away from the Catholic Church during Henry VIII's time and was burned at the stake for his beliefs."

"Good Lord!" AJ stopped in mid-step. "Really? Like Joan of Arc?"

Isabelle nodded. "When Queen Mary, the one they called Bloody Mary, came to power she tried to do away with England's reformation movement by killing hundreds of Protestants, including our Reverend Morgan."

"What did he do to make her so mad?"

"It didn't take much. He believed the Bible should be in English, that priests shouldn't have to be celibate, and—"

"I sure can go along with that," AJ said, laughing. "But dying for it seems awful. I never would'a been that strong."

The two continued down the rows with Isabelle giving AJ a quick bio on each inhabitant of the family plot. One, Forrest Elias Morgan Sr., she admitted, had been a slaveholder. And his son, Forrest Elias Jr., had died fighting for the South in the Civil War when he was very young. Another, Ben Hutchinson, she described as a WWII pilot who'd been captured by the Germans, suffered horribly in a prison camp, and committed suicide after he came home. His wife, Molly, who lay beside him, was actually the Morgan family member. Some had elaborate marble markers; others were granite slabs flattened into the ground as if they were slowly disappearing. One, in the rear corner, had no marker, only a worn, wooden cross. It seemed out of place among the other stone markers. On each of those, most of the names were clear; however, a few were worn badly. Reeves, Archibald, Mariah, Mildred—names she'd never heard of on the West Virginia side of the family. Husbands, wives, and several children rested there. Fascinated, AJ wondered who kept the moss from overtaking them. As they reached the recent grave of Jack Morgan, Isabelle stopped. A pristine red-granite tombstone marked the place, but the grass hadn't fully grown in to cover the settling earth.

"How'd you learn all this ancient stuff?" AJ asked.

"Mr. Jack loved genealogy, you know. It was his hobby. I helped him record it all. Between that and the estate's business, he kept me bustling, believe me. But, I enjoyed it . . . loved it, really. Genealogy was important to him. It was his way of surrounding himself with family. Their stories were his history. And it's why he was so eager to find a member of the family to inherit Langford Hall.

"I understood and came to think of Jack's family as my own. Now, with him gone, I'm not sure what will become of me. I just can't see myself retiring, even though I'm old enough, Lord knows." From the corner of her eye, AJ thought she saw tears glistening on Isabelle's powdered cheek. *Is she that worried about losing her job, or were they closer than she's letting on?*

As she watched Isabelle staring silently at Mr. Jack's marker, AJ thought about the cemetery that held both her husband and her father and, she presumed, would also hold her someday. It too was a family plot, high on Turkey Knob, though not nearly as well kept. Suddenly, the memory of Jeff's funeral hit her like a tsunami. As the preacher said his rambling prayers over Jeff, she'd cut her eyes toward her daddy's grave, just a few feet away. Five years earlier, she'd had no tears for him, and she didn't the day of Jeff's funeral, either. D. Ray had been a mean drunk when he got into the 'shine, which was too often, and he was bad to hit her mother. AJ wondered if any of these Morgans had beaten their wives.

In a roundabout way, the 'shine had eventually killed her father. One night, after what he liked to call "a few beers with the boys," he'd apparently drifted into the wrong lane of Rt. 119, and a coal truck hit him head-on. The impact decapitated him. Alice said her greatest comfort was that he never knew what hit him. AJ's solace was that he could no longer beat her mama. She remembered looking at his open casket, hoping to feel some sorrow, but all she could think about were the blue shadows in the creases of his bruised, still hands, and that he was wearing a coat and tie for the first time in her memory. With a sigh, AJ had turned and walked away from the casket.

Truthfully, she hadn't really been surprised his life ended that way. She'd half expected it. She knew the moment her mother called her at school to say he'd died that her life had changed. With the call, her dreams of graduating and becoming a veterinarian slipped as far away as his head had been thrown from his body. Girls weren't supposed to hate their daddies for dying. But she had.

"In his prime, Jack was such a handsome man. Those warm brown eyes . . . and he loved his horses. I used to watch him with them. You could see that it was a mutual love affair. Bless his heart,"

Isabelle said, almost to herself. She turned, now dry-faced, and headed for the gate. "We'd better get back to the house. Morton will think we've fallen in."

AJ followed her, wiping away her own long-delayed tears.

"By the way, I've got some things I think you should read that belonged to Jack," Isabelle said as they made their way to the library. "But I'm not sure if I should give them to you now or when you come to live here, though."

"What makes you so darn sure I'll come? It's a lot to ask, you have to admit."

"It is," Isabelle agreed. "But I just have a feeling." She smiled and let her words hang in the musty air before she continued. "Maybe what I want to give you will help persuade you. It's part of what Jack had me working with all these years—part of the Morgan family history. Down through the generations, they were always writers, recorders of their lives, some remarkable, and others rather ordinary. And they were also hoarders. They kept all those papers—journals, diaries, and letters, lots and lots of letters—and passed them down. They tell an inspiring tale of the Morgans' struggle to keep this land and the home in the family. I think if you read them, you'll fall in love with your Virginia family. And I hope they will convince you that you need to take up the Morgan mantle and carry on the family tradition here at Langford Hall."

AJ started to ask how much stuff there was, but the sound of ragged snoring met them at the library door. Both women laughed, waking Mulgrew, who quickly cleared his throat and stood to greet them. With a start, AJ noticed a painting near the bookshelves she hadn't seen earlier. It could have been her grandfather but for the cut of the frock coat, the stiff, high-collared shirt, and the cravat. Before she could ask, Mulgrew spoke.

"Tour over?" he said, straightening his tie and tugging at his shirtsleeves in an effort to reassemble himself.

"Yes," said AJ. "Isabelle gave me the scoop on every single Morgan out there. I had no idea there were such important folks in the family.

They make my branch look like pikers. 'Scuse me, but who is that on the wall over there?" AJ pointed over Mulgrew's shoulder.

"That's Jack's father. Why?" answered Isabelle.

"Lord, he looks just like my daddy's paw. I guess I really am kin to these Morgans," she laughed. "Maybe granddaddy should have taken his daddy up on his education offer instead of heading off to West Virginia and becoming a old farmer. I started college, but had to drop out when my daddy . . . well, I told you all about that, didn't I?" She fell silent, realizing she'd spoken ill of her own kin, something her mama would have worn her out for.

"I also told AJ about Jack's papers, " Isabelle started. Mulgrew interrupted.

"Dear Lord, you aren't going to burden this girl with all those musty files just yet, are you? Let her make her decision, then she can read them."

"Well, I want her to know, want her to see just how important Langford Hall was to all of them."

Her curiosity piqued, AJ said, "If some of those folks out there wrote them, I'd love to read them." She jerked her head toward the graveyard. "But I really don't want to be responsible for whatever it is, especially if I ain't keeping the house. Maybe I could take the stuff and bring it back before I leave tomorrow."

"There's the ticket," Mulgrew said. "Give her the slave journal. It's not the oldest, but the earlier letters are too easily gotten out of order. I'm with AJ. Better to let her read them here."

AJ stiffened slightly at the inference she wasn't bright or careful enough to keep the letters in order, but since she really didn't want them on her hands, she said nothing.

"No, I think it will take you longer than one night to absorb it all," said Isabelle. "Besides, you'll be back. I just know it."

Placing her hand on AJ's arm, Isabelle said, her Southern accent thickening, "My dear, it was such a pleasure to meet you. We look forward to your return, to you living here." She winked at Mulgrew.

AJ caught the wink and felt somewhat relieved to not be responsible for what were obviously treasured artifacts. "It was real nice to meet you too. And thanks for taking me all around to see the place. If you been keeping it up, you done a good job. It's beautiful."

Isabelle laughed. "Oh, my no; not me. We've got several staff members who do that sort of thing."

AJ's stomach rumbled as she tried to cover her *faux pas*. "I didn't mean—"

Isabelle looked shocked but, recovering her manners, gave a short laugh. "Oh dear, those ham biscuits must not have been enough."

"God, I'm so sorry. I guess I'm used to a farmhand sort of noon meal. I didn't know how long a drive it would be, so I didn't stop for lunch. I'll get an early supper in town."

"It's all right, dear," Isabelle replied as she followed Mulgrew and AJ to the porch. After another round of effusive goodbyes between Isabelle and Mulgrew, the visitors were headed down the driveway. Isabelle waved until the car passed under the shadowy canopy and through the stone gates.

The sun had begun to set, and, tired from her trip, AJ found herself slipping into sleep. Mulgrew was quiet too, until they reached Hadleigh.

"So, what did you think? Ready to take up the mantle of mistress of Langford Hall?"

She woke with a start. "Hell no, I'm not ready," she said more forcefully than she intended. "I mean, I don't know. As I told Ms. Collins, it's a lot to ask. I can't make a decision like that at the drop of a hat. I got to go home, talk to my family, and think about it. I'll get in touch with you when I've figured it out."

They pulled into a parking space in front of his office, and Mulgrew turned to her. "I do understand, but we can't wait forever. The farm has to have someone besides Tom Beckett in charge. He's a competent manager, but he can't make the big decisions. It needs a new Jack, or Jacqueline." He laughed at his own joke. "How about two weeks? Could you make a decision in that length of time?"

AJ sighed, weary. "I suppose so. I'll have to before Annie starts back to school—that is, if I was going to bring her with me. Hers starts about then."

"Fine. Take my card. It's got all my contact information on it, including my email and cell number. I look forward to hearing from you, hopefully sooner rather than later." Again, he chuckled.

After thanking Mulgrew, AJ opened the car door, picked up the folder, and walked toward her truck. On the window was a parking ticket. "Damn," she muttered as she headed for the diner.

∽ Chapter Four ∽

"Oh my God, Dew, you ain't going to believe this freakin' house. It's ginormous! I couldn't count the bedrooms, and I didn't even see the third floor where all the servants used to live. Downstairs it's like a freakin' museum. All these old paintings, antiques and shit. I swear, I don't know if I could live there like it is."

AJ was nearly breathless as she told Dew about her visit to Langford Hall. She had FaceTimed him so she could talk and eat at the same time. She'd been starving by the time she got back into town. Even if it wasn't as good as her mom's, the fried chicken dinner she'd picked up from the diner near the train station tasted delicious. Now, she sat crosslegged on the hotel's bed, her phone propped up on the to-go box of chicken. It was a small room with lace curtins tied back from the window air conditioner that was working overtime. Glancing up at the reflection in the dresser mirror on the opposite wall, she noticed a significant tear in the cabbage-rose wallpaper on the wall behind the bed. *That design and the pink chenile bedspread are sure to turn off any traveling businessman.* On the other hand, she was grateful for the cozy room, however shopworn. Somehow, it felt more real than the bedrooms at Langford Hall.

"Slow down, gal," Dew chuckled. "You're going to choke on that drumstick."

He was always amused at AJ's gullywasher of words when she got excited. Dew, on the other hand, was a man of few words. "So, what's deal with the inheritance? You going to move down there and become a Southern belle?"

AJ wasn't sure if he was kidding or serious. "I don't know, Dew. I've got to talk to Alice and think about how I'd do it. It is tempting. A gal don't turn down twelve million every day."

"Shit, I was only kidding, but you're serious. You'd really move? Leave the farm? Me? Everything?" His face was suddenly crimson from top to bottom. Apparently he thought she'd reject the idea out of hand, that the trip was just a lark.

"Dew, I said I haven't decided yet. Of course I don't want to leave home or you. But this place is part of my family, too. Maybe I need to ride this out, see where it goes." She saw his scowl as his lips mouthed, "Shit," but she continued. "I saw a painting of Mr. Jack's father. Looked just like my grandpaw. And his secretary, Isabelle, has all these diaries and letters and shit she wants me to read from my family way back."

"Look, alls I'm saying is you've put your blood, sweat, and tears in that farm. It's part of your family, too. It's your mom's only home, and Annie's. What about them? And what about me?" His voice cracked a bit.

"I know all that, Dew; don't think I don't. But don't pressure me. I've got a lot to think out. I said that before. Look, it's late. I'm tired. Let me finish my dinner and get some sleep. I'll be home tomorrow and we'll talk then. Love you." She made kisses at the phone.

"Love you, too," Dew said perfunctorily, and signed off without returning her kisses.

AJ sighed as she stared a moment at the dark screen. She knew she should call Alice, but she was too tired. As she finished the second biscuit, she studied her face in the mirror. *Maybe Dew's right. Leave Gimlet Hollow? It's home. It's all I've ever known. Sure would be a different kind of life. One I never dreamed I'd have. And I could give Annie stuff I'll never be able to give her if we stay on the farm.*

She rose with purpose, threw away her dinner mess, and took a shower. When she returned, she climbed into the crisp sheets of the four-poster bed and lay back on the fat, down pillows.

"Damn, this feels good," she said to no one but the walls.

⌐

The next morning, AJ downshifted into first gear as she threaded her truck up the switchbacks of the mountain below Turkey Knob. She'd lowered her window as she began the climb in order to take in the familiar smells of home. She loved the sometimes-cloying fragrance of honeysuckle that covered the pasture fence in spots, and the rich scent of the earth turned often to disrupt the weeds' attack on her crops. As she climbed, she noticed that the temperature was at least ten degrees cooler than it had been in Hadleigh when she left. There, she'd been uncomfortable with the smothering summer heat; at home the air was crisper, even on hot days.

She'd tried to find a country radio station but gave up in frustration. Aside from hard rock, or religious programming, all she could find was National Public Radio. It was just as well; she really needed the quiet drive to think. She sighed and mentally ticked off her list of concerns. She wasn't sure what Dew would do. He'd softened after they talked it over again, but she didn't know if leaving for a year would be a relationship deal breaker. She hoped not. As for Alice, she didn't know yet what AJ was required to do before she could sell the estate. Truth to tell, AJ still didn't know what she'd do in the long run, but she knew this might be her only chance at something more. The chance to be her own person.

On Turkey Knob she knew everyone, and there was comfort in that. On the other hand, everyone knew her too, and her background. She always felt they saw her as the poor daughter of that drunk, D. Ray, or as the sad little widow whose husband had died so tragically, leaving her to run a farm and take care of her mother and daughter. If she moved, it would be her chance to build a new life, one where people would only know her for herself and her ability to manage the large estate known as Langford Hall. She wanted that life, to at least try it. That would sound selfish to Dew and Alice, but she couldn't deny how she felt. Instinctively, she wouldn't know if she wanted to accept her inheritance unless she gave life in Hadleigh a try. Besides, she rationalized, the road ran both ways. She could always go home again. She couldn't explain those feelings to them in that way, of course. So how?

I know I could run that place; it'd be like here, only bigger. But Alice can't handle our farm herself. Maybe Uncle Jimmy can help her. Maybe. I know Annie'll have a fit and want to come with me. If she stays, Alice will have her at church at least twice a week. She'd hate that. And she won't be able to ride Gunner, neither, except when Uncle Jimmy's here. God, if I decide to go, what'll I say to convince them it will be okay? Ain't looking forward to talking to none of them.

The steep climb ended. The familiar crunch of the gravel driveway never failed to sound like a welcome home. Today, the honeysuckle scent she loved almost took her breath. Gunner was grazing in the pasture, so she stopped to watch him for a moment. Tears stung her eyes when realizing how much she would miss him, the farm, and all of Turkey Knob. She blinked them away, circled the oval flower garden, and parked near the house, facing back toward the road. Before she could get her bag from the truck, Annie was running toward her, her coal-colored pigtails bouncing on her shoulders. As AJ hugged her daughter, she saw Alice, in her favorite apron, standing on the porch with her arms crossed over her ample bosom.

"What a welcoming committee," she said to Annie as she released her. "I love your hello hugs, sweetie." As she walked toward the house, she called, "Hey, Alice."

Straight faced, Alice responded, "Glad you're home safe. Thought you mighta called while you was gone, though."

AJ shrugged, knowing no excuse would satisfy her mother. "Sorry, I was just really busy. I'll tell you all about it, promise. Let me put my things away, go through the mail, and check on Gunner. We can talk at dinner." AJ knew she was stalling.

Later, in the kitchen, AJ saw that the table's usual oilcloth covering had been replaced with a yellow tablecloth that looked freshly ironed. Alice put the bowls of green beans and fried apples down and went to get the potato salad and ham.

"Annie, did you wash your hands?"

"Yes'm," she said, placing her napkin in her lap. To be certain, AJ reached for her daughter's hands and looked them over, then smiled. "Good job."

Unsure how to start, she began to serve Annie's plate.

"Mama, tell me about the farm. Is it as big as ours? Do they have cows? Or sheep?"

"It's way bigger. I didn't see no cows, but I heared they do. I know they got horses. I saw the barn. It was huge. Bigger'n ours for sure."

"Can I go see it and ride their horses?"

"We'll see," said AJ.

"What's the house like?" asked Alice, hoping to start the discussion.

"You won't believe it," she said.

Throughout dinner AJ described the town, the house, its cemetery, Mr. Mulgrew, and Isabelle, drawing a frown from Alice and a laugh from Annie with her descriptions of both her new acquaintances. She said Isabelle's hair looked like the straw in Gunner's stall as it poked out from under her hat, and that Mulgrew's yellowed moustache looked like he had a paintbrush stuck to his lip.

"Don't mock your elders, Audrey Jane. What was the big deal about the inheritance?"

"Don't you think that's a talk for adults? Little pitchers have big ears, you know." She jerked her head toward Annie.

"I'm not a pitcher," Annie snorted. "Tell me, too!"

"I will, honey, but I want to talk to your granny first. Okay? Why don't you help clear the table? And I'll bet you've got a book you'd rather be reading, right?"

Annie nodded. "Yeah, I guess," she mumbled and shuffled out of the kitchen. As she went, AJ noticed her skinny little legs. *Gotta get that girl to eat more. Put some meat on those bones.*

After she left, AJ explained the inheritance and the stipulations that went with it to her mother as they cleared the table. "I gotta go live there before they'll let me decide what to do with the property, Alice. I know that sounds crazy, but that's what the will says."

"I hear you, but can't you just refuse the whole shebang? Or sell it?"

"Refuse it? Why would I do that? One year, that's all, and then I can do whatever I want with it. Sell it or go live there."

Alice sighed. "I understand, but just how am I supposed to manage without you here?"

"Maybe Uncle Jimmy could come do the chores? His farm ain't much to look after. Few gardens is all." AJ looked carefully at her mother's expression. *So far, so good*, she thought.

"Suppose that's possible, what about Annie?" Alice asked as she ran water in the sink.

"Actually, I'm all tore up about what to do about her. I know she'll want to go with me, but I hate to take her out of her school here to put her in one where she don't know a soul. My hands will be full trying to manage that place, anyway. It's a lot of property, with a lot of details, I 'spect. Could you manage if I left her here?" AJ went to the sink and began washing the glasses. She checked Alice's expression again.

"That'd be fine if she'd stand for it. But she's pretty sold on having her mom around. She don't always cotton to my ways, you know? I don't want no constant arguing and fussing."

"I know. She'll just have to get used to it. I'll give her a big talking to."

Plates and silverware clinked in the soapy water, filling the quiet. Finally, AJ broke the silence. "So, you'd be okay with me going? I still ain't sure how you feel about it."

"I ain't happy about it, but it don't sound like we've got much choice. Didn't I hear you say that?" Alice grabbed a dishtowel.

"Yeah, but if you'd had a conniption fit about me leaving, I'd have figured out something, no matter what. I hope Dew doesn't throw one on me. I bet he won't want me to go no way, but I've got to convince him. Damn, I can't just walk away from all that money. It would be stupid. Think what we could do with it."

Alice hissed through her teeth. "Sssst. No cursing, Audrey. Not on my watch."

"Sorry." She handed Alice a plate to dry. "I'm supposed to give the lawyer an answer in two weeks. If I got my act together, I could go back right after Annie starts school. That way, I could be sure she's happy with her teacher, not that I could change nothing if she ain't; but I'd be here to maybe get her over the rough patches."

"I've got to talk to Jimmy before you can make a decision. If he can't help out, you can't go. It's just that simple. I'll call him in the morning before he heads out."

AJ hugged her mother, surprising Alice. "I knew you'd be my champion. Despite our differences, you've always been there for me and I appreciate it." Alice smiled, but said nothing.

Dew called just after AJ had gotten Annie in bed. Instead of her usual bedtime story, AJ told her daughter all about the presidents who had visited Langford Hall. Afterward, Annie said it was the best fairy-tale ever. AJ had stopped short of saying she was going to live that fairy-tale for a while, however. First of all, she didn't know if Jimmy would agree to help her mother run the farm, and secondly, she didn't want to upset Annie right before bed. *Better to let her dream.*

"Hey, Dew, I was going to call you as soon as Annie was asleep. How were sales at the market? Good! That's terrific. Thanks for doing that for me. I needed the money. How about you coming over instead of going to Pies & Pints? I've got all sorts of stories to tell you." She sat on the edge of her bed fingering the fringe on her worn Martha Washington spread.

"I know you're tired, but I really want to see you. Just for a little while." She stroked the bed thinking of the chance to be with Dew under that cozy spread and quilt. She could see his hair fanned across her pillow, his well-muscled arms above his head.

"Great, I'll see you in about thirty minutes."

AJ washed her face and sprayed on some rarely-used cologne. She added a touch of lipstick, and finished unpacking. All the while, she stewed about how the evening would go. *Lord, I hope he don't throw a shit fit on me and leave.* She went down to tell Alice that Dew was coming and would likely spend the night. As usual, she gave AJ that look she knew too well. AJ knew her mother liked Dew and probably thought of him as a potential son-in-law. Nevertheless, Alice didn't approve of them sleeping together, especially under the same roof they all shared.

⌒

By the time she heard Dew's Grand Cherokee in the driveway, AJ had put on Willie Nelson's *Stardust* CD and checked on the beer situation. Nervous energy fueled her actions. She was sensitive to Dew's feelings and didn't want him to think she would callously leave him. She really cared for Dew and thought he felt the same way, but this move, however temporary, could really test the depth of their relationship.

As Willie began to sing about "when our love was new and each kiss an inspiration," she remembered the day they met, over a year ago now. He'd been in town and stopped at her booth at the farmer's market. She'd seen him strolling through the stalls and tables, expertly assessing the corn, beans, and peppers. Trim and muscular, his jeans had fit him like a second skin. His light-brown hair, parted in the middle and drawn into a ponytail just like Willie's, framed his tanned angular face. By the time he reached her stall, his canvas bag was bulging. She remembered wondering if he was shopping for his wife. He hadn't looked to her like the type who would cook for himself.

He had grinned at her. "Fine-looking tomatoes you got there. You grow 'em?"

"I did," AJ said. As he lifted one to test its firmness, she noticed that he wasn't wearing a wedding ring and returned the grin. He'd hung around longer than it took to buy the tomatoes, and she'd enjoyed the conversation. It had been the first of many. She smiled at the memory as she opened the door.

"Hey, babe," Dew said as he came in. "I missed you."

AJ threw her arms around his neck in a deep embrace and kiss. "I was only gone a day, sweetie, but I missed you too."

His comment worried her, knowing the point of the looming conversation.

"Want a beer?" Without waiting for the answer that she knew too well, she headed to the kitchen. Dew followed.

"So, tell me about Virginia. I want every detail. Am I dating a rich girl now?" He encircled her waist and pressed himself into her backside.

AJ laughed. "Well, sorta." She opened two Pabst Blue Ribbons and handed one to Dew. "Come on; I'll tell you all about it."

As they often did, she sat on one end of the couch with her feet propped on the old trunk she'd converted to a coffee table, Dew lay with his head propped against the pillows on the other end, his sock feet in her lap. As she described Langford Hall, Mulgrew, and Isabelle, she massaged his feet between pulls on her beer.

"But what's the deal with the inheritance?" he said after she'd finished her monologue. He held up his empty bottle as a second question.

"You go get it, okay?"

Dew nodded, got up, and padded to the kitchen.

"Well?" he said as he resumed his former position.

"According to the will, I got to live there a while before I can do anything, like sell it, if that's what I decide to do. I know neither of them wants me to sell it. I think it's why Isabelle wanted to give me that slave book. Trying to hook me with the family tales."

She'd spat it all out without taking a breath, fearful that if she didn't, she wouldn't be able to at all. Now she watched Dew's expression turn from curious to incredulous.

"What do you mean, *if* you decide to sell it? I thought that was the plan all along. You told me that's what your mom wanted you to do. Now you saying you might not? How you going to manage two farms when one of them is in Virginia?"

"I wouldn't. I'd stay there and sell this one. Coal companies want it anyhow. But I ain't saying I've made up my mind. I ain't. I am saying I'm probably going to go live there for a year, maybe less." She took a swallow of her beer, glad to have the taste of those words washed out of her mouth.

Dew's face fell. She'd expected anger; instead he looked as if she'd just slapped him in the face.

He jerked his feet from her lap and sat up. "Probably? *Probably,* hell! You mean you made this decision without talking to me? I thought I mattered to you more than that. We talked some about it before you left, but I thought you wasn't going to decide until we discussed it again."

"Dew, you matter lots to me. Lots. But that's what the will says. I didn't know that before I left. I ain't for sure yet, but Alice is going to take care of things here if her brother Jimmy Jenkins can help her out. Annie's staying here too. I'll come home real often. We can talk and

FaceTime every day. Besides, I ain't that far away. You could come on weekends I can't get home. It's only four hours. Like I said, I ain't for sure yet on account of Alice ain't talked to Jimmy yet."

"Shit, I knew going over there was a bad idea. Now I'm sorry I watched your damn stall for you."

Now AJ looked surprised. "If you hadn't, I'd still of gone, Dew. A body just don't ignore a letter like that. You wouldn't have, I know. Besides, it's a chance, maybe my only chance to live an easier life, at least for a little while. I love my farm, but it's damn hard—"

Dew interrupted. "Hell, I know it's hard work. Life is hard work. Hard work and responsibilities. I work hard too, but you don't see me going off to follow some damn fairy-tale life."

She put her beer on the table and moved to put her arms around him, but he jumped up and began to pace. "Dew," she pleaded, tearing up. "Don't be that way. It won't be so bad, really."

"The hell it won't," he yelled. Then lowering his voice, he sounded perplexed. "What's wrong with life here? I thought you loved this place, these hills. Plus, you got responsibilities here. You need to stay and take care of them."

"Please, Dew," she begged again as a knot of dread grew in her guts. "Don't tell me—"

"Don't tell you what?" He jerked away from her outstretched hand. "Tell you how I feel? *Bullshit!* I can't tell you what to do, AJ, and I ain't gonna beg, but I will tell you this. You can go off and play princess if you want to, but I ain't guaranteeing this Prince Charming will be around when you get back. *If* you come back, that is."

He lunged for the door. AJ tried to stop him, but he beat her to it, and left.

"Dew!" she yelled, as the door slammed in her face. After a moment, she slumped on the couch, too stunned to cry. She tidied the living room, and went to bed, now more unsettled than ever. Sleep came uneasy, and she woke earlier than usual, tired from thinking and reliving Dew's angry outburst.

⟋

By the time Alice and Annie rose the next morning, AJ was in the kitchen fixing pancakes like she'd done every Sunday for years. Annie loved it when her mother dotted each one with blueberries trying to form a face in the fresh batter on the griddle. The way they slid into comical expressions as they cooked always made both of them laugh. Today, however, AJ wasn't in a laughing mood, and she certainly didn't want to have to tell Alice about her argument with Dew. Thankfully, Alice didn't ask how the evening went, but AJ was sure she would later.

While Alice was at church, AJ planned to talk to Annie about the move. Alice had called her brother Jimmy first thing, securing his promise to help out so AJ could leave. Now, knowing there was nothing stopping her, not the farm chores or Dew, she needed to explain to her daughter. As they ate, she prayed this conversation would go better than the one with Dew.

"Hey, sweetie, you know the farm in Virginia I told you about yesterday?" AJ said casually, laying her fork on the plate of half-eaten pancakes.

"Uh-huh," Annie mumbled, her mouth full.

"Well, one of these days it could be ours. Yours, mine, and Alice's. What would you think of that?"

Annie swallowed and looked up. "Would we move there?"

"Well, sure, but you could have your own horse, and a much bigger bedroom."

"Really? That sounds cool. But what about Gunner? Can he go too?"

"Absolutely," AJ said, picking up her fork again.

Annie gave AJ a long look. "Are there woods? And a creek?"

"I ain't for sure, but I'll find out. But here's the deal. If we want to live there, I'm going to have to go live there by myself a while first; then we'll decide if you and Alice are going to come too, or if I'll come home."

Annie dropped her fork and burst into tears. "*Nooooo*, Mama, I don't want you to go without me. Take me with you. I don't want to wait. I want to go now," she wailed.

AJ put out her arms, motioning for Annie. "Come here, sweetie." Annie ran to her and, big as she was, climbed into her mother's lap like a toddler.

"Why? Why can't I go with you?"

She wiped her nose with the back of her hand. AJ reached down and cleaned the snot off with her napkin.

"You've got school, and since I might not stay, I don't want you changing schools if we ain't going to move. Let's call it, uh, a practice move. You know how you practice your spelling words before you take the real test?" Annie sniffed and nodded. "Well, we can say I'm just practice-living in Virginia until I decide if I really want to do it all the time. So, while I'm gone, you and Alice will be in charge of our farm. Can you do that? It's a big job, but with Uncle Jimmy here to help, I'll bet you can. You'd still be in charge of Gunner, and you can ride him every day as long as Uncle Jimmy is here. Okay?"

"How long will you have to practice-live?"

"What if I stay while you're in third grade? I'll come home when you get out of school. And if you guys are going to come to Virginia, we'll move during the summer."

"A whole year, Mama? That's too long. I'll miss you too bad." She looked as if she might cry again.

"I know it's a long time. I'll miss you too, sweetie. What if I come home every time you get your report card? And we can FaceTime every evening before you go to bed. Oh, wait, you don't have a phone, do you?" She feigned shock, as Annie shook her head. "Well, how about I fix that? I'll buy one for Alice and teach her how to FaceTime. Secretly, we'll call it your phone, but since you can't take it to school, we'll let Alice keep it during the day, okay?"

"My own phone?" She jumped out of AJ's lap, squealing. "That would be totally cool. None of my friends' moms will let them have one. Okay, you can go as long as I get my phone."

AJ laughed. "I promise. Now finish your pancakes. They're getting cold."

After breakfast, AJ went to the barn, partly out of necessity, partly because it gave her solitude. With each heft of old straw in Gunner's stall, she replayed the scene with Dew. *I hate what happened last night. How could I have said it so he wouldn't have gotten so mad? I guess I couldn't. There weren't no other way to say it. And Dew's gonna do what Dew's gonna do. But we never argued before. Maybe it was my fault. But, damn it, I deserve to try that life, and he shouldn't have acted that way, like he thought he had the right to make my decision. Alice and Annie are okay with it, so screw Dew. I'll decide for myself, thank you, Dewey Bennett.*

By the time the stall was clean and she'd led Gunner back into it, AJ was sure she'd made the right decision.

~ Chapter Five ~

On Monday, AJ called Mr. Mulgrew to say she would come to Langford Hall for the trial residency. She saw no reason to delay telling him. She had some conditions of her own, however. She wouldn't arrive until after Labor Day so she could get Annie settled in school, and she wanted Isabelle to keep her job if she wished. Her gut told her the older woman would be an invaluable source of knowledge and support, at least until she could manage on her own. Mulgrew readily agreed to both.

As she hung up the phone, AJ's eyes fell on a photo of Alice, Annie, and her that Dew had taken last Christmas. She swallowed hard, realizing that with that call she'd turned her family's life upside down. And she figured Dew was gone from hers. Things would never be the same, even if she returned at the end of the trial period. She'd be a different person, for certain, and Dew would probably be with someone else. That thought made her as sad as any other. She wondered if her grandfather James had had a similar feeling when he struck out for West Virginia all those years ago. Knowing her thoughts could turn into rethinking the decision, she focused on what she needed to do in the next few weeks.

Make sure the truck and all the other equipment work; set up a bank account that Jimmy can access for incidental expenses; arrange for the regular bills to be sent to Langford Hall. The mental list began to grow until she gave in and committed it to paper.

Over the next few weeks, as she checked the items off her list, AJ felt like a child on a seesaw. First, she would excitedly dream about the opportunity ahead; then she'd see Annie playing in the creek and agonize over what she was going to miss in her daughter's life in the next year. Sometimes it hit AJ like a gut punch. Annie was at an age where change came rapidly—lost teeth, new interests, new skills, and the potential shattering of childhood myths like the tooth fairy and Santa Claus.

She had to admit she also longed for Dew. Besides being a good lover, he'd been fun. They bowled, ate out, and enjoyed hanging out at Pies & Pints. He never failed to make her feel attractive and sexy. She missed the feel of his strong arms around her almost as much as their dates and his flirtatious ways. She'd thought he would rethink the situation and call, but he hadn't, not once. Not even a text.

Before their first conversation about Virginia, she hadn't thought her decision would send him running like it had. Sure, she knew he might get tired of her absence and find someone else, but his unwillingness even to give her a chance was a bit of a shock. While the turn of events had saddened and even angered her a bit, it *had* exposed a crack in Dew's otherwise charming facade. *Will that quick temper surface again?* Still, she missed him. Despite the ache, however, she knew going was the right thing to do.

⌒

The day after Labor Day, in a steady drizzle, Annie watched teary-eyed as AJ put her belongings in the truck. "Are you taking everything, Mama?" Annie sniffled.

"No, baby, just stuff I might need and things that will remind me of you." She blew her daughter a kiss, but Annie didn't return the gesture.

Plastic covered everything AJ carried, and she wore a yellow slicker to protect her and her belongings. At the end of the sidewalk that abutted the driveway, Annie huddled under Alice's umbrella with one arm around her grandmother's legs. She should have been at school, but AJ had allowed her to stay home just this once. AJ's face was wet too, but not entirely from the drizzle. After she put in the last load, she wiped her eyes, approached the pair, and knelt in front of Annie.

"Sweetie, don't cry. I'll talk to you tonight when I get there and every other night. You can tell me about Gunner, school, and all your new friends. You and Alice will have a good time without me always giving you chores to do. And I'll be back when you get your first report card. I have to sign it, remember?" She laughed and tried to get Annie to smile by poking her in the ribs. It didn't work. Annie, stone-faced, merely grimaced.

"That's a long time from now," Annie said, wiping her nose on her sleeve.

"I know, honey, but I got to go. Give me a kiss; I got to get on the road."

Annie threw her arms around her mother's neck and stayed locked there until AJ reluctantly pried them loose. Finally, she stood, gave Alice a hug and whispered, "Thanks, Mom. I love you." After a kiss on Alice's cheek, she got in the truck, circled the center garden and drove down the gravel driveway. In the rearview mirror, she saw her mother and Annie waving. Their arms seemed in rhythm with the windshield wipers.

AJ took her time winding down the mountain, reluctant to leave her known world behind. She blamed the snail's pace on her tears and the rain. But by the time she merged onto the interstate, the rain had stopped, the sun had reappeared, and her thoughts had shifted to the new world she was approaching.

What have I gotten myself into? I sure hope I ain't bitten off more'n I can chew.

⟵⟶

The sun slanted slightly westward as AJ turned into the driveway of Langford Hall. Isabelle had told her to call so she could open the security gates, since AJ didn't have a remote control yet. The motion of the rolling gates broke AJ's worries, and she started down the tree-lined driveway. Somehow, the trip felt different to her; this time she wasn't just visiting. She lived here. It was her home even if it might only be a temporary one. Again, Isabelle—wearing the same hat— stood waiting on the porch. That was comforting, at least. *Suppose she sleeps in that hat?*

"Welcome home, AJ," she called as AJ reached the porch. "How was your drive?"

"Just fine, thank you. I got a bunch of stuff in the truck. Where do you want me to put it?"

"Let's leave it for now. I'll get the yardman, Eddie, to bring it in later, after you've settled in a bit. Want some iced tea?"

As the two walked through the house to Mr. Jack's den, AJ couldn't help looking around as if she were again in a museum. Now it was her museum. She wondered if she'd ever get over that feeling.

"I certainly appreciate your wanting me to stay on with you, AJ. I know we'll get on famously." Isabelle gripped AJ's hand and held it a bit too long for AJ's comfort. She wasn't used to such displays of emotion from strangers, and in her mind, Isabelle was still that.

"I know we will, too. I'm glad to have you," AJ replied as Isabelle's grip loosened enough for her to break free.

In the den, Isabelle pointed to the massive antique walnut desk on their left. AJ looked at the ornate carvings on the sturdy corners and the large brass drawer pulls and imagined Mr. Jack hunched over a pile of papers, sorting through them one by one.

"This is where Jack usually worked each day," said Isabelle, as if she were reading AJ's mind. AJ also thought she was insinuating that AJ should take up the reins immediately. "My desk was, uh, is, in the sunroom," she continued as she poured tea at the glass-top tea table.

"I think it would be weird sitting at Mr. Jack's desk. Do I have to work there? It's kind of dark in here, too. I'm used to being outdoors most days. Isn't there anywhere else?"

"Well, I suppose we could switch desks and move the computers. I love this room, probably because it is so, I don't know—Jack, I guess." Once again, AJ sensed that their relationship was more than professional. "I'll have Eddie move all the files and so forth. We'd better go find you a bedroom before he brings in your things and dumps them in the front hall. I suspect if you wouldn't feel comfortable at Jack's desk, you sure wouldn't want his bedroom, either." She laughed.

"No, I sure wouldn't. Sleeping in the bed of a dead man totally creeps me out." AJ shivered for effect.

"Well, he didn't actually die there, but I take your point," Isabelle said as she led the way up the broad stairway. "And it is very masculine, to boot."

AJ nodded, recalling the darkened room from her earlier tour.

The second-floor hallway stretched the width of the house, intersected by the upstairs landing, which was furnished like a small sitting room. Two club chairs flanked an octagonal table that held a horsehead lamp and a short stack of books. Portraits that AJ presumed were of family members dotted the walls between each closed door.

"That's the way to Jack's room, if you recall," Isabelle said, pointing to their left. "Let's go this way." She turned in the opposite direction. "Remember the lovely room at the end of the hall? It is a mirror in layout to Jack's with large windows and an attached bathroom. In older times, it must have been the lady of the house's suite. Jack thought of it as a special guest room, but it should be yours. I think you'll like it."

Isabelle opened the door, and AJ stepped past her into a light, airy room with sheer gauze curtains, a four-poster bed, and an overstuffed chaise lounge upholstered in fabric dominated by bright-yellow cabbage roses. The bed's coverlet of yellow and lime-green irregular stripes was topped with more pillows than AJ had ever seen on a bed. They occupied a full fourth of its surface. A plush, white area rug hid most of the floor, but AJ saw gleaming, wide oak planks.

"Yes," she said to Isabelle. "This is wonderful. I do love it."

"I thought you would. Let me show you the closets and bathroom so you'll have an idea of where you can put your things. Did you bring a laptop? It could go on this old dressing table, assuming you don't use one." She looked questioningly at AJ.

"Lord, no. I'm lucky to get me a turn at the bathroom mirror with Alice and Annie around. I get up at the crack of dawn just to have hot water in my shower. And having a toilet to myself is a total luxury." They both laughed as Isabelle gestured for AJ to look inside the bathroom. It had been decorated to match the bedroom. Striped shower curtain, yellow tile, and a vanity longer than any AJ had seen except in the movies.

"This'll do just fine, Isabelle, more than fine. Thank you."

"Great, I'll go tell Eddie to bring up your things. Clara will have dinner ready about six. Will that suit you? I'll join you, if you don't mind, then head home so you can get some rest. Okay?"

"Sure, that's just fine. I'll be down in a little bit. I just need to check in with my family, to let them know I'm here."

When AJ sat on the chaise, she felt like she was sitting on a pile of feathers. *Boy, I could sure nap here.* She dialed the new cell number, hoping to surprise Annie with her first real FaceTime call.

"Hey, Alice," she said as her mother answered the phone. "I just wanted to let you know I'm here. Everything okay?" AJ listened to her mother give her the details of the day's chores and how Jimmy had handled things.

"Dew called? Really? After all this time? What'd he say?" AJ grinned and felt flushed. "Why didn't he call my cell? Oh, I was probably in a dead zone. Did he ask you to have me call him?" She had jumped from the chaise and was now pacing the room.

"Okay, I will after I talk to Annie. No, it'll have to be after dinner. I can't call him at work. Can you call her in, or do you want to call me back? Okay, I'll wait."

While Alice went to the door to call Annie, AJ looked out the windows of her new bedroom, then at herself in the mirror. *I didn't realize I missed him so much, but why should I jump up and call him just because he's suddenly decided to get in touch with me? Hmmm. Maybe I'll just make him sweat it out. Or maybe I won't call him after all. He deserves to stew in his own juices a while like I did.* Soon she heard her daughter say, "Mama?"

"Hi, sweetie. Turn on FaceTime so I can see you too. That's better. Hi, again." She laughed.

"Hi, Mama. You look funny on the phone. What're you doing?"

"Well, I'm talking to you, silly. Want to see my room?"

"Sure. Is it pretty?"

"You bet," her mother said. "Look for yourself." AJ walked around again, pointing out things to Annie. "I can't wait to have you visit. This bed is so big we can share it if you want. Or you can have your own room." The two chatted a while longer.

"I've got to unpack, but I'll call tomorrow night and you can tell me how you did on your spelling quiz. Love you."

She kissed the phone goodbye and Annie did the same. AJ hung up and flopped onto the bed, realizing suddenly how inadequate the phone call was. The inability to hug her daughter, to read to her, or listen to her practice those spelling words ached like the phantom pain of a missing limb. *What the hell have I done?*

A knock on the door brought her to her feet, and she rushed to open it. "Hey, Miss AJ. I'm Eddie. I've got some of your things. I'll get the rest on the next trip. Where shall I put them?" As he entered the room, a familiar earthy smell wafted past AJ, making her homesick all over again. His lanky gait reminded her of someone back home, too.

"Thank you, Eddie. You can just put them on the bed or the couch. I'm not sure yet just where I want things. You take care of the yard, Isabelle says. I did that and more back home in West Virginia. You ever live on a farm?"

He set the boxes down and looked up at her quizzically. "This *is* a farm, Miss AJ, but I don't live here. Some days it feels like I do though," he said as a wry grin crossed his long face. "I do enjoy working in the dirt, yes."

"Me too," AJ said, "but I guess I won't have much chance now. At least not for a while."

Eddie laughed. "Oh, you can come help me any day. Matter of fact, I'd best be getting back to it after I bring up the rest of your things."

He turned to go as AJ said, "Thanks again. I might just take you up on that offer."

AJ spent the better part of the afternoon unpacking and putting things away. The longer she worked, the more the room began to feel like hers. The activity had pushed Annie, Alice, and West Virginia to the back of her mind, and she began to wonder what each day here would be like. Isabelle had been right; the dressing table made a perfect little desk. She was sure she'd spend most of the time at a computer downstairs, but for her personal use, this was her own little office.

Just as she finished, Isabelle knocked. "AJ, do you have time to come meet the farm manager before he leaves?"

"Certainly," AJ said as she opened the door. "I'm just fussing with things now. Where is he?"

"His office is down the walkway. We'll meet him there."

AJ grabbed her cell phone, jammed it in her back pocket and closed the door. "I'm looking forward to meeting him. What's his name again?"

"Tom Beckett." Isabelle chuckled. "I always think of the guy they canonized for standing up to the King of England. Thomas a' Becket? Remember the movie? Richard Burton played him? Anyway, he's no Richard Burton." She laughed again with more gusto. This was one movie AJ didn't remember, but as soon as she saw him, she knew what Isabelle meant by her last remark.

Seated at the desk, the man's balding head glowed under the overhead lights. As Beckett rose to greet them, his expression suggested he didn't like being interrupted. But when Isabelle introduced AJ, he reached to shake her hand with a smile that could have melted snow.

"I'm so glad to meet you, Miss AJ. Morton has told me all about you," he said. AJ met his eyes, which didn't smile like his mouth did. She'd met men like that before, and her first impression was that he wasn't going to like working for a woman. Eddie's smile had been much more genuine.

"It's my pleasure. I've got a lot to learn, so I hope you'll be patient with me. We never kept a lot of records back at my farm. I know farming, but I'm not fond of keeping records," AJ said.

"Don't you worry. I'll handle all that for you. And if you really want to, I'll show you the books whenever you want." He sat back down in the chair and stretched his legs. They reached almost to where AJ stood. As she stared at them, he whirled the chair around to his former spot and hunched over his papers again, clearly dismissing the women.

"Oh, I *will* want to see them, and to learn what you do, but we can start later. I need to learn my way around first," she said to his rounded back, determined to let him know she was in charge now.

"Fine," he muttered.

"Nice to meet you," AJ said as she and Isabelle left. "Man, he's a piece of work," she said as soon as Isabelle had closed the door. "What the hell's his problem? Doesn't he like women?"

"I think he just resents having someone else in charge. He worked for Jack for so long that he got used to his ways. He's probably afraid of someone new changing things. He's a real curmudgeon and a control freak. You'll get used to him, though. Don't worry."

"Huh! He better get used to me," AJ huffed. She could be just as stubborn and wasn't going to be intimidated by this man.

After a scrumptious dinner of shrimp scampi, which AJ had never eaten before, and asparagus, Isabelle left saying they'd drive around the farm tomorrow. AJ went to the kitchen to thank Clara, then headed upstairs. It felt odd, being in that huge house almost alone. After Clara left, she would be alone, and the thought unsettled her. She couldn't recall the last time she'd ever been alone in her own home. Until she married Jeff, she'd lived on the farm with her parents. Then there was Jeff; and after he and her father died, she had Alice and Annie. Even at college she'd had roommates.

She decided not to contact Dew right away to give him a taste of his own medicine—until loneliness hit her. She grabbed the phone and called, pacing while staring at Dew's number as it continued to ring. Just as she was about to hang up, she heard that familiar twang.

"Hey, babe. I was afraid you wouldn't call back. I called you, but your mom said you'd left," Dew drawled.

"Hey, yourself. It's good to hear your voice."

"I should have called sooner, but my old stubborn streak got in the way. I want to apologize. I ain't very good at it, and it ain't my normal way, but I am sorry I stormed out that night. I shouldn't have did that. You were right. It's your decision, and I didn't have no right to demand to be in on it. It's just—"

AJ interrupted. "It's okay. I know you didn't really mean it. I should have at least talked to you before, you know, before making the final decision. I'd said I would, and then I didn't. God, I miss you, too." She melted. "Why don't you come over this weekend? We could make up proper like, if you know what I mean." She laughed softly, hoping she sounded sexy.

"I know you'll think I'm still mad at you, but I really can't. I promised Ralph Long I'd help him harvest his wheat. Maybe the next weekend though, if we get done or it don't rain."

"No, I don't think you're mad, and I understand. We'll see about next weekend. I just knew I wouldn't know enough by this weekend to feel like I had work to do. By next week, who knows? But we'll talk all week, okay? I'm alone in this huge house and it's a comfort just hearing your voice. Put on FaceTime. I want to see you." The phone face was black for a moment, and then she heard Dew again.

"God, it's good to see you," AJ said with a face-splitting smile.

"You too, baby."

They spent the next thirty minutes catching up with events of the past two weeks. Dew told her about running into some old buddies at Pies & Pints, and she told him about the farm and her premonition that Tom Beckett was going to be a force to reckon with.

After they disconnected, AJ took a long, hot shower and fell into bed, the euphoria she still felt visible in the grin on her flushed face.

~ Chapter Six ~

The following morning, when AJ opened her eyes, a soft light bathed the room. She glanced around, unsure of where she was. Her bedroom in Gimlet Hollow had only one window, and it opened onto the shadow of the surrounding oaks that had always felt to her like a protective fortress. But the room was always dim, even under the noonday sun. As soon as she spotted the cabbage roses on the chaise, she knew it was the first day of her new life in Hadleigh. She stretched the full length of the king-sized bed, which felt enormous compared to her old double bed, then reached for her cell phone: 7:20. She couldn't recall the last time she'd slept so late.

She washed her face, re-braided her hair, and applied a smear of lipstick, a nod to her new position and an effort she wouldn't have made at home. The morning had the feel of a fairy-tale life until she had to decide what to wear. Opening her closet, she realized she had few clothes she considered appropriate. *I gotta get some new clothes. Isabelle will know where to shop, I guess.* She sighed and pulled on her well-worn jeans and boots, and a clean, pale-blue T-shirt. As she did, she was back in West Virginia. At home, she'd have already accomplished several chores, including getting Annie off to school. With a pang of longing, and unsure of what to do until Isabelle arrived for work, she went in search of coffee.

The house was as still as if it had been abandoned. Out the arched front windows, however, she spotted Eddie spreading rich-looking, black mulch. *Well, someone around here keeps the kind of hours I'm used to.* Remembering Isabelle's admonition about Clara's proprietary claim on the kitchen, she knocked before pushing open the paneled swinging door.

"Anyone home?" she called as she stepped over the threshold.

Clara, a stout fiftyish woman in a white uniform, looked surprised to see anyone in the doorway; then she smiled. "Good morning, Miss AJ, I didn't expect you so early. I hope you slept good. What can I fix you? Coffee? Some breakfast?"

"I'll get it myself, Clara. I sure don't expect you to fix it."

"That's my job, hon. If I didn't cook, what would I do to earn my keep?" As she laughed, her bosom rolled under her apron.

AJ laughed too. "Well, if you say so. How about coffee, and maybe some scrambled eggs and bacon? If it ain't too much to ask. With cream and sugar, if you got it? Thanks."

A cup of coffee, along with the white pitcher of cream and the sugar bowl, appeared as if AJ had conjured them simply by asking. The blue stripe around the middle of the set reminded AJ of a blue chambray shirt she had left at home. As she doctored the black liquid, she asked, "Do you know what time Isabelle usually comes to work?"

"Her schedule changes day to day. If there's a school group coming through, she's here by nine. She told me there is one today. I'm baking cookies for them."

"I thought I smelled something good. Can you save me one?"

Clara laughed again. "Sure, hon. I'll save you two."

As the laughter floated around the room, AJ warmed to the affable woman Isabelle had depicted as stern. Quite the contrary, AJ was finding her easy to talk with. Perhaps it was because she sounded like some of the folks she knew back home.

AJ blew on her coffee. "I think I'll go walk around a bit. I'll be back in about an hour. I'll eat then if that's okay."

"Don't matter to me; I'll be here whenever you want it."

Clara laughed again as AJ headed for the back door. She stood on the back porch for a moment, recalling her earlier trip to the cemetery with Isabelle. This time she intended to look at it by herself, to study the names of her new ancestors. Sipping the hot coffee as she walked down the long path, she glanced around to see if anyone else was working. In the side yard, she spotted Eddie again. *He sorta reminds me of Jeff. Maybe it's the grin or the way he lopes across the yard.*

She reached the cemetery before she remembered that the gate was kept locked. *Shit. Wonder why they do that? Who's gonna go in there anyway without Isabelle?* Leaning over the fence, she could read several of the gravestones on the perimeter. She saw young Eli's tombstone next to that of his parents. She remembered Isabelle talking about him dying during the Civil War. Said something about his slave going with him. In the corner was a slightly sunken spot the shape of a grave. The wooden cross she'd noticed when Isabelle took her there earlier was its only marking. *Maybe that's his grave back there. Ask Isabelle. She'll know for sure.* As AJ approached the house, she made an impulsive turn and headed across the yard to the barn on the other side of the driveway. She had wanted to see the resident horses since her first trip to the farm.

The barn was, in comparison to hers, an equine mansion. Its pristinely white clapboard siding gleamed in the distance. As she approached, she inhaled the perfume of hay, horse feed, sawdust, and manure. It was the sweetest smell on earth—next to that of Annie's skin when she was a baby. She knocked, then slid the heavy door open. "My God, a paneled barn," she said more loudly than she meant to. She'd never seen anything like it. This barn was better built than her home. Certainly, the knotty pine paneling was of higher quality. At home, they had Lowe's sheet paneling of questionable wood—if it really was wood. This was a tongue and groove installation by a master craftsman.

As she walked down the broad center aisle, she read the names engraved on the brass plaques on each stall door. Before she reached the cross aisle, a door opened, and a dark-skinned, compact-looking man in fawn jodhpurs and gleaming oxblood boots approached her.

"Excuse me, but the visitors' tour doesn't include the barns." He spoke with an accent that wasn't familiar to AJ and certainly not a West Virginia twang.

AJ stuck out her hand, which he took hesitatingly. "I'm not exactly a visitor. I'm AJ Porter. I'm the new, uh—" She started over. "I'm Mr. Jack's great-niece. I live here. At least I do now." She watched as his expression changed from annoyance to surprise.

"Uh-oh, screwed that one up, didn't I? I'm so sorry. I'm Santos, the stable master and trainer."

"It's okay, Santos. Nice to meet you."

"Did you come to see Mr. Jack's horse?"

"Truthfully, I came to see any horse. I miss mine back home already."

"I get that. Mr. Jack's horse, Merlot, is an American Thoroughbred. He's got a fancy registered name, but the boss always called him Merlot. He's a splendid jumper with a room full of trophies and ribbons. Mr. Jack jumped when he was younger. Of course, that was with another horse. It was almost a profession with him, they say. Until he broke his hip, he loved to compete. After I came, Mr. Jack hired a professional rider for Merlot. You ever jump?"

AJ watched Santos's brown eyes twinkle as he talked about the horse. It was as if he had trained him single-handedly.

"Never did on purpose." AJ laughed. "Once my old gelding, Democrat, took a fence, but it sure wasn't my idea. I never thought it was something folks did on purpose. I just get a kick out of trail riding and mucking stalls."

Santos laughed. "You like shoveling that shit? Sorry . . . I mean manure? I gotta say, I wouldn't do that unless I had to."

"So, give me a pitchfork and wheelbarrow and I'll do it."

"*Dios mio*, Miss AJ, I'd never hear the end of it. We've got stable hands to do that. If I let you, the guys would rag on me for sure. Let's go see that horse instead."

Santos pointed down the aisle toward a large stall with a blue ribbon hooked on the brass nameplate. AJ followed him, but her eyes were in constant motion taking in the grandeur of the spacious barn. The door to the tack room was open, giving her a glimpse of dozens of wooden pegs laden with some of the cleanest saddles and bridles she'd ever seen. *God, compared to those, mine look like something I should throw out with the shit.*

As they approached Merlot's stall, he nickered and stuck his head over the stall door. Santos put his hand out, and the horse nuzzled it affectionately. "Aww, he likes you," said AJ. She could see why Jack had called him Merlot. His coat reminded her of a shimmering glass of the red wine. AJ considered him a sorrel. His long mane, however, was as blond as Lady Gaga's locks, although *his* color was natural.

"Yeah, he does, but he's really looking for a sugar lump. If he could, he'd dig it out of my pocket." As AJ watched the interaction between the man and the animal, she suddenly longed for Gunner. Of course, he didn't compare in stature or breeding, but he was hers, and Merlot would never be. Tears stung her eyes, but she wiped them away before Santos could catch her.

"He sure is a beauty. I'd love to ride him sometime if fences aren't involved," she said.

Santos laughed and gave the horse a pat on the head. "We'll see. He can be a handful."

As he gave Merlot the sugar lump, he murmured, "Later, buddy," then turned away from the stall. "I'll be exercising him later if you'd like to watch. I may even put him through his jumps," he told AJ as they headed toward the door.

"Thanks, I'd like that, but I'm not sure what all I've got to do today. It's my first day, you know."

"Okay, it's a daily ritual, so another day will work just as well."

"Thanks for introducing me to Merlot. I'll be back often. I might even sneak in and muck a stall." AJ laughed at Santos's shocked expression. "Just kidding, Santos. See you later."

As the barn door closed behind her, she poured what was left of her cold coffee on the ground and returned to the house. Reaching the porch, she saw Isabelle's car in the driveway. *Shit, hope she don't expect me to start in doing something before I eat. Starving.*

AJ passed through Mr. Jack's office—she wondered if she'd ever think of it otherwise—and headed toward the kitchen. She had expected to find Isabelle hard at work, but the room was empty. She pushed open the kitchen door. Isabelle sat in the breakfast nook, her hat firmly in place, eating scrambled eggs. "Come join me, dear," she said without preface.

AJ slid into the bench on the other side of the table. "Morning, Isabelle. Those eggs look good. Clara, could I have the same thing?" She turned back to Isabelle. "I hear you've got a school tour scheduled today. Could I tag along, unless you had something else I needed to do? I might learn something." She laughed.

"That's a good idea. You'll need to change, though," Isabelle said, indicating AJ's T-shirt. "We always try to look professional even if there are only children on the tour."

"Uh-oh, that could be a problem. I don't exactly have professional-looking clothes. Except that outfit I wore on my first visit. I'm not partial to skirts, either, as you can see. I've got work jeans and better pants. That's it."

"Maybe we should go on a shopping trip this afternoon. After the kids leave. Or I can tell you where the good shops are and you can go by yourself. Do you know Chico's? Or j. jill? They've both got clothes I think you'd like, and they're both in Charlottesville, which isn't too far away."

"I guess those stores ain't come to West Virginia yet. I was going to ask you where I could get some new things, but I'd like it if you'd come with me. I don't know what's right for here. My clothes usually come from Walmart. Their jeans worked fine in my old world."

"Okay, sounds like fun. We can grab a frozen yogurt while we're there. Right now, I gotta run. The school bus will be here shortly. Why don't you change into some good slacks and a nice shirt and meet us in the front hall in about fifteen minutes?"

"Sounds good; I'll hurry."

⁓

AJ heard the kids before she saw them. At the foot of the staircase, a group of about fifteen eighth-graders, dressed in school uniforms of navy-blue pants or skirts and white shirts, chattered and laughed among themselves. A few looked in awe at their surroundings, their heads on a swivel. Isabelle, her hat making her look taller than she was, stood on the lowest step and clapped her hands. The group went silent except for a snicker or two. AJ stood in the back near where the laughter had originated.

"Welcome to Langford Hall. I'm Isabelle Collins. Today you are visiting a home where presidents have danced, and history has been made. If you'll remain quiet, I won't have to use a microphone." The snickering stopped abruptly. "But I'll be happy to answer your questions as we go along. And after the tour, we'll have some cookies and lemonade." As Isabelle began talking, AJ realized her words were almost the same ones she'd used when she showed AJ the house a month ago. It was as if she'd written and memorized a script.

Why didn't she introduce me? Maybe I'm too hard to explain. "This is AJ Porter. She *might be the new owner." Yeah, I can see how that would sound weird.*

After the group toured the cemetery, they entered Mr. Jack's study. Isabelle stopped them here and began to talk again. AJ listened to a story she hadn't heard before.

The students settled on the leather couch and the chairs that had been gathered for them. Isabelle leaned on Mr. Jack's desk and started. AJ could tell that the *cheerful hatter,* as she'd begun to call Isabelle, had said these words scores of times. And she delivered it with such enthusiasm AJ wondered if she'd once been an actress.

"When you first arrived, I told you that history had been made in this house. Well, it might have been made right here at this desk." She ran her hand tenderly over its polished surface. "The second owner of Langford Hall was Langford Elias Morgan, and two of his close friends were the third and fourth presidents of the United States. And who were they?" Isabelle asked in her best teacher voice.

After a few moments of awkward silence one brave girl answered meekly. "Jefferson and Madison?"

I would have sounded just like her when I was a student—if I'd had the guts to open my mouth, that is.

"Right. Thank you. Thomas Jefferson and James Madison." Isabelle continued, "We know they were friends because several letters between Mr. Morgan and each president still exist. We had the ones they wrote to Mr. Morgan in our files, until Mr. Jack Morgan donated them a few years ago to the University of Virginia. Some of old Mr. Morgan's letters are in the collections of each of the presidents' papers. And of course their homes, Monticello and Montpelier, are within a day's ride on horseback or by buggy from here.

"Mr. Morgan and President Jefferson corresponded often on several matters of state. In the beginning of his presidency, Mr. Jefferson was still trying to work out details of things like the term of his office and that of members of Congress. About that time, Mr. Morgan sent him a long essay he'd written, probably at this very desk, regarding the necessity of preventing the wealthy aristocracy from either running the government or dictating who would. As you know, only adult men who owned property—but not women or Negroes, as they were called back then—were granted the vote. But because most men who were *elected* to office were usually wealthy, Mr. Morgan felt that should change. He thought men should be able to stand for election whether or not they were wealthy.

"Mr. Jefferson replied that while he hadn't read the entire essay, he agreed with Mr. Morgan's point. He agreed the current situation did not fully represent those who were simply common men and that it needed to change. Eventually it did change, and perhaps because of Mr. Morgan's essay.

"So, you are standing in the home of a man who no doubt influenced how our government evolved. Think of it. However, there could be some argument that we've drifted away from some of Morgan's and Jefferson's ideals. Today, it costs so much to run for elected office, especially on the national stage, that we often do have the rich running our government, despite the Founders' wishes."

AJ noticed that some of the students were looking around the room, apparently bored with Isabelle's political science lecture. Evidently, she noticed it too, suddenly switching gears.

"All three were farmers, too. We don't usually think of our early presidents as such, but that's what they were, despite their involvement in the formation of our country and its constitution. So, on a more personal note, most of their letters were about farming. All three exchanged plant seeds and shared ways to graft nectarines and peaches onto other fruit trees. They discussed new farm equipment inventions, as well. And once Mr. Morgan sent some dinosaur bones to Mr. Jefferson during a trip west and received a letter of thanks in return."

That brought the students' eyes back into focus. "Where did he get a dinousaur bone?" came a question from an arm-waving boy near the doorway. Another boy up front had raised his hand, too.

"That's a question I can't answer. Mr. Morgan was touring the American West when he wrote Jefferson telling him that he had one for him. The letter also mentions seeing the Grand Canyon, so he may have gotten it near there.

"As I said earlier, the three men visited each other's homes often. Several letters also thank Jefferson for playing his fiddle at parties the Morgans held. He would sit up on the upper landing above the staircase in the front hall. The furniture in the living room would be moved out for dancing. They say he was a fine fiddler until he had a few too many drinks. Then he would abandon his music and begin flirting and dancing with the ladies."

Hormonal giggles broke out among the girls. Some of the boys high-fived each other as if they'd have done the same thing.

"Mr. Morgan also bought hard cider and new varieties of wine for Mr. Jefferson on more than one occasion. Once, Mr. Jefferson took almost three months to pay him. He wrote to apologize for the delay, saying he'd been out of the country and would send it immediately upon his return. What do you think the wine cost? Seven hundred dollars. That was a lot of money back then, so it must have been a lot of wine."

An African-American boy who had raised his hand earlier asked, "Did Mr. Morgan have slaves?" *The slavery issue again. Doesn't go away, does it?*

"Sadly, yes, he, like most Southern farm owners, did. They couldn't have raised their crops without that human labor. He and Jefferson talked about the issue often. I've read in their letters that both of them thought the practice was abhorrent, and, of course, it was Jefferson who espoused that all men were created equal. But, as practical men, they realized they couldn't maintain their businesses any other way."

"They could have paid them!" he said, in a decibel louder than his question.

"Way to go, kid," muttered AJ.

Isabelle replied. "That's very true, but it wasn't the practice at the time. We don't condone it now, of course, and we see the tragedy of it; but it was a fact of life then. I wouldn't have approved of it back then either, so all I can do is apologize for Mr. Morgan. In his heart, I think he knew it was wrong. It is a mystery to all of us that Mr. Jefferson didn't free his slaves, either." Isabelle suddenly pointed to the tea cart laden with oatmeal-raisin cookies and a huge cut-glass pitcher. "Are we ready for cookies and lemonade?"

AJ watched as the kids milled around the tray. Toward the back of the group, the boy who asked the question was whispering to a female classmate. AJ wanted to go to him, congratulate him for his brave question, but since Isabelle hadn't even acknowledged her, she didn't. As AJ watched his face, her mother's saying about "looking madder than a wet hen" sprang to mind. The girl looked as if she were trying to calm him down. But, for the most part, Isabelle's diversionary tactic had worked.

Fifteen minutes later the house was theirs again, and blessedly quiet. AJ watched a cloud of dust billow behind the mini-bus as it made its way down the driveway; then she turned back into the room where Isabelle sat on the couch sipping lemonade.

"Isabelle, you think the Morgans were good to their slaves? I mean, I heard how slaves were whipped, or worse. And I seen *Twelve Years a Slave*. Remember telling me that one of the Morgans took his slave to war with him? Is that his grave out there, the one with no marker except a wooden cross?"

"Yes, that's his. His name was Moses. Years later, he wrote his life story in that slave journal we wanted you to read."

"Why doesn't he have a marker, then?"

"Well, Eli's brother was a bit of a bastard, not literally, of course, but despite his father's wishes, he never freed Moses. I guess burying him without a marker was another way of expressing his racism. Terrible, huh?"

"Wow! Yeah, that's pretty bad. Do you think Langford Morgan, Jefferson's friend, was like that, too?"

"Well, I've got no proof other than the letters between Mr.

Morgan and Jefferson and Madison. It's clear they all thought the practice of holding human beings in bondage was evil, but they continued to do it. I'm not sure how you reconcile that, but I'm hopeful Langford didn't mistreat them."

"Me too. It bothers me to think this place was built on slave labor. Least my granddaddy didn't hold with that. Family says he was a kind man that never said a bad word about blacks. Reckon he left here to get rid of the taint of slavery? Maybe he chose West Virginia because it broke off from Virginia and became a Union state because of that. What do you think?"

"Hard to tell. He never wrote back. As you know, no one knew where he'd gone until Mr. Mulgrew found those records."

"Well, that's what I'm choosing to believe," AJ said, crossing her arms as if to put a period on the matter.

Changing the subject, Isabelle asked AJ if she'd like to ride around the farm to see what crops they produced. That way, she said, AJ could see the scope of their operations. AJ agreed, and the two set off in Mr. Jack's somewhat-the-worse-for-wear Range Rover.

After dinner, AJ went up to her room to call Annie, Alice, and Dew. AJ told Annie about Mr. Jack's horse, but she also had to tell her disappointed daughter she wouldn't be allowed to ride him. Annie said she'd found another dead frog in the creek, and that Alice had told her not to go there again. After AJ blew goodnight kisses to Annie via FaceTime, she dialed Dew. She'd touched up her lipstick, unbraided her hair and brushed it into long waves. She never did that at home. *I miss him more than I thought I would.* She listened eagerly for him to pick up.

"Hey, gal. I was hoping you'd call." Dew's deep voice boomed over the phone's speaker, and she grinned widely. "What'd you do today?"

"Hey, Dew." AJ grinned, glad he cared what her day was like. "I had a good day. No work, really, but I spent some time at the barn, listened to Isabelle tell a bunch of middle-school kids about how one of the Morgans was friends with two of our presidents. Can you believe that? My family, friends with US presidents? He might have even had a hand in how our government works. Who knew?"

"Seriously? That's some heavy shit."

"Ain't it though? And I toured the whole farm. Holy shit, you should see what all they grow here. Wheat, soybeans, cattle, and even some corn. It's a real slick operation. Makes me look like a piker going to the farmer's market. My place ain't nothing but a old dirt farm; this here is a real business. They export stuff, even. And I'm gonna have to learn how to run it." AJ sighed as if overwhelmed.

"Babe, you'll be just fine. Hell, you've run your farm for years, since long before I been knowing you. One day at a time; that's how you do everything, ain't it? You'll do fine. What about that manager? Ain't he supposed to teach you?"

"Yeah, I'm meeting with him again tomorrow. I got the feeling he ain't going to cotton to me meddling in his business."

"It ain't his business; it's yours, remember?'

"I know, but I also got the feeling he thinks it *is* his. You know Mr. Jack was an old man. He probably left this guy alone to run things his way for a long, long time. Should be interesting. I'll call you tomorrow night and tell you all about it." She stretched out on her bed. "How was your day? Same old, same old?"

"Pretty much, but I did get a call from old Dave Lovett. Remember him? We're going to get a beer and maybe pizza next Friday. That is unless you've changed your mind about me coming over then." AJ could see his grin spreading as he chuckled seductively.

"Oh honey, I'd love it, but I still think I gotta work next weekend too. After I meet with the manager, I'll probably have lots to study. I feel like I'm having to take tests to be here, you know?"

"I hear you. Maybe the following weekend, huh?"

"Maybe so. I'm thinking of coming home for Thanksgiving, but maybe I could come take Annie for Trick or Treat, too. That's probably about report card time. I done promised her I'd come ever time they came out. We'll see."

"That sounds great, babe."

"I miss you. Love you, Dew."

"Love you too, babe." Dew made kissing sounds into the phone. AJ returned them. "Miss you, too," Dew added at the last minute. "Night."

⌐ Chapter Seven ⌐

By the time AJ headed to her ten o'clock meeting with the farm manager, Tom Beckett, rain had settled on the day. *A miserable way to begin my work life,* she thought before silently thanking whichever ancestor had added the slate roof over the long walkway to his office building. The brass door knocker was smaller than that on Langford Hall's thick front door—nevertheless, still impressive. She lifted it into a light knock. No answer. She banged it solidly this time. Again, no answer. *Where the hell is he? He set the meeting. Damn it! All dressed up for nothing.*

It had taken her twenty minutes to decide which of her recent purchases from Chico's to wear. Her shopping trip to Charlottesville with Isabelle had produced an entire new wardrobe. And, best of all, at no cost to herself. She had finally settled on black pants, a hot-pink silk top, and large hoop earrings—an outfit she'd have been laughed at for wearing back in Turkey Knob. She'd even brushed her hair into a side-parted flowing style she'd seen on CNN's Erin Burnett that was way too impractical for work on the farm back home. She knocked several times more, but there was no answer.

Feeling purposely snubbed, she marched back into the house and straight to Isabelle's new office where Mr. Jack's used to be. "Do you have any idea where Tom Beckett might be? I had an appointment with him at ten, but the office is locked up tight as a tick and he doesn't answer." She felt her face flush as she talked, a visible sign of her irritation.

"I don't, actually, but he called early this morning. Said he would be gone all next week, but not where he was going. Maybe he had an emergency that caused him to forget your meeting."

"Oh," AJ said, her righteous anger suddenly deflated. "I didn't think of that. Still, I feel sort of lost with nothing to do. I was all set to get my hands on those books so I could begin to understand the workings of the farm. When you introduced me to him the other day, I got the notion he wasn't going to be too happy to have me looking over his shoulder. I hope he didn't diss me, leave on purpose so he didn't have to deal with me."

Isabelle laughed softly. "Well, I told you he was a control freak." More seriously, she continued. "But if this is his idea of maintaining control, we'll put a stop to that." She contemplated AJ's new look. "Since you're all dressed up in your new duds, let's go have brunch at the country club. It's a lovely drive about thirty minutes away. You'll get a chance to see some of the countryside, and they've got a wonderful buffet. I'll tell Clara not to fix us anything." She stood from behind her desk without waiting for AJ's response. "I'll grab the umbrella and meet you at the car in about ten minutes, okay?"

"Sure," AJ said, hoping her insecurity didn't show. She'd never been in a country club and could only imagine what to expect. *Old ladies in feathered hats like Isabelle wears? Extra forks and spoons I won't know when to use. High-society girls looking down on me like those stuck-up sorority girls at Tech? Lord, when I tell Alice where I been, she's going to tell me I'm getting above my raising.*

⟋

The Hadleigh Road Country Club's main clubhouse sat a good mile off the highway through acres of a golf course with the most manicured grass AJ had ever seen. Even with all Eddie's hard work, Langford Hall didn't hold a candle to this. Here, it hadn't rained at all. AJ wasn't surprised, however. She'd often seen that back home. It would be pouring in town and not even cloudy by the time she arrived home.

As they crossed the gently rolling terrain, AJ spotted a bank of tennis courts on her right with white-clad women intently hunched over the clay surface in anticipation of their opponents' volleys. In front of the low portico that marked the clubhouse entrance, Isabelle pulled into the first parking space she found. AJ surveyed the low brick building that spread across the knoll. Six abandoned golf carts rested in the lot set aside for them like parked horses waiting for their riders to return. Two uniformed young men opened the carved double doors as Isabelle and AJ approached.

"Welcome to Hadleigh Road, Ms. Collins. Good to have you with us today."

Isabelle nodded. "Boys," she said, her voice a singsong greeting. Mimicking Isabelle, AJ nodded at the two African Americans as well, but said nothing. *Boys? That's demeaning. Those guys could be in college.* In the foyer, a black woman wearing a starched pink dress stood in what looked to AJ like a closet. The sign over the door read CLOAKROOM. *Don't hardly need that today. It's in the seventies.* To AJ the foyer smelled stuffy, like old dust trapped in the damask draperies, overstuffed chairs, and thick Persian carpet. Isabelle marched ahead into the dining room, nodding or waving to acquaintances as they went. The club's maître d' crossed the room to meet them. She, too, was African American, and wore a gray uniform so stiff AJ wondered how her arms could bend.

"Good morning, Ms. Collins. Where would you like to sit? By the windows?"

"That would be fine. I'm sure my guest, Mrs. Porter, would enjoy that view of the course. Thank you."

AJ turned hesitantly as the woman pulled her chair out for her; then she smiled at AJ. This wasn't something she was at all used to. On the other hand, Isabelle seemed to expect it as she waited until the woman returned to her side of the table.

"This is really pretty, Isabelle. You must come here a lot. Everybody seems to know you." AJ looked around the richly appointed room, which now swarmed with guests being shown to their linen-covered tables.

"I used to come here often with Jack. It was one of his favorite places to eat. On the nights Clara was off, he always ate here since he didn't know how to boil water." She chuckled. "Most of the time he invited me merely for companionship, of course."

AJ thought she detected a slight blush creeping across the older woman's face, though it was hard to tell under her omnipresent hat. As Isabelle spread her napkin on her lap, AJ leaned in more closely against the chatter that had suddenly filled the room.

"Tell me about him. Would I have liked him?"

Before Isabelle could answer, a black waiter, also uniformed, approached and greeted Isabelle. "Good afternoon, Ms. Collins. Can I get you a cocktail before you order? Ma'am?" His eyes swept to include AJ in the question.

"Good morning, Manny. Good to see you again. AJ, would you like a glass of wine or something stronger? I usually have a glass of wine."

AJ paused. "I'm not much of a wine drinker, but I'll try whatever you're having. Thanks."

Isabelle ordered them both a glass of pinot noir, which AJ had never even heard of.

"Who is your guest, Ms. Collins? I don't believe I've seen her before?"

"Manny, this is AJ Porter. She's the new owner of Langford Hall, or she will be soon. I suspect this won't be the last time she'll come to the club." AJ blushed as Isabelle talked about her as if she weren't there.

Manny then turned to her and smiled courteously. "It's a pleasure to meet you. I hope to serve you often, with or without Ms. Collins."

"Thank you," AJ said. While that last phrase sounded to AJ as if he were flirting, she soon realized it was probably the way he talked to every stranger to the club. She'd sure never heard such a pleasant greeting from a West Virginia waiter, and she had to admit it was nice.

"Before I get your drinks, will you be having the brunch buffet, or would you like to order from the menu?"

"What's your pleasure, AJ?"

AJ opted for the buffet, thinking she'd be more likely to know what she was eating than if she had to order from the menu without knowing the names of some of the dishes. Manny gave them the option to get their food while he got their drinks. Isabelle said she had eaten only a croissant and coffee for breakfast and that she was hungry, so AJ agreed, and the pair of women headed to the buffet. As they crossed the room, AJ realized she hadn't seen a single white waiter.

Wonder if all the staff's black? Bet there ain't a black waiter in all of Fayette County. Hell, I ain't sure there're any blacks there period. Sure ain't any on Turkey Knob. Looks like they got a corner on the jobs here. Carryover from slavery, likely. Isabelle's Southern roots show when she talks to black folks. Not sure I can ever get used to that.

There were so many food choices on the long buffet that AJ's head spun. The mixture of smells could have caused a migraine in someone sensitive to scents. To AJ it was heavenly. She'd never seen so much food in one place. Scrambled eggs, an egg casserole with something green in it, and a made-to-order omelet station; bacon, sausage, and ham; fresh fruit trays with some varieties AJ couldn't identify; pancakes, French toast, a waffle-maker with two huge bowls nearby—one full of whipped cream, the other with strawberries—as well as the pitcher of batter; biscuits, croissants, sweet rolls, and an array of spreads for the biscuits more extensive than on the grocery shelf at home. In front of each heated chafing dish or chilled tray stood a small hand-lettered label in a silver stand. AJ walked around the tables twice, trying to decide between the French toast and an omelet.

Just as she lined up for an omelet, Isabelle motioned for her to step out of line and join her near the coffee station. As she approached, Isabelle said, "AJ, I want you to meet some of the gals from our little town." Two thirty-something bottle-blondes stood next to Isabelle, half-filled plates in hand. In AJ's estimation, both wore too much makeup and one needed a touch-up of her dye job.

"AJ Porter, this is Juliette Jarrett," she said, placing her hand on the arm of the one wearing an apricot cotton sweater and madras plaid slacks. "And this is Bunny Watson," she said, turning to the other, plumper girl. "Both have lived in Hadleigh all their lives and can introduce you to nearly everyone in town."

Juliette laughed, then extended her hand and gave AJ a limp handshake. "I don't know about everyone. The Junior Leaguers, sure. But Bunny knows the rest." She laughed again.

AJ turned to Bunny, the one whose brown roots had crept a good half-inch into the blond waves cascading from her part, and offered her hand. "Glad to meet you both. Isabelle's been telling me I need to get off the farm and meet some folks. I hardly been here long enough to find my way around the farm, and I ain't . . . uh . . . haven't tackled the town, yet." The two women shot each other sideway glances.

"Where y'all from, Mrs. Porter?" asked Juliette. "Your accent sure isn't one we hear much around here. Is it Tennessee? Southwestern Virginia?"

"Nope, I'm from a town in West Virginia you probably never heard of called Turkey Knob?" Her voice rose into a question mark.

"Is that near Roanoke?" asked Bunny. "I've got cousins there."

There it is, the same old shit I've heard all my life.

"No, it's West 'by God' Virginia. It's a different state, *Bunny*." She emphasized the girl's name, thinking it too childish for a grown woman. Bunny seemed oblivious to her tone, but AJ could see both young women now wore embarrassed but somewhat dismissive expressions.

You think West Virginia is so damn backward that no one from there would possibly go to a country club. How does that give you the right to ignore West Virginia as a real state? Damn!

"Oh, right. Sorry, hon," she muttered, as AJ stared her down.

Isabelle, trying to cover the *faux pas* and AJ's obvious disgust, interrupted. "AJ is the heir of Langford Hall. She'll be taking over its management as soon as she learns the ropes."

The girls stole another condescending glance at each other, which AJ caught again. It was patently clear they didn't consider her—a hillbilly from a backwoods state—capable.

"Bless your heart. That's a big job, especially for someone who isn't from around here. Good luck. You're going to need it," said Juliette, pretending to sound sorry for AJ.

AJ's voice cracked with anger. "Oh, I think I can manage just fine. I been running a farm in West Virginia for eight years. Langford Hall ain't so different, you know, just bigger. Now, excuse me, but I'm hungry, and I want to get an omelet before they're all gone."

With that, she left Isabelle and the blondes and returned to the line. Isabelle flushed slightly. "I'm sorry. You ought to know West Virginians are very sensitive about their home state. After all, they *did* become a state nearly two hundred years ago. Enjoy your breakfast."

As she left the now speechless girls and joined AJ in the omelet line, Isabelle could see AJ was fuming.

"Stupid girls. Why in the hell is West Virginia still looked down on? You can't make political jokes about Muslims, or blacks, or whatever. But it's still okay to think of us as stupid hillbillies. They're the stupid ones. They don't even know it's a different state. It's ridiculous. Everyone I meet away from home thinks we marry our cousins, drink moonshine for lunch, and go barefoot all the time. I'm sorry I lost it, but damn, I just get sick of it."

"Not everyone here is like Juliette and Bunny; believe me. I'm sorry. Truly. If I'd known, I'd have avoided them instead of drawing you over. Let's forget them and enjoy our breakfast. Okay?"

AJ agreed, but she couldn't help brooding throughout the meal about her introduction to Hadleigh's society. *Geez, if everyone's like those bitches, I ain't never gonna like it here.*

As AJ chewed silently, Isabelle tried to resurrect the earlier mood. "You were asking about Jack before Manny came over. Yes, I think you'd have liked him very much. And I know he'd have liked you, especially your spunk. He'd have been as furious as you were at their stupidity and their lack of tact."

"Really? Gosh, I thought you'd be furious at me. And that I'd embarrassed the *family.*" She made air quotes as she said *family* because she still didn't consider herself part of it.

"Honey, what you said is nothing compared to some of the shenanigans others in this family have pulled. We're . . . I mean they're not all high and mighty like you might think. I mean, look at Langford. He owned slaves. That's not so admirable. And Robert, the brother of young Eli? As I said before, he was a real bastard. Maybe now that Tom will be gone awhile, you ought to read that slave journal. You'll see what real bigotry is."

⤚ Chapter Eight ⤙

With little to do but read, AJ went downstairs late the next morning. When she asked to see the slave journal, Isabelle grinned. "Actually, I'm going to bring you the whole box of stuff. That ought to keep you more than occupied while Tom is gone. And they'll be a lot more interesting than the financial reports, that's for sure."

"What all is in there?"

"Well, besides the slave journal there's Ben Hutchinson's war journal and Molly's diary. Old deeds, some personal letters from way back. Plus, the letters between Ben and Molly while he was gone. Her name was short for Margaret. Margaret Elizabeth."

"And whose daughter was she? I'm trying to keep this family straight." AJ laughed.

"She was the great-granddaughter of Eli's *bad* brother, Robert. The one I called a bastard. Maybe the apple didn't fall far from that tree." Both women laughed. "Her father was named Richard, though. He and Reeves were twins."

AJ frowned. "You lost me," she said.

"Sorry. I'm confusing you, I know. I'll find you the family tree so you can fit all the players in their respective decades or centuries," Isabelle said, partially as a mental note to herself.

"I always thought a twin sister would be so cool," AJ said.

When Isabelle failed to respond, AJ continued. "Okay, so, where do I start? The letters?"

"Wherever you want to. I'll put the box on your desk while you eat breakfast."

AJ thanked her and headed toward the smell of fresh biscuits.

When she returned with a mug of coffee, she found a banker's box on her desk. Near the top were a small bundle of ribbon-tied letters, a floral clothbound diary, and a journal about the size of a child's composition book. The diary's leather lock-tab showed signs of wear, but it was open and looked like it had been forced that way. The journal, which she guessed Ben had carried throughout the war, was stained and dirty. On its cream-linen cover were a liberty bell, a pilot's insignia, and the words *A Wartime Log*. She moved those aside, as well as the yellowed envelopes from long ago, until she found what had intrigued her since Mulgrew mentioned it—the slave journal. AJ carefully lifted out the tattered book.

It might have been linen-covered at one time, as well, but only one reinforcing leather corner and the cardboard under the binding remained, and it was peeling at the edges. Through the open spine she could see the cords holding the well-worn volume together. As she carefully placed it on the desk, a letter fluttered to the floor. Curious, she picked it up and saw elegant, deeply slanting but slightly shaky handwriting that had faded to sepia. Inexplicably, she began to read it aloud.

> My dearest Robert,
> As you must be most painfully aware, I have struggled since last winter to recover from the

grippe then contracted. Unfortunately, I fear it will be the cause of my demise.

Therefore, being of Sound mind and of the Current belief that it is Wrong to hold Negroes in Bondage, I do hereby Convey in the strongest terms my desire for the Manumission of all Negros at Langford Hall upon the occasion of my Death. Further, you are to Provide each with the Sum of $20 to assist in their Resettlement. However, should any Negro desire to Remain at Langford Hall, you are to pay them fair Wages commensurate to their Work.

As to the Negro fellow known as Moses, he is to be given the Sum of $50 for such Resettlement or allowed to stay at good Wages, if he desires. Furthermore, he is in Possession of the Morgan family Ring previously worn by your brother and my dear Son, Eli. He is forthwith allowed to Keep and wear it, as I awarded it to him for his Bravery while serving Eli on the battlefield at Cold Harbor.

Further, when the aforesaid Moses departs this earth, his remains are to be buried in the Morgan family Plot at Langford Hall.

While my last Will and Testament fully describes the settlement of my entire Estate, these wishes were not included. Therefore, I take Pen in hand to record my aforesaid wishes this day, the 18th of May, 1865, in the County of Dillard, in the State of Virginia.

Your most loving father,

Forrest Elias Morgan, Sr.

AJ sat back, stunned as a chill ran up her spine. *This letter is more than a hundred years old and one of my ancestors wrote it. If he thought slavery was so damn wrong, why hadn't he freed his slaves earlier? He certainly should have. I wonder how Eli died?* She opened the frayed cover. Inside, the handwriting was the same as in the letter, but the words were more perfectly formed. Bold letters that were no doubt black when they were inscribed announced that the journal was "The Property of Elias F. Morgan, Owner of Langford Hall." For a moment, AJ studied the strong hand, wondering exactly what kind of man this ancestor had been.

Turning the page she saw that the book was a columned journal. Beginning in 1826, it listed farm purchases by date, seller, product purchased, and amount paid. The wording of the entries was odd, unlike the way AJ would have written them. *"21 June; to Joseph Knox; 1 bag seed; $.15." "To Joseph Knox . . ."* sounded to AJ as if Morgan had sold the seed, not bought it. On some pages, a child had penciled crude drawings of ladies in Victorian dresses and arithmatic sums over the entries. Others recorded recipes—one for a poltice to be used on the livestock—and still others held directions for bleeding a sick animal.

Fascinated, she continued turning pages until she came to one with different headings: *Date of Acquisition, Name, Age, Value.* Below the double red lines under these headings was a list of first names only: *Daisy, Tom, Henry, Peter, Moses, Sarah, Rachel*—more than twenty in all. Some were mere children, twelve or thirteen years old when they were bought; others were in their prime. Concrete evidence, not just the tales Isabelle had shared, that her family, at least one branch, had owned other human beings and made them work without pay or any hope of living out their own dreams. It made her half sick. What struck her most deeply was that they were listed as property like she would have listed her tractor, plows, or tools, if she'd made a similar inventory. Although their purchase price was high, they had no last names—no identity other than as part of the equipment. Yet they must have been the most valuable part of running the farm. *God, that's awful.* One, Peter, had cost $800.

No wonder my granddaddy left. Probably hated the stain of having family who used to treat people like they was cattle or machinery. Makes me ashamed of them.

Each subsequent page looked to AJ as if it were an annual inventory of Morgan's slaves. Sometimes a name would disappear, and another would take its place. *Did he sell them or did they die?* The last entry listed the year as 1866. *I thought the Emancipation Proclamation was signed before that.* She reached for her phone and Googled Emancipation Proclamation. Talking to the room again, she said, "That old bastard. Isabelle was right. He didn't free his slaves when he should have!" Then she noticed that year's entries were in a different hand, no longer graceful, but back-slanted as if the writer might have been a southpaw.

"If that's Robert's writing, neither of them obeyed the law; plus, Robert disobeyed his father's wishes, too. No wonder Isabelle called him a bit of a bastard."

I'm glad granddaddy came to Turkey Knob. I know Paw never had nary a bad word for black men. Bet he learned it from his paw. Proud of him, but not the slaveholders. Hate that.

The next few pages were blank save for more childish scribbles, but by now she couldn't put it down. Suddenly, she saw a full page of writing—not journal entries, but a narrative of some sort. The writing had changed again, this time to tidy printing. Flipping the page, she began to read again.

⌒ CHAPTER NINE ⌒

Didn't wanna come. But, here I is. Massa brung me. He signed up with the militia. Say it were what he had to do. Say he be a proud Son of Virginia, and if Virginia be fightin, he joinin up. Say all the mens was fightin to keep havin things their way. No Federals gonna tell them how to do they business. And if the Yankees was comin to Virginia to fight, he gonna defends her. Tell me if'n I wants to keep a warm bed, I best be prayin the South wins. Say, Yankees win, they gonna turn me out so's I got no home. Then he say I'se goin with him. Couldn't tell him no, no how, on account of I'se his. Now we's out in this field, I shore wish I'se back home.

Couple times we got to go back when we was close by. But it cause me no end of grief to leave again. Ever time, my sweet Sary laid on my neck and cried, and my boy Thomas hung on my legs like a fox hound on a catch. I'se afraid ole

Massa have 'em both whipped for takin on so. Might've been better if I hadn't gone back a'tall.

We got here that first day 'bout suppertime. Massa ridin his sorrel mare, but I had to walk near ten mile from over at 'Canicsville pullin his supplies. Long the road, bunch of slaves standin by a fence holler at us, but we never answer. All that marchin make it too hard to hear. Them horses kick up dust so thick I feels like I been eatin it. Our 'federate boys in high spirits 'cause they drove back them Yankees over there. But ever time they commence fightin I feels all mixed up. I doesn't want Massa to git kilt, but if'n them Yankees wins, I be a free man. 'Fore that we fought near home, at Spotslvany Courthouse. Same thing. Mixed up. I loves Massa Eli, but I shore wants my freedom. It were a fearsome fight, but they gave them Yankees the scare. When I knowed they's near by home, I'se afraid Yankees'd hurt my sweet Sary, or take the animals and food, but Massa say they's too far off.

Now they say we's at Cold Harbor outside Richmond 'bout a mile from Gaines Mill. Some says they's haints still round here from that fight few years back. They's a tavern nearby, but no one's lookin to go there. Be shot for a deserter, most like. Soldiers found a clearin in the woods where I set up Massa Elias's tent. After I cooks his supper, I found me a place to throw my bedroll. Good thing it near summer now, cause us slaves gots to sleep on the ground. I puts my bedroll a piece from the campfire, so's I be a bit cooler, but I'se still hot. All them soldiers got tents, but we's lucky to have a blanket to sleep on. Massa Eli gots a cot, so he be all set. Back home, I sleeps comfortable, cause my bed's in young Eli's room. Out here, we gots skeeters, and ticks and they's bitin somethin awful. Gots welps all over my arms and back. I'se wore out. Between scratchin, pickin off ticks, and some fool dog barkin out yonder, I don't reckon I'll sleep a wink.

Massa Eli 'bout two years younger'n me, but he still my Massa. I'se lots stronger'n him too. S'pose that's on account I chop wood, haul water, and tend his slop jar while he done nothin but read. He a fine one for readin. Taught me, too, but never let on to his pa. Let me ride he horse too.

Once Tom, the overseer, caught me tryin to read a letter from my mama. Laid into me with his whip. 'Fore he could blister my back, Massa Eli come runnin. Grab his arm. Say, "Don't you lay a hand on Moses. He mine to boss, not yours. You whip him, I'll tell my Pa." He wink at me and shoo me off. Tom so mad he kick a chicken plumb to kingdom come when he leave. Sometime I sneaks and reads Gramma's Bible. Don't know why she gots it. Cain't read herself.

She a house slave but she walk tall like a queen. When I'se just a young'n she told me that story of baby Moses, say I'se just like him, cause my Massa took me into his big house to live with his boy, Eli. My gramma say that was like bein in the Pharaoh's house and someday I'd grow up like him and take my peoples to freedom. She used to sing to me about it. We be sittin on a bench and she be rockin back and forth singin. Tears be droppin on my face the way she held me so close. I could see inside her mouth when she sing. "Tell ole Pharaoh, let my peoples go." She had a pretty, high pitch voice, but it got sorta trembly when she sang. Her eyes look like they did when I'd done somethin bad and she about to switch me.

AJ swallowed hard. She could almost hear Moses telling it. She took a deep breath, wished she had another cup of coffee, and continued.

Massa Eli let me read the news sometimes. He never mind if'n I listen to he talk with other white mens, neither. Most often they cover they mouth and talks sideways like they don't wants me to know what they's sayin. But when I be servin dinner, they acts like I'se not even there. Then I listens real good. When Massa at that university them boys talkin bout this war all the time. After they attack that fort, them boys whoop like banshees how they gonna whip them damn Yankees 'fore breakfast next day. They braggin they goin fight to keep us slaves. Some of 'em went off and join up that very night.

Didn't join up hisself, ol' Massa. He still home. Paid the fee for some other poor soul to git shot up in his place so's he could stay and run the plantation. Run his niggas, more like it. He a harsh man who think nothin of gittin out the whip. Forrest Elias Morgan. Such a fine name shouldn't belong to such a mean man. Gramma say not 'pose to hate, but I comes close to hatin that man. He a proud one, too, the old Massa. All puff' up boastin to guests all time bout how Massa Thomas Jefferson come to he house when he granddaddy was alive. Bout how Massa Jefferson play the fiddle for dances. And old Massa all time showin off a fine pair of lady's white silk shoes he say Dolley Madison done left behind when her feets hurt from dancin so hard. Magine havin enough shoes to leave 'em like a dirty rag.

She stopped again. *Were those the same shoes Isabelle showed me? Good Lord, she wasn't kidding.*

First pair boots I recollect gittin smell like a fine saddle. I'se 'bout ten. So proud to finally have shoes. Ever New Year's Day, Massa give out new shoes. Young Massa say I'se gittin some that year. Said time I look like a young gentleman's proper slave. We's all lined up a-waitin our turn. Tom the overseer did the givin-out while old Massa stood on the porch, grinnin and watchin. Gots mine, runned over to the edge of the porch, and pull 'em on. They was way too big. I came near to cryin. I'se afraid to say anythin, so Gramma stuff 'em with rags.

Still, if'n I had my way about it, I'd druther stayed on the place, where I could be with my wife and boy. If'n I done stay behind without young Massa, I wouldn't had house duties no more. They'd of put me out to the fields, instead. Since I been workin like a field hand anyway, didn't help me none to come. I'se dug breas'works 'til my shoulders groan and my arms feels stiff like tree stumps. Now some fella over yonder coughin like his chest gonna splode. Sleep gonna be hard to come by.

We's rousted out fore dawn the next day. They's a cavalry battle last night over to the crossroads 'bout a mile away. Our boys tried to push back them Yankees but didn't make no ground. Say some got kilt, some hurt, but Massa Eli, he fine. Grant headed our way, tryin to take Richmond, so we'uns gots to git these breas'works done lickety-split. We's dug 'em under the trees a ways from camp. Look like them Yankees gonna have a bad time crossin that field yonder. Look like cows done chewed up all the brush. Open flat field out there. Look as big as Massa's 'backy fields.

Me and three other slaves out here in the woods again cuttin down saplins to pile a'top the breas'works so's our soldiers be hid good from them Yankees. I don't reckon that'll stop 'em, but it might slow 'em down some. One of them niggas complain all yesterday sayin we don't gots be out here 'cause Lincoln done sign some paper sayin we's free. Say he sign it last year. I never heard such, but if that be true, why they still here, I wants to know? I ask the one called Josiah. He look to be older'n me but he work hard. He say he been some Richmond family's butler 'fore the war.

Josiah, he a skinny nigga, but he gots a fine pair boots. He start up fussin again today. Talkin 'bout that free paper again.

"If'n you's so free, how's come you ain't left? How's come you still here workin like a field hand?" I say, restin on my axe.

"Ain't gonna be for long," Josiah answer. He carryin a armful of branches to the breas'works so it hard to hear him.

"What you mean?" I say, walkin toward him.

Other fella, Jacob, say, "Hush your mouth, Josiah." He keep swingin that ax, talkin 'tween strokes so's the soldiers won't pay us no mind.

Josiah never stop, but he say, "You don't know dis nigga. He might tell he Massa."

"Lord, no. Wouldn't do nary thing," I say. "You runnin? Where you fixin to go? Canady? You gots peoples up there?"

"Me, Jacob, and Tobias, over yonder, we's leavin tonight. We's thinkin on joinin the Union Army. Say they's just up the road a piece. They lets us slaves fight 'stead a workin for a Massa. We's free men. Why we still slavin? Come along, Moses. You's free too," Josiah say.

I reach down to git the tree Jacob cut, head low to the ground. "Lord, I cain't do that. If'n I runs, my wife and boy be left behind. Don't you gots family?"

"We all do, but we's gonna send for 'em when the war's over," say Jacob. "That's why we's runnin. We wants our children raised free."

"You decide. Let us know by supper. We's leavin when it git good and dark."

"I'll think on it," I say. And I did. All day. Ever swing of that axe remind me of all the whippins I seed. I thinks on how ole Tom look like he take pleasure in them whippins. How them slaves looks half dead when they cut down.

Bein free! What a sweet dream. No more fetchin for Massa Eli, a'feared of one a them whippins from Tom. My girl free to take care our house 'stead of some white woman's. Free to have my own land someday. My boy growed up a free man. Sweet Jesus! I heerd tales of some who fled north, how they found work in Boston, sent for they family. They say niggas treated regl'r up there. Just like white folks.

But they had help along the way. Didn't run off to fight no war. Don't know a soul up north. Where I find work? I 'spose I could hire out. It be hard. How I lets my Sary know where I'se gone? I know old Massa, he send the paterollers after me, hear I'se gone. Done that once. Peter, big, strong mule driver ran north. Next mornin old Massa send for the paterollers. They come with them mangy bloodhounds a'sniffin round. Two days later, they's back. Gots Peter in chains. Tom, that bastard, whip him till the skin on he back striped like blood raw meat. Then he pours salt water on it. Still hears Peter scream in my dreams. Now, if'n I runs, he whip Sary, too, or worser. I'se sure of it. Make my blood run cold. He be thinkin she know where I gone. I might be free, but it be harder on my gal. Then who gonna raise my boy? In a way, I'se sorry he be borned. All I did was make another slave.

AJ's hand flew to her mouth. She gagged. *Ugh. Gross.* It made her blood run cold. *God, how could someone be so cruel? Poor Moses. I can see why he'd be sorry he had a child.*

How I know them fellas is right, besides? If'n we runs, and they ain't no papers sayin we's free, then we's dead niggas. How we even know where they army is? What if they army don't wants us? Could be runnin in the dark for nothing. Shot for the enemy. If'n we does join up, could git kilt just like them Yankees we kilt at Spotslvany. We's settin up pretty good defenses hereabouts for our men. What if them Yankees lose the war? We be right back bein slaves. It sure go worser for us then.

Still, it don't seem right, me bein name Moses and all. I suppose to help free my peoples, not fight to keep 'em slaves. I 'members my gramma tellin me 'bout Moses. He don't have it easy, no how. He done what he 'sposed to do to free his peoples. He even kill a man and had to run. If'n I really be like Moses, I'd a kilt ole Tom long ago, but I'se too skeered at what he do to my Sary. Bible Moses don't have no Sary. I does know how to shoot, tho. If'n them Yankees gives me a chance, I be a good soldier. Might help my peoples more by fightin. Might git new boots, too. Better rations. When this war be over, I send for Sary and my boy. We starts a new life. Sweet Jesus!

By time I gone fix supper for Massa Eli, I'd made up my mind. We don't gots much to eat but fatback and biscuits. Still, Massa Eli lets me eat with him. Most other slaves goes off somewheres else to eat. Lord, I'se hungry. Massa say he plumb wore out marchin and fightin all day around the crossroads. Say long 'bout suppertime, the Yankees back off. He laugh, say they musta got hungry and gone back to eat. After supper, I asked if'n I could take a walk and Massa Eli allow it. I went lookin for Josiah. Found him out in the field across from where I been campin. He and Jacob settin by the cook fire, pokin it with a stick. Josiah look up. "You made up you mind?"

"I done thought on it all day, and I gonna go with you," I say.

"You be a free man by mornin," Josiah say. He look hard at me. "Didn't let on to no other niggas, did you? It go hard if'n you did."

"Lord no. You take me for a fool?" I say.

He say, "Go git you bedroll, some biscuits and water, if'n you kin find some, and when it good and dark meet us where we's cuttin trees this mornin. Don't you tell them other niggas. Hear? Too many folks make a ruckus. Yankees might not take whole passel niggas, neither."

Where I gonna git biscuits, I thinks? Ain't gonna steal 'em from Massa. I never steal from him 'fore. I ain't gonna start now. I gonna have to go without, I reckons. Back at camp a bunch a slaves sittin round the campfire singin like my gramma does. One real black nigga whistlin through his hand, like I seen a old white haired nigga do back home. They's singin, Swing Low, Sweet Chariot. Make me sad to think I might never see my gramma again if'n I runs.

I growed up with her, my gramma. Never knowed my mama. When I'se older, I heerd stories 'bout the Massa and my mama. They say he my real daddy cause I gots light skin and my hair sorta reddish-like. Maybe so. Maybe that why he sold her. Cover up dat shame. Never saw my mama's husband, so it be hard to know if'n I favors him or not. Hard for me to recollect how my mama look, too.

Good Lord, that makes Moses a Morgan, too. He's related to me as much as Mr. Jack is.

One thing I do recollect is how warm her belly feel when I curl up beside her. I tries hard not to think on the day she got sold off. Still, I recollects it sometime at night. The man what come for her was fat and smell like too many flowers. I went and held fast to her legs. Wouldn't let go.

My gramma pull me off and hug me tight so's I couldn't run back to Mama. Gramma was cryin and that set me to cryin. Mama just stood there with her head down, then she climbed in the wagon and they drove away. When she gone, that bed colder'n sleepin on the ground last winter.

I lays down on my blanket, wonderin 'bout what I'se about to do. How I pack up without these other niggas askin questions? It gittin long bout dark and I'se still layin there. Somethin' tell me: "Don't go." It like my gramma tellin me stay out'n the fields when I'se little. I 'members that song I heered when I'se small. "Run, nigga, run; paterollers git you. Run, nigga, run, almost dawn." I kin hear my gramma singin. I gits up. Start walkin toward the trees. I reach the meetin spot but no one there. It good dark. I thinks maybe I cain't see 'em. I whistle low. No answer. I waits and waits. Moon movin across the sky. Smell of wet dirt remind me of plowed fields back home. Them boys don't come. Look like they done left without me. Might be best, I says to myself. I weren't gonna go no way. Came to tell 'em I'se changed my mind. But if'n they was waitin I might'a gone. Might'a been bad tempted to git to freedom.

Next day they say Grant blowed up a bridge over the South Anna and whipped our boys nearby. He holdin Cold Harbor now, but our boys don't plan to give up. Reinforcements come overnight, Massa say. If'n them Yankees come acrost that field yonder, our soldier boys think we win 'cause we's dug in good in that big stand of trees.

Massa move out with his company 'fore dawn to wait for the fightin. He had some biscuits. Say they's mealy, but they have to do. It turn fierce hot dis morning.' Too hot for choppin trees. I'se glad that job done. Sun's already so bright, hurts my eyes to look at the sky. I'se tied a rag 'round my head to keep sweat out'n my eyes.

Massa Eli musta thought dis'd be a bad fight. 'Fore he leave, he sittin on he cot twistin that fancy gold ring he wear. Look like he twist he finger off. Instead he pull the ring off and hold it out to me. He say, "Moses, I wants you to keep this ring 'til I comes back. If'n I don't, if'n I gits kilt, don't let 'em bury me here. Take me home. Give this ring to my daddy. He'll want to pass it on to my little brother, Robert. And if'n I gits shot, don't let me die on that there battlefield. Take me home to die. Promise?" I say, "Massa Eli, I cain't wear that ring. It a family ring b'long only to a Morgan. Lord, don't put a curse on you self. You gonna be just fine. You see." But he say it again. Wouldn't stop 'til I promise. So I did. He been good to me. Leastwise, good as any Massa. I reckon I owes him that. He walk away. I puts it on, and stands there twistin that ring, just like he do.

Spent all day waitin to hear the fightin but it were quiet as a graveyard, 'cept for the rain. Came late in a day. First drops so big put holes in the dust. Look like bullet holes. Then it got right steady. Still quiet. Scary quiet. Make a man wonder where them Yankees are, why they not fightin. Maybe they stayin dry some'ers. 'Long about suppertime, I be thinkin Massa come back, but he never. Then we hear the battle. Sound like thunder rollin down the road. Sometimes feel like ground gonna open up, shake so hard when them mortars land. Fightin so hard, we seen flames shoot through the trees way off. I'se afraid for Massa Eli. 'Fraid I'd have to make good on my promise. I went to Massa's camp to wait, 'fraid he come back hurt.

Long after dark, he drag into camp. Look like a whipped pup. Face all dirty, smeared with ashes and mud, eyes all funny lookin. Look like he lookin at somethin, but not me. Say it were a terrible day. Lots of fellas kilt or shot, but he say he lucky. Say curse didn't work, look like. That the only

thing he say make me know he alright. I ask, "Did we win"?
He say, "Hard to tell." Tomorrow be more of the same, he
'fraid. Sleep don't come easy that night, neither. Dream I
hear fightin, muskets, growlin dogs, Uncle Peter screamin.

Next mornin I goes to camp to cook for Massa Eli. He
gone already. Tents near empty. I find couple biscuits
and wrap 'em up. Figure I'd best find Massa. Be sure he
got somethin to eat. I walks acrost the field tryin to figure
whoro ho be. Dirt's a sea a'mud. In that long stretch of trees
ahead, it quiet. I knowed the trenches be full a soldiers, but
theys quiet as kin be. I gits closer. Under the trees it feel like
eyes everywhere. Like theys haints out there like they say.
I stops. Broad daylight, but it dark under them trees. Lord,
don't look like a good place for this nigga to be. I turns and
runs. Hope Massa taked food along.

When I'se close to my camp a big fuss commence among
the other slaves. I starts runnin thinkin they's a fight, or a
whippin. I gits to the edge of the clearin, see three niggas
a'swingin from the trees. Other slaves tryin to git to 'em,
cut 'em down. Oh, Lord. Don't let it be them boys, I thinks.
I slows down, walks calm like, stand away from the crowd.
They lowers them bodies careful-like to the ground. Shore
'nuf. It Josiah, Jacob and Tom. They been whipped, too, and
flies was already buzzin round. I'se so mad, I'se hot all over.
'Mind me of poor ol' Peter after he whup and left to the ants.
All the slaves talkin, sayin they heerd theys fixin' to run.
I didn't say nothin, but I knewed it to be true. Shore glad I
didn't go along. Lord, Lord! Look like that free paper done
'em no good a'tall.

AJ put the journal down. *Damn! They lynched those poor boys.
All they wanted was freedom. Sounds like shit the Klan did.* Repulsed,
but still curious, she picked it back up. It was like watching a horror

movie; despite the scary parts you kept on because you had to know how it would end.

One nigga, boy been sleepin nearby, holler at me. "Moses, come help us bury these boys. Ain't you got a shovel?" Nodded I did and went to fetch it. Runnin through the mud I thought, gonna be easier to dig this than dry clay. We dug them three graves, tied sticks to make crosses. Then that boy what been singin t'other night sang Jacob's Ladder. Lord, he do have a nice voice. We's quiet. All 'round it quiet. Too quiet. I couldn't git them hung boys out my mind. They's drippin bloody water. T'warn't the first time I seen a hung nigga, though. Old Massa never done such, but when we's marchin, I seen one hung 'long side the road near 'Canicsville. Wondered what he done, figured he been caught stealin. Maybe he try'n run, too. I reckons them soldier bosses hung those slaves out in the open to show all us what happen if'n we tries the same.

I stays mad all time we's buryin them boys. Look like white folks let us be. Them fellas just wants to be free. If'n this war end and that paper real, we's free anyways. Still, look like in a way, my gramma warn me not to go. If'n I ain't heerd that singin remind me of her, I might'a packed up and gone t'other night.

All day we hears shots ever now'n then. Cain't tell who's shootin though. They say sharpshooters on both sides hid in them trees. Make me jump out my skin when I hears them muskets. Some these white mens make they slaves load muskets and the like. Mine don't make me go on the battlefield. Say I'se too valuable to lose. He hunkered down somewhere out 'dere I reckons. I 'spect he's skeered but he never let on 'cept when he ask me to bring him home if'n he die. When I'se 'round the tents this mornin soldiers be writin they names on papers, pinnin 'em to they jackets. Must be 'spectin 'nother fearsome battle. Wonder if Massa done that?

Old Massa be mighty mournful if'n he boy die. Don't know how he take it. Puts great stock in that boy. 'Spects him to take over some day. Massa little brother too young, now. He a mean one, too. Saw he tie a dog's back legs together and then make it run. If'n the South lose, might be nothin to take over. How he run that place with no slaves? We be free! Free to leave. Go north. Look like we leave with nuthin though. If'n we don't gots peoples up there, where we s'pose to go, come to think on it? Where we work? If'n we stays, maybe Massa hire us for pay. Give us our own land. I 'spects he'd be mighty bitter 'bout havin to do that. Ol' Massa, that is. Young Eli think on it better. I recollect he say us slaves could stay for wages. If'n old Massa still runnin' things, likely we be turned out.

It hard to sleep knowin young Massa out there somewhere. I knows he must be hunkered down in the breas'works, but it be hard to say where. They's lots of trenches out there. Fog settle over us 'till I cain't see trees. Middle of the night, awfulest blast wake me. Ground shakin so hard I thinks it might open up. Skeered the livin daylights out me. It plumb pitch black in camp. Over near the trenches it bright as day. Look like trees on fire. Cain't hear myself think, shootin so loud. Cain't hear nothin but cannons and guns. Firing seem like it go on forever. Screams comin from everywhere. Lord, I hope young Massa be safe.

By daybreak, it quiet as a tomb 'cept for a few shots now and then. Fightin seem over, so I figgers Massa Eli come back soon. All day I waits, but no Massa. Long about supper some soldiers comes stragglin in lookin like they seed ghosts. They say it were the worst fight they'd been

in. But no Massa. I gits a empty feelin in my belly wonderin
if he kilt. Would I be free? But them soldiers what made it
back say most the dead be Unions. Say they stacked like
cordwood on the field. I asked round bout Massa, but nobody
know nuthin. If'n he never come back, if'n he dead, I could
just up and leave. Sneak off in the night. Send for Sary and
my boy when I gits North. Be hard, but who look for me?
It be a long time 'fore old Massa come lookin. By then, I be
North. Be free. And if'n what them hung niggas say be right,
I'se already free now.

By dark I figgers Massa be hurt, maybe dead. Make me
feel kindly sad. I'se a'feered to go lookin though. I figgers to
wait 'til mornin. Tryin to sleep, I thinkin 'bout home. It's a
fine place. Massa gots 'bout a thousand acres in Spotslvany
County where he raise tobacco and cotton. That brick house
take two weeks to whitewash ever year 'cause it so big. My
poor Sary don't fare so good. Our cabin don't even gots a
floor. I always worries that I lives better'n her and Thomas.
Ol' Massa mean to everyone but me. Maybe I is his boy. That
make me his oldest, not Eli. Huh! Lot of good it do me, me
bein a nigga. Wonder if houses up north be like Massa's?
They gots plantations there? Kin a body farm up there?
Wonder if they's jobs for niggas?

AJ remembered reading that lots of masters had children by their
slaves. *Poor women had no say-so over what happened to them. Even
old Thomas Jefferson had a slave mistress. How could those old guys
make their own children slaves? That's just wrong. Pisses me off.*

In the mornin Massa still ain't comed back. But them
soldiers what did, say they's still some fighting, so I 'spects
he's just doin his duty. I seed our rations near gone, what
they was left. Guards in camp gittin hungry too. I heerd 'em

speculatin 'bout goin to that tavern to see if they could beg some food. Wondered if they's goin bring us slaves some, too. When they got back say there weren't no food. Unions had strip it clean. So I goes out to find me some berries, maybe some greens to eat with my hardtack. Still gots coffee, praise God.

By afternoon, it so hot we just settin and sweatin.

More boys back in camp today. Say they's dead men all over that field out yonder. Say Lee and Grant won't let nobody go git 'em to bury, neither. That don't make no sense to me. Look like if a body just hurt, they'd want to go git him. Soldiers say neither generals wants to call a cease fire. Be like admittin they lost.

If Massa out there, wounded or dead, his daddy shore want to know. Bring him back either way. I reckon they's countin on me to go git him. Bring him home. But they's still fightin. I kin hear it ever oncet in a while. That no place for this nigga. I ain't come to this war to fight, nor gits myself kilt. I'se just here to cook and build battlements. If'n I'se fightin to free my peoples, like Bible-Moses, that'd be a different kettle of fish. Gittin kilt to keep 'em slaves ain't this nigga's job.

Last night I heerd a few of the other Massas' slaves took off. Figgered they Massa be dead. Said it were they chance to be free. I could do that. I could'a done it days ago, come to think on it. But if'n I had, if'n I did, I'se a'feered I never see my sweet Sary nor my boy Thomas again. Nor my gramma. And this war ain't over, neither. If'n the south win, old Massa send them paterollers after me soon's he kin.

Boss generals finally calls it quits. By noon time, the boys say we kin go find our Massas now. We gots two hours 'fore fightin start again. I sets out with a canteen of water, some rags, and a few berries figgerin he be near starved. Didn't bring no cot nor wagon. I'se afraid all that slow me down. Closer I gets to them trenches, the skeereder I gits. Smell like slaughterin been goin on. Smell like hog guts rottin in the sun. I tie my kerchief across my nose. Hard to breathe. Dust kick up with ever step. Sun blisterin down. Hotter'n hinges of Hades, as my gramma used to say.

I reach one trench, jump in, see soldiers lyin out down in there, look near dyin of thirst or starvation. They's blood on the ground, but they don't look to be too bad hurt. I say, "You know Massa Morgan? He with Virginia Militia?" Two soldier boys look up, shake they head, say, "You gots water?" I give one a drink, but I worries I run out 'fore I finds Massa.

I trots through the trenches, seem like for miles. They's more'n one row, some places. Keep askin. One soldier say he think he on the south flank. Don't know where that is, so I just keeps goin. Smell is somethin awful. Cain't see the battlefield. Prolly best. Oncet I spot a body on top the breas'works. He so swole up he the size of a horse. I ain't never seen such. I stops and pukes. Feel bad for them boys nearby but I cain't helps it.

Zigzag over to 'nother trench. Still cain't find Massa, so I starts hollerin. "Massa Eli, if'n you's out here, holler so's I kin find you. Massa Eli Morgan. Massa Eli. Massa Eli. Lord, where is you?" I hears a man say, "He down here. He shot. Keep on comin." I runs now, steppin on soldiers' mess, almost trip on one soldier's leg. I holler, "Sorry," but I keeps runnin. "Massa, I'se comin. Hold on. I be there directly."

Finally, I hears he voice. "That you Moses? Lord, I thought you'd left me." I sees him laid up against the trench walls. Leg all twisted, bloody. Look like it shot half off. He gots a belt tight round it. I drop down beside him. "Lordy Massa, I wouldn't leave you, but I'se here now. They never let us come finds you. You gonna be fine. I git you out here, git you back home." After I say it, I wonders just how I gonna do that. Gots no wagon, no cot to put him on 'til we back at camp. He shore cain't walk on that leg. I guess I'se gonna drag him on a blanket.

I lifts him out the trench and he scream, "My leg, my leg." I ties a clean rag 'round he leg, but it smell. 'Nother soldier, shot in one arm, help me drag Massa onto a blanket with t'other. He screamin all time. I makes a sling out it and tie one end round my waist. Take a hank of rope and wrap Massa up inside like a dead hog. He quiet now. Must'a passed out. Stood up to get my bearins. Then I sees that battlefield out 'cross the breas'works. Dead Union soldiers all swole up lyin all over the ground, stacked on each other like a wall of bodies far as I kin see. I even sees a arm in a ditch. Just a arm. It so black, I done thought it were a nigga's. Grass soaked with blood. Dried red puddles. Began to gag again, but there ain't nothin left to puke. Put my kerchief over my nose again and start walkin. It were a sight I never wants to see again.

Walk what seem like a hour draggin Massa. I worries I'se hurtin him worser ever bump we hits, but he don't say nuthin. Most likely still passed out. When we gits to camp, I holler, "Where's a doc? Massa need a doc real bad." One soldier jerk he thumb yonder toward back of camp. Holler, "They's a field hospital set up beside the road." I keeps walkin through camp, but they's wounded soldiers layin all over the field. Lord, it hot. When I sees a tent near the road, I holler, "Massa here need a doc. He shot bad in the leg. Kin somebody help him?" No one answer, so I drags him clean up to the tent. "Massa here need help," I says to one man's back. He leanin over a boy on the ground what gots no arm. Wailin' for he mama. 'Nother man in a coat what should'a been white, but's mostly red, point out in the field a piece and say, "Just put him over there; we'll get to him."

"No sir," I says. "I ain't leavin him. He my Massa. I takes him over there, like you say, but I'se stayin with him."

"Do as you like," man say, but he never look at me. Soldiers all over cryin out. Wantin water, somethin for pain. He pay 'em no mind. Just keep talkin to that boy on the ground with no arm.

I takes Massa to the edge of the tent, figger'n close by folks git help first. I unwrap Massa, and he groan. I lift up he head, rest it on my knee. "Massa Eli? You don't worry none now; we's at the hospital." Massa eyes blink open; he whisper, "Water, give me a drink, Moses." I try, but he choke on it. Commence groanin when the coughin make that leg hurt worser. I sits on the ground, put Massa's head in my lap and wait.

Long 'bout suppertime, doctor fellow come round, look at Massa's leg, say, "That leg has got to come off. It's infected bad, might turn gangrene and we've got no sulfa to treat it. You best let me take it off 'fore that happens." Massa hear that, he scream, "No, you're not going to take my leg. I won't let you. Moses, get me home to my Pa. He's got good doctors. They can treat it. Please, Moses, don't let 'em."

"Massa, I'se 'fraid you die if'n you pay no mind to that doctor. You gits gangrene, I cain't help you none."

He say, "Moses, I rather die at home or on the road than lose my leg. If'n I die, I don't blame you none. Let's go!"

Oh, Lord, don't let him die. AJ wanted to skip to the end of the journal. She knew he had died during the war, but hoped it wasn't this way. She forced herself to continue.

He grab my hand so hard that ring he give me cuttin my finger. "Lord, Massa, you ask a hard thing of this nigga, but I do as you say. I go fetch our wagon. Be back quick as Jack Robinson."

'Fore I leaves, I drags him outta that hard sun and puts him under a tree. I takes off my kerchief and ties it to a branch sos I can find him when I gits back. I leaves him there, runs across camp to fetch the wagon. I'se tryin to harness up Massa's mare, but she don't take too kindly to the traces. Boy nearby say, "Trade you that mare for my mule. She no pack horse. She ain't gonna pull that thing. You needs my mule. He pull good." I 'spects Massa Eli wear me out I gives away that fine mare, so I says, "No, thanks." Told him Massa put great store by that horse. Took me three tries, and she near bolt oncet, but she finally settle down. I figger if'n I rides her, she do all right.

Massa sleepin when I gits back. I hates to wake him, but knows we got to git movin 'fore it full dark. "Massa, I gots to put you in that wagon," I say. He bolt up, act like he gonna stand up, climb in. Oncet he move, he yell out and fall back. 'Nother slave see us, come over to help. We lift Massa inside and he pass out.

One ol' boy grab my arm, say, "You leave him die on the road, you'se free, boy. You know that, right?"

"Reckon I cain't do that," I says. "He countin on me."

He let go just a shakin he head. Once I'se mounted, I does wonder what happen to ole Moses if'n Massa do die. Paterollers come for me, thinkin' I'se stole that mare and this fine ring? I studies it shinin on my finger with that helmet and all them fancy words on it. Wonder what it say and why he never asked for it back? Guess he done forgot.

We travel 'bout three hour. Massa talk some then fall asleep. Say he think we's goin lose this war. Pass one or two boys in gray limpin home. Maybe they know'd it, too. One shout, "We's done for. Gimme ride!" I hollers, "Gots no room," and keeps on goin. Long 'bout dark I pulls the wagon off the road to a stand of trees. Let the mare graze, but I'se a'feered to turn her loose. Leave Massa in the wagon too. He wake up when we stop, start to groanin. Say, "Moses, how soon we be home?" I say, "Lord, Massa, we's just gittin started. Might take couple days."

I digs in the wagon for a biscuit, and hand it to him. But he wave it away. "You eat it, Moses. I'm not hungry," he say. "Lord, Massa, you gotta eat, keep up you strength." But he shake he head. "You eat it. You got to get me home." I did, then crawl under the wagon to sleep a bit.

Woke sudden-like when I hears the horse whinny. She dancin round in the traces. "Lord, don't let no one steal that mare," I says to myself. Massa hear it too, grab he pistol, try to sit up. He cry out, fall back. I jumps up, take Massa's pistol, and move quiet-like to the mare. Cain't see nuthin in the dark; don't hear nuthin neither. I puts a arm around that mare's neck and whisper to her, like I seen Massa do. She calm down directly, and take a bite of grass. I tuck the pistol in my belt. Should'a kept it there all along. Seem like Massa must'a pass out. He ain't sayin nuthin. Hard to sleep after that.

'Fore dawn, we's on the road again. Massa too quiet. He moan some, 'specially when I rewraps he leg. We all outta rags, so I takes off my shirt, use it. He leg stinkin now. Lord, I hopes that gangrene ain't set in. Wish he'd a let that doctor take it off. He die, what ole Massa gonna say 'bout the way I takes care of him? He let Tom take de whip to me?

'Bout suppertime, I spots a farmhouse a piece up the road. Tries to hurry that mare, but she movin slow as molasses. I stops on the road, gits down, and walks up the lane. Cain't see no one. House look empty, not burned though, just empty. It not a fine house like ol' Massa's. Just a white farmhouse. First I holler, "Hey there. Anyone home?" Gots no answer so I steps up on the porch. Door hangin open, so I pushes it back, and goes in. Gots Massa's pistol ready, but the place like a grave. Like the family just up and leave. Maybe them Union folk chase them off. I looks in the kitchen for something to eat, feed Massa, but if the Yankees was there, they taked that too. Out back they's a garden plot. I drops to my knees and start scrabbin with my hands in the dirt. Found one tater and a carrot. I eats the tater and near pukes it up. Taste like dirt. Carry the carrot back to Massa, but he not even awake. Leg smell worser, too. Smell like the leavins off a deer done got kilt for food. Good stuff gone, entrails left to rot. Hot to touch, too. I tries to wake him, say, "Massa, I brung you a carrot. Come on, wake up now and eat this here carrot." But he just toss and moan. I'se a'feered to sleep there, 'cause them owners might come back, take me for a thief. So, we moves on down the road 'til mare plumb gave out. Slept under the wagon again.

Next mornin when light broke, I goes to the back'a the wagon. Massa sound 'sleep, so I leaves him. He need that sleep. I could see we's gittin' close by home. Mare seem to know it too, and start pickin up her feets. Wagon bouncin somethin fierce, but Massa not makin a sound. 'Bout noon, I stops to give Massa water. Soon as I gits 'side the wagon, I knowed somethin wrong. Stink worser and he still as a church mouse. I shove he shoulder, but he don't wake up. Just lie there. I reaches over to lift he head, but I ain't heerd him breathin. "Massa," I says, "Gots you some water." But he face gone gray and he fingers looks kindly blue. I knowed then he gone.

I sits on the ground, starin at that ring 'til I cain't hardly see. "Lordy, Massa, you almost make it home. Lordy, we's so close. So close. I done tole you I'd git you home, and that's what I'se gonna do. You cain't know it, but you be home directly." I wipes my eyes, cross he hands on he chest, and puts he ring back on. Then I covers him up so them buzzards won't git drift of him, git back on the mare, but I cain't make myself go. Seem like I'se lost in my mind. Massa always been there and now he gone. Finally, I wipes my eyes again and head home.

AJ lowered the tattered book, tears welling. Reading of Moses's loss and the guilt he felt for not being able to save Eli. She knew that kind of guilt. She recalled the day she got the visit from the mine boss who told her Jeff had been killed in a slate fall. *That old man just stood in the doorway twisting his neckerchief in his hands.* After he said it, AJ collapsed on the porch. He carried her into the house. Alice came running when she heard him shouting. She couldn't console AJ because Jeff was her life.

I let him down. He never knew he was going to have a child. I never told Alice neither, so she didn't know it was guilty crying as well as mourning.

Good thing that mare know the way home, 'cause I'se not payin much mind. Thinkin 'bout Massa Eli and all he done for me. Treat me like a brother. Wish I could'a tole him. Sure sorry I ever thought 'bout runnin. Too, I'se worrin 'bout ol' Massa now; wonderin if'n them Yankees stole everything. Hope that place not burnt up. Sure hope my sweet Sary there, my boy Thomas too. Don't even know if home folks still alive.

Long 'bout supper time, I sees our fences. Lord, it feel good to be back. Fields empty though. Not a slave in sight. No horses neither. Lord, I hope's my family still there, ain't been runned off. 'Bout half way up our road I spots two nigga boys runnin toward us. I yells, "Hey boy, go tell Massa Moses back. We's home." Boys stare like they seen a ghost then heads back toward Massa house. I gits a cold feelin in my belly, scared what ol' Massa gonna do when he know his boy dead. But I'se 'cited too, keep lookin for Sary and Thomas but don't see nary soul. Barn still standing; so's slave cabins. That good.

House come in sight soon's I round the bend past the big oak. Don't look burnt a'tall. I sees ol' Massa on the porch like he always stand, hands behind he back. Missus in doorway with they boy Robert. Massa see Eli's mare, start down off the porch. Then, he stop in the yard like he don't understand why I'se ridin it stead of Massa Eli.

I gits off, walk up to Massa, and looks him square in the face. "Massa, I brung your boy home, just like he say. Massa Eli—he home now." Then I looks down. Tears in my eyes.

Massa grab my arm, look 'round kindly wild, say, "Where is he? Why wasn't he riding the mare 'stead of you?" But I think he know 'cause he heading toward the wagon while he talk. I steps in front of him. "Massa, I tried. Lord knows I did, but he die long 'bout noon. I reckon that gangrene set in like that doctor say."

Massa flung off that blanket, cryin "Nooooooo" 'til it break your heart. He lay he head 'longside Massa Eli face, sobbin. Others hear him hollerin, come runnin. I seen the Missus fall on the porch. I cain't watch no more. Turns and walks toward my cabin.

The tears AJ had blinked away several times now rolled down her cheeks. It was too much. Hearing or reading about any death always brought her right back to the two she'd suffered within a year of each other. Thinking about Mr. Morgan's reaction to his son's death dredged up the terrible memory of the night her mother called her at college with the news of her father's death. The jangling phone had awakened her. She'd been studying for mid-terms and had just fallen into an exhausted stupor. Alice had been almost incoherent, forcing

AJ to ask her several times what she was trying to say. Finally, she understood, and she cried too—not for her father, but for Alice. Even though her dad had treated her mother terribly in his later years, she heard the agony of loss in her mother's voice and wished she felt the same. But all AJ could feel was relief for Alice and sadness for herself knowing that her college days were over.

Sary sure a sight for sore eyes. She say supplies scarce, but Yankees didn't never come. They just runned out of stuff. Some slaves still there, some gone when they hear 'bout that free paper. Ol' Tom, that bastard overseer, gone, too. Just took off one night. She glad of that. Thomas stickin to me like a burr on a dog. He growed, but still act like a little'un.

Family hold young Massa's funeral next day. Slaves work all night making his box. Put him in that family plot out back. Missus throwed herself on the dirt after he's covered up 'til ol' Massa pick her up. They's a mess of Morgans buried out there. Now he with 'em. We's all at the funeral: me, Sary, Thomas, and the rest of the slaves what's still on the place. I done tole ole Massa how young Eli comed to be shot. Fightin like a true son of Virginia. I think that make he proud, but when I tells him Eli won't listen to the doctor, he say, "He stubborn, like me." When I tells him 'bout holdin on to young Massa's ring, he reach in he pocket, pull it out and give it to me. Tears roll down he cheeks. "You cain't wear it," he say, "but I wants you to have it. Eli would have wanted that too." I cries too, but that do make me feel mighty special. Ol' Massa seem old, really old. I don't ask him what happen whiles we gone, but he look whipped.

That night, Sary say that free paper real and we's free. Say we oughta' leave like some the others done. I knowed she's right 'bout the free part, but freedom don't seem so temptin no more. Look like them hung niggas make me think hard on what it take. Look like Massa gonna need all the help he kin git after this war over. Who know, maybe we gits to farm our own plot. Maybe my boy know freedom someday, real freedom. I teach him about real freedom. 'Bout how you kin be free in you mind, even if you body b'long to a Massa. 'Cidin to stay, makin my own mind up, that a kind of freedom, too. We see. For now, I just wants to rest a bit.

Moses Morgan, February 20, 1896

AJ quickly wiped the stream of tears with the back of her hand, afraid they'd splash on the page and smear the delicate ink, or that Isabelle would walk in and see them. After gently touching Moses's childish signature, she closed the book.

Damn that Robert for burying Moses with no marker, just that wooden cross. He should have given Moses a proper marker considering that he was a real Morgan. I bet he knew that and resented it. Isabelle was right. He was a son of a bitch!

⌐ CHAPTER TEN ⌐

A J slipped the journal and the letter back into the box and picked up one of Ben's letters. But it lay in her lap, the image of Moses and Eli too fresh in her mind. The long history she was beginning to learn swirled in her mind. *Now that I know all this stuff, not sure I can ever turn my back on a place that's been in my family for so long.*

After a delicious lunch of chicken salad with grapes and almonds, a recipe she'd never had back in West Virginia, AJ went back to her office and reopened the bankers box. This time she removed the packet of letters between Ben and Molly, his journal, and her diary. It was a lot to read, but she wanted to know more than Isabelle had told her.

AJ smiled as she untied the satin ribbon that held the letters. She admired the tender way Molly kept Ben's letters. *Don't remember ever receiving a letter from Jeff or any boyfriend, for that matter.*

As she fanned through the envelopes, she saw they were addressed to both Molly and Ben. On those to Molly, the handwriting was an amalgam of printing and script. The others, in flowing Palmer script that Molly must have been taught in grade school, were to Ben. Each had a red number in the corner. *She musta numbered these after Ben brought home her letters to him.*

Careful to keep them in chronological order, she read each one. Slowly, their lives unfolded—from Ben's capture in Germany and ultimate imprisonment to Molly's long wait for his return, and the affair that cost her the only chance she had at being a mother. Both touched AJ, who wondered how she would have handled Molly's situation, and how Jeff would have fared in a German stalag. Puzzled, as was Molly, about the abrupt end to his letters, she opened Ben's war journal and read with horror of the death march he was forced to endure when the Germans thought the Russians were on their way. *Bet Jeff would have survived that too, but wonder if he'd have been the same man when he returned.*

All of the documents gave her a personal perspective of war that she'd never had to face before. It all seemed so senseless. Lives lost, families shattered. War seemed somehow to have defined the lives of her Morgan kin: the Revolutionary War; the Civil War; World War II. She knew some had to be fought for freedom's sake, but not all. Vietnam was certainly an unjust war. And Desert Storm? Wasn't that all about oil? *Maybe we need to butt out of other people's problems.*

⁓

Dusk had begun to fall when AJ returned Ben's diary to its box. There were many more entries, but AJ had read enough for now. A rustling from the sunroom reached her, and she walked toward it. Isabelle was closing the draperies across the tall arched windows.

"Looks like another stormy night," she said as AJ entered the room.

"Possibly," she said. "Got a minute?"

"Sure. You been reading?"

"Yes. Some of their letters, parts of her diary, and some of his journal. He had a terrible time, didn't he? I don't see how he survived that march. No wonder he had a reaction after he got home."

"Me either," Isabelle said. "I guess back then there wasn't any treatment for PTSD. Soldiers were just supposed to suck it up and move on when they came home."

"Isabelle, how do you feel about Molly's affair? Would you ever do that?"

Isabelle blushed. "Not if either of us were married, but a relationship out of wedlock? Maybe, if it were the right person."

AJ wanted to find out if Isabelle and Jack had a thing, but she stopped herself. "Yeah, I can see doing that, too. But that's not adultery. It's just romance. But even that probably would have been frowned on back then. Nowadays, it ain't . . . isn't a big thing."

"Well, in some places it still is." Isabelle laughed with a tinge of bitterness. She snapped off the lights, leaving them in semi-darkness. "Night, AJ, see you in the morning."

At breakfast, she was still haunted by scenes of fighting. She'd dreamed about the young soldiers in Ben's story, only it was Jeff she saw on the battlefield. Off the landing craft he came, charging through the pulling current onto Omaha Beach, a hill just in sight across the flat sand, the white cliffs beyond. The moment his feet hit dry sand, he was struck. His rifle fell and was grabbed by another soldier who stepped over him. AJ had awakened with her face awash in tears.

No more of that. Too hard. Enough Morgan suffering.

As AJ left Clara's kitchen, she stopped to chat with Isabelle, to see if she'd found that family tree, but she wasn't at her desk. Clara could have told her whether there was a school tour, but AJ decided not to go back to ask. She settled at her desk, coffee cup at hand, and waited for Isabelle. She'd closed the box and set it aside, determined to focus on the future. It seemed only a few minutes before she heard Isabelle's unmistakable footsteps.

She approached AJ's desk and without preamble said, "If you don't have any plans this morning, I'd like to introduce you to the guy we've always considered our crop manager. He's called Hank, but his real name is Henry O'Sullivan. Good old Irish boy. Well, not a boy, really; he's been with us for years. He's free this morning and I said you ought to meet him. He agreed. Okay?"

"Sure," AJ said. "I'm not dressed for any formal stuff, but maybe he won't mind these jeans and a sweater." She looked down at her comfortable clothes, but Isabelle didn't acknowledge the remark or the style she'd criticized when AJ first arrived. "Let me grab another coffee and we're out of here," AJ called as she headed to the kitchen. Ten minutes later, the two women were in the Range Rover heading through the fields to the storage barns and out of sight of the house. A breeze ruffled AJ's hair and fluttered Isabelle's hat brim, carrying a hint of damp dirt being churned up by the machinery that was plowing under the spent crops.

"So, what's his job, again?" AJ asked.

"He manages all the planting and harvesting. Oversees the farm hands, and reports on the output of each crop. It's a lot to handle, but he's been doing it, like I said, for years. Jack hired him when he was about twenty-five. I think he'd like to retire, but we won't let him. He's too valuable. Still, Jack always checked his reports before they went to Beckett. He felt that was a way to keep them both honest. Since Jack's death, no one has done that. Hank thinks someone needs to. And I agree with him."

"Why? Does he think there's something funny going on? Do *you*?"

"No, no. It's just a good practice to continue. And you're the logical one to do it. So, lucky you." Isabelle laughed.

"Right. Lucky me."

They alighted from the car and walked up the gravel driveway to the enormous metal barn. "Wow," said AJ when they stepped inside. "I expected crops, not equipment and machinery." From a small walled-off room came a large, florid man with a shock of the most unruly auburn hair AJ had ever seen. It grew with no rhyme or reason. It flopped over his brow, except for where a cowlick shoved it to the right; it skimmed his ears and stood like a rooster's comb at his crown. He stuck out a paw that could have belonged to a sideshow giant and grinned.

"Hello, hello. Welcome to the heart of Langford Hall."

AJ's hand disappeared into his grip. "Thank you, Mr. O'Sullivan. My pleasure. Ms. Collins says I need to get to know you.

"No, no, no, missy. No Mr. O'Sullivan here. That's my dad. He's gone, God rest his soul. I'm Hank, and I don't answer to anything but. Do I, Isabelle?" He laughed and winked at her.

"If you do, I've never heard it. I guess you'd better get used to Hank, AJ."

"Okay, Hank it is." AJ smiled.

Hank was by far the most genial person she'd met at Langford Hall, aside from Clara.

"I know I have lots to learn, and according to Isabelle, you can teach me. Trouble is, I'm not a hundred percent sure what questions to ask yet. I've got a small farm back home, but this is an industrialized operation. There's a difference. On the other hand, farming is farming. And I'm willing to learn how you do it on a scale this big."

Isabelle, who had been standing behind AJ as Hank greeted her, now took a step forward. "AJ, how about I leave you with Hank for a while so you can begin to get an idea of what he's doing? I've got a tour group in thirty minutes. If I come back just before lunch, will that give you a good start, Hank?"

Hank said, "I think that's a grand idea. Miss AJ and I will be fine, won't we?"

AJ nodded. "Sure, that's just fine. See you later."

Isabelle smiled at Hank, patted his thick forearm as if he'd just done her a huge favor, and made her way back to the Range Rover. AJ shook her head.

"How does she do it? I couldn't walk in the gravel on those heels without falling all over myself."

Hank laughed. "Don't know, but I've never seen her in anything else."

"She's been such a big help," AJ said, surprised at herself for confiding in this man she'd met only minutes earlier.

"Well, I hope you'll say the same about me after we get through here. Come on. Want another cup of coffee? I've got a Keurig in the office."

"I'd love one."

AJ followed Hank through the door and into the paneled office. "Wow, this is pretty ritzy. Almost as fancy as the horse barn."

Hank muttered, "Thanks" and handed her a chipped coffee mug. AJ lowered herself into the captain's chair next to the desk while Hank plopped into the worn, leather, swivel model behind it. He began to rifle through the deep file drawer on his right, pulling out files and stacking them on the desk.

"You know, some days I think we produce more reports here than we do farm crops." A deep chuckle rumbled up his throat. "These are reports on machine maintenance. These are personnel records. And these are crop reports." As he spoke he slapped a meaty hand on each of the three stacks he'd built. "Want to talk people, machines, or crops first?"

She laughed but knew this was serious stuff. He seemed to take it all in stride, exuding a love of his job and desire to share the details.

"Let's talk about the crops. I need to know exactly what we grow, who our customers are, and what our output is or should be."

"Wow, smart girl, you know *exactly* what questions to ask. Don't kid me; you're a natural."

For the next few hours, they talked like two old farmers comparing notes about their harvests. Hank was a good teacher, and AJ an engaged learner. By the time Isabelle arrived, AJ was excited, her mind full.

"Hey, Isabelle. Hank is an excellent teacher. I'm ready to run this place, thanks to him." AJ laughed, then demurred. "Not really, but I sure have learned a lot." She turned back to Hank and stuck out her hand. "You've been a huge help, Hank. Really," she said with a wink.

Hank flashed an *aw shucks* grin. "Glad to help, Miss AJ. Take these file folders with you and come on back after you've studied the reports in them. You may have more questions by then. And I'll be more than glad to answer them." They shook hands like close friends.

"Well, that looks like it went well," said Isabelle as she started the car, and pulled away.

"It did . . . it really did. He's a great guy. So easy to talk to. Not like Tom at all. *He* didn't make me feel like a dumbass—sorry, dumb bunny—even once." AJ smacked her own mouth lightly, then laughed. "Gotta get rid of this potty mouth. Sorry."

Isabelle just smiled and nodded, as if tolerating a slow learner. "You think you're ready to face Tom when he gets back?"

"I learned a lot, but I'm still not so sure about that. He'd just love to find a way to put me in my place. He don't seem to like me meddling in his business. But we'll see."

"I think you'll manage just fine. Don't worry about him. Remember, I've got your back."

"Thanks, Isabelle. I appreciate that." They rode in silence for a few minutes. "Hey, did you find that family tree?"

"I did, and I put it on your desk while you were with Hank." *Oops, here I go again. Focus on the future.* As they made their way back to the house, she wondered why Beckett couldn't be as nice as Hank.

AJ spent the rest of the afternoon reading reports and making notes, getting prepared for her meeting with Tom. By dinnertime, she knew what the farm's output was for each crop. And she knew the revenue each should produce. She still needed to read the equipment inventories, and the personnel records. After that, all she would need from Tom would be the financial reports.

⟿ Chapter Eleven ⟿

That night, when AJ turned back the covers, the sweet lavender scent from a sachet she'd found in the linen closet wafted from the fresh sheets, and she climbed into the luxurious bed worn out from reading Hank's reports. However, since she wasn't actually sleepy, she'd brought the family tree upstairs with her, hoping to figure out where all the members she'd read or heard about fit in each generation. Now, nestled into the four feather pillows piled against her headboard, she unfolded the delicate document. The creases in the paper threatened to break apart, so she gently spread it open on the bed.

There they all are: old Langford, Reeves, poor Eli and his daddy, and there's Moses. I'm stunned that they put him on there. Obviously wasn't Robert who did it. Bet it was Isabelle. And there's Daddy. Wow! She must have added him after Mulgrew found our branch. Now she can add me and Annie.

She studied it for a long time as if she'd feel a stronger connection by memorizing their names and relationships. Finally, her eyes began to glaze over. She folded it carefully, placed it on her bedside table, and fell asleep.

Wrapped in a lace shawl, she stood shivering in the dusk on the back portico at Langford Hall. A cold wind stung AJ's face, and she could smell the approaching winter. Annie was running down the tree-lined path toward the cemetery. Leaves swirled under her feet, and her hair trailed behind her. AJ called for Annie, but she refused to turn around, or respond. From between the trees, a man stepped out, caught Annie's arm, swooped her up into his muscular arms, and started walking. For a moment, AJ thought it was Dew and that he was bringing Annie back. As he drew nearer, she saw that it was not Dew, but Moses. He reached the porch and set Annie down. "I brung your chile home, Miss Audrey," he said. AJ smiled and touched his arm. "Thank you, Moses. I appreciate it. Come inside and we'll have some cocoa."

She woke with a start but wasn't frightened. *Strange dream. Moses brought Annie back just like he did Eli. Even if he was still a slave, he came back home instead of runnin' north.* He was a Morgan, and Langford Hall was his home, too. And now it was hers as well. *Yeah, I can live here, least for a while.* She tossed and turned for an hour before finally sinking back into the deep pillows.

⌒⟶

AJ's head jerked up as the phone on her desk chirped. She'd been trying to read Hank's machinery inventory reports as her third cup of coffee cooled nearby. But her dream had taken its toll and her mind was foggy. Lists were boring in any case, and with two hours less sleep than usual, she could hardly plow through them. She grabbed the phone, checking the caller ID as she did. It was Alice. *What the hell? She don't ever call during the day.*

"Mom, is everything okay? Is Annie alright?"

"I hated to call you, AJ, but I knew you'd want to know. Annie is running a high fever, and she's got a really sore throat. I called Doc Hubbard and Jimmy's gonna drive us down there, but I thought you'd want to know. Her face is bright red all except around her mouth. I'm thinking it's scarlet fever. I seen that face before, long time ago on my sister's boy. Don't mean to scare you, but . . . I'll let you know what he says as soon as we see him. Gotta go."

"Okay. Keep me posted and give her a big hug." AJ paused a moment, then added, "You want me to come home?" But by the time she asked the question, Alice had disconnected. Now AJ was wide awake, and worried.

I got no business over here fooling with this damn farm and these freakin' reports. I oughtta be home taking care of my own affairs. Shit. Why'd I say yes to coming here? Need to get home . . . now.

She dashed into Isabelle's office. "I gotta go home," she blurted. "Annie's sick and Mom just called. She thinks Annie's got scarlet fever."

Caught off guard, Isabelle said, "What? I'm sorry. I was concentrating on something else. Annie's your daughter, right? How old is she?"

"She's eight and she needs her mama." AJ was on the verge of tears.

"Come on, honey. Sit down. You can go if you want, but I'm sure she'll be fine. Your mother is pretty capable, isn't she? Is she taking Annie to the doctor?" AJ nodded. "Then why don't you wait to see what he says. You can't do anything now by jumping in the car and taking off."

AJ sighed, the emotion going with it. "You're right. It's just the first time I've been away from her when she's been sick. I know Alice is doing the right thing. I'll wait until she calls back to decide what to do. I guess I just feel guilty not being there with her. Truthfully, Alice does most of the caring for Annie anyways. I'm out workin' all day. I wouldn't be nursing her hardly at all even if I was there." She managed a weak smile and shrugged. "By the way, did you put Moses on that family tree?"

"I did. After reading his story, I thought he deserved to be included. After all, he really was a Morgan, even if Elias never claimed him. That just wasn't done. Plus, it never set right with me that some of the Morgans were slaveholders. I thought adding Moses was a sort of apology, you know?"

"I'm glad you did. I felt so bad for him. He was a hero in my eyes. And it sounds like his old master thought so too," AJ said.

"I agree. Back to Annie; she'll be fine, AJ. Trust me. Kids get over these things."

"I know," AJ responded. "She's gone through all the other kid's stuff: ear infections, hand, foot, mouth, and croup. She even had chicken pox, but it was a mild case 'cause she'd been vaccinated. I'm going back to work, but I'll let you know what I decide."

AJ returned to her desk intent on looking over Hank's reports again. It was Friday. Monday and Tom's return fast approached, and she wanted to be prepared for a possible confrontation. She shuffled the papers, but she couldn't concentrate.

Maybe I oughtta go home this weekend, at least. I need to see her even if I'm not staying to take care of her. Bless her little heart. I ain't been gone that long, but I really miss her.

Two hours later AJ's phone came alive. "Mom? What did the doctors say? Is Annie okay? What did they give her?"

"Calm down, Audrey Jane. She's okay. The doctor said it weren't scarlet fever after all, just strep throat. They gave her a prescription, so it likely won't turn into scarlet fever, but she's gonna be out of school until the fever goes away and she's not contagious. I got her lozengers for her throat and she's in bed readin'. She'll likely sleep a lot. I'm making chicken soup and Jell-O. Don't worry. She'll be right as rain in a week or so."

AJ sighed. "I'm so relieved. Thanks for handling ever'thing so good, Alice. I'm sorry I weren't there to help. If you want, I'll come on home for the weekend, though."

"Ain't necessary. Stay there and do what you got to do. You were coming home at the end of the month, anyway, wasn't you? Wait 'til then. You and Annie will have more fun when she's better. You and her can go to the Turkey Knob Halloween party."

"Thanks again, Alice. Give her a big smooch and lots of hugs. Are you taking anything to keep from gettin' it? Can't afford for the nursemaid to get sick, you know."

"Yeah, I got a prescription too. I don't think it likely, though. I've nursed worse and never got sick."

"You are a tough old bird. I'll give you that," AJ said with a short laugh. "Bye, Mom. Love you."

She put the phone down and smiled as her screen saver picture of Annie popped up. She kissed her fingertips and laid them on Annie's cheek. *Look how worried I was over a simple sore throat. Shoulda known Alice could handle it.*

After lunch, AJ worked on studying the crop and inventory reports again, determined to master the information by the weekend. She'd been working for about an hour when Isabelle walked in.

"Busy doing your homework?" She laughed. She had a new hat today, AJ was sure. Brown felt with a turkey feather in the brim. *Must be her fall hat.* The weather had cooled, and the leaves were beginning to show small patches of gold and red. AJ knew that back home the fall color was probably setting her hills ablaze, or soon would be. She would probably miss it by the time she got home for Halloween, so she was glad to see a bit of color here.

"Hey there. Yeah, I'm determined to know this stuff if I have to study over the weekend. Tom's due back Monday, and I want to be ready."

"Well, I think you need a diversion. The Charlottesville Ballet Company has a performance Saturday night. Actually, it's kind of an unusual event. They call it *Beer and Ballet*." Isabelle chuckled and wrinkled her nose. "I'm not a beer fan, but I have season tickets to the ballet. Have you ever seen one?"

"No, I never. I guess the closest place I could have seen one at home is Charleston, and anyway, I could never have afforded tickets. I do love my beer though. Sounds like fun. What do I wear?"

"One of your new outfits will be fine, dear. Just add some jewelry. These things are pretty casual. Lots of college students attend this one, as I recall, and they never dress up. I don't like to drive into Charlottesville at night, so I'll ask you to. We can have dinner first and then go. And I promise to avoid snooty girls." The two laughed at the memory of AJ's run-in at the country club. "We can take my car. I'll come out about five and we'll drive in. I'm glad you want to go." She smiled warmly and turned to leave.

"Thank you, Isabelle. I look forward to it."

As Isabelle walked away, AJ realized how much she truly liked the woman. Granted, Isabelle was at least thirty years AJ's senior, but her spirit was youthful, vibrant. That's what made her seem much younger than her years, AJ decided. She smiled, thinking how different her life had been in the weeks she'd been there. She'd changed her hair, worn more stylish clothes, eaten food she'd never imagined, been to a country club, and now she was going to the ballet.

Fairy-tale life. Think of what my ancestors did to keep it going. There's old what's-his-name who was friends with Jefferson, and Eli, bless his heart. Then there's that bastard Robert, and then Reeves. Mr. Jack worked hard to preserve Langford Hall, too. No wonder he wanted to be sure to pass it on to another family member.

AJ rose, put her phone in her pocket, and went to the kitchen for one of Clara's oatmeal-raisin cookies and a cup of coffee. *This ought to get me through the rest of the afternoon. Wonder what she's cooking up for dinner tonight? Hope it's salmon.*

She closed the folders and locked them away just as Clara announced that dinner was ready. Late dining was new, too. At home, supper was always at five; Clara served her delicious meals around seven.

Tonight, she was eating alone because Isabelle had an early meeting in town with some of her friends. Her mind was a million miles away when Clara entered the dining room. AJ jumped when she heard her footsteps. She hadn't heard her enter. Clara reached for AJ's empty plate.

"Damn, Clara, you scared the poop out of me. Sorry."

As she set a piece of apple pie in front of AJ, Clara chuckled. "That's okay, Miss AJ. I should have called from the kitchen."

AJ looked at the pie, its scoop of ice cream melting into the crust. "Looks delicious, Clara. Thanks. My mama makes great apple pie. I'll see if yours stacks up." She laughed to let Clara know she was only half serious.

Deciding to make it an early night, AJ went upstairs, flopped on the bed, and called home to talk with Annie. Alice told her Annie might not want to talk because her throat was so sore, but she did. It was a short conversation that ended in AJ promising to be there for the upcoming Halloween party in Turkey Knob. AJ lay back on the pillows, worn out.

I'll shower in the morning. Sleep, here I come.

⌣ CHAPTER TWELVE ⌢

Thunder woke AJ before dawn. Her first thought was to be sure Gunner was okay. She'd heard of horses accidentally killing themselves by running spooked into a fence post. She sat up and in the dim light realized she wasn't home. Sighing in relief, she lay back on the pillows and listened as the storm swirled around the sturdy house.

This house has been here for generations. Wonder how many storms it's withstood? Not just the weather kind—family storms. More than one. Today I'm just gonna read. There has to be a book in the library I'd like. Next week could be a bitch. Thank God it's gonna be quiet all day. No school or public tours. No meetin's. Nothin'. Isabelle won't even be here until time for dinner and the ballet.

AJ pulled on a robe over her nightgown and padded downstairs for coffee and a bagel if there were any. "Hey, Clara, how you doing this morning?" she said as she entered the cook's domain.

"Doing just fine, Miss AJ. Pretty robe. Are you ready for some breakfast?"

"Thanks. Have we got any bagels?" she continued, heading toward the coffee pot. "I think that's all I want today. I'd like to take it to my room so I can read in bed. I was going to see if I could get Santos to let me ride one of the horses, but the weather stinks, so I'm gonna find a good book in the library and just relax. I can get my own, though, if we have some."

Clara gave her the look that said, *"Fixing your breakfast is my job."* Aloud she said, "That sounds like a good way to spend a rainy morning. I'll fix you one. An everything bagel with cream cheese?"

"Sounds wonderful. You know, I never had one of those until I came here. They are the bomb."

"The bomb?" said Clara, puzzled.

"It's an expression; means awesome." AJ laughed.

She walked into the library, the sash to her robe trailing behind her. Most of the books were leather bound, their gold titles faded. Walking down the shelves that reached the ceiling, she realized Jack had organized them as if it were a lending-library. Biographies shared space with autobiographies. History books competed for room with books on politics. *Where the hell are the novels? Need something besides real life. I've read enough of that in these Morgan papers.*

Finally, she located a section of literary classics: Shakespeare, Whitman, Faulkner, Fitzgerald, Hemingway, Steinbeck, and Dickens, all in alphabetical order. She was surprised to find, on the shelf below, George Orwell, William Golding, J. D. Salinger, and Harper Lee's *To Kill A Mockingbird.* She pulled it from the shelf and headed back to bed. *I love this book. I could read it again and again.*

A few hours later, she'd read until her eyes hurt. She ate her half-finished bagel, cold though it was, and went to take a shower. As she crossed the room, she noticed that the rain had stopped, and it was sunny. *Maybe I can go riding after all. Maybe Santos will let me pick a horse that I can take out on a regular basis.*

∽

In less than thirty minutes, AJ was knocking on Santos's office door. No one answered, so she yelled, "Santos? You here?"

Santos stuck his head out of the tack room. "Hi, Miss AJ. I didn't expect to see you today. How can I help you? I'm not exercising Merlot today. It's my day to clean the tack."

"I wondered if I could talk you into letting me go riding? I miss my horse, Gunner. I miss riding, period; and since I don't have anything to do this afternoon . . . is there a horse in this fancy stable that is just for trail riding? And is there someplace *to* ride?"

Santos took a moment before he answered. "Hmmm, I could let you ride Topper. He's an older horse that we retired some years back. He's sweet, gentle, and a comfortable ride. Can you use an English saddle?"

"Sure, I like them better anyhow. Where can I ride? Out in the fields?"

"Well, yes, but I think I ought to go with you until you learn the trails. Give me a minute to finish up what I'm doing," he said as he started back toward the tack room.

"Want some help on that? I love the smell of saddle soap. Nuts, huh?"

"Well, I shouldn't, but sure. Come on. I'll put you to work since you've got all this time on your hands."

AJ dashed toward the table where a can of saddle soap sat with a damp cloth beside it. "What needs cleaning first?"

Santos pointed to a saddle on a sawhorse. "I was going to do that next. Dig in. Nice to know I don't have to train you." He laughed. His laugh sounded like a bass guitar. She grabbed the rag and the can of soap and began cleaning with a practiced hand.

"How long have you worked at Langford Hall, Santos?"

"I guess it's been about ten years. Mr. Jack hired me. My parents came from Guatemala when I was a kid, so I've grown up here. They had a farm out in the country and I always had a horse. Seem to have an instinct for what makes them tick. Mr. Jack was looking for a stable boy back then, and somehow he'd met my dad. Mr. Jack knew everyone in the county, rich or poor. We were in the poor group." He laughed again. "He must have mentioned it to Papa 'cause he sent me here and Mr. Jack hired me on the spot."

"Wow. What a story. I grew up on a poor farm too, only now it's mine. Sometimes that's a good thing, sometimes not. I wouldn't have it no other way, though." Then she laughed and continued cleaning. Suddenly, she stopped, looked up at her surroundings, and said, "Guess I would, though, huh? I'm here now, ain't I? And this sure is another way." She laughed again. "And I like it . . . lots."

The pair continued for another forty minutes, exchanging small talk, and the stories. AJ told Santos the details of how she came to Langford Hall, and he told her of his ongoing fear of being sent back to Guatemala, a place he barely remembered. By two, they were saddling up to ride. AJ had spent a few minutes letting Topper get to know her, smell her, as she fed him sugar cubes and carrots. She liked feeling his gray muzzle on her hand. He reminded her of Gunner. Of course, it was his coloring; Gunner had more dappling and Topper had black leggings, unlike Gunner. Still, she felt an instant rapport with the gelding. Santos had chosen Merlot's next-door stable mate, Chia, a striking bay mare with white socks and a blaze on her forehead.

Over his shoulder, Santos yelled to AJ as they left the barn and crossed the driveway. "I'll lead since I know the trails. Topper doesn't mind following, so just keep a little distance and we'll be fine." They walked until they'd gone beyond the yard and the cemetery; then Santos yelled, "Let's go!" and kicked Chia. AJ did the same, and the two horses leapt into a canter and disappeared into the woods.

Before long, Santos slowed and pointed to his right. AJ followed his direction just in time to see a red fox trot into the thicket. She grinned, pleased to see wildlife running free. She hadn't seen a fox in years. Back home, many of the native animals had fled with the encroachment of mountaintop removal mining.

They resumed their pace, following the trail across the gently rolling terrain. In some places, the dense woods ended and they rode across a broad vista of lush green fields.

Reentering the woods, Santos held up his hand. "Stream up ahead, AJ. Give Topper his head and he'll cross it easily."

Looking down as Topper waded through the stream, easily dodging the occasional rock, AJ marveled at the crisp, clear water it held—a real contrast to her creek back home. *Bet I could see fish in there if I watched long enough.*

As they continued, AJ became more attuned to movement in the bushes. Without Santos saying a word, she spotted a doe and three fawns standing in a patch of sunlight ahead of them. As they drew closer, the small tribe disappeared.

Two hours later they were back. AJ was flushed and grinning broadly as she dismounted. "That was the most fun I've had since I got here. I loved seeing all the wildlife. Thank you so much, Santos."

"No, thank you, Miss AJ. It was good to get out and ride. I rarely have the chance. Well, I just don't take it, I guess. I should more often." They began unsaddling the horses and wiping them down. "Just put the saddle over the sawhorse and hang the bridle over there; I'll clean them up later."

"You sure? I can clean them," AJ said, but Santos waved away her offer. She shrugged. "Okay then, but anytime you want company, I'll go with you. Matter of fact, could we make this a weekly thing? I really miss being able to jump on a horse whenever I want and just take off. Somehow, it calms everything else down. It's just us, our breathing, and the movement of our bodies together, you know?" AJ led Topper to his stall, as Santos did the same with Chia.

"Yeah, I know." He laughed with a sort of wicked grin.

"What's funny about that?"

"Sounded like you were describing sex," Santos said, blushing.

AJ laughed and blushed. "It did, didn't it? Well, can we do it again? Ride, I mean." She giggled like a schoolgirl, but Santos didn't.

"I think that's a good idea," said Santos. "You help clean tack, and I'll take you riding. Fair exchange?"

"Absolutely, but I'm getting the better deal. I love cleaning tack too, you know. And if you ain't careful, I'll be mucking stalls before you know it."

"Don't think so. That's still my job. See you next Saturday?"

"You couldn't keep me away. Thanks again, Santos. I had a blast."

AJ turned and walked through the barn, scuffing her boots in the thick sawdust. That warm, familiar smell floated up around her and she smiled, content with herself, pleased with her rapport with Topper, and happy about the prospect of another afternoon with the horses.

⌒

Promptly at five, AJ heard Isabelle's car crunching the driveway gravel. She met her on the porch.

"Hey, Isabelle. I'm ready if you are."

"Ready as rain," Isabelle replied. "Let me see you. What a great outfit. I love the long necklace. Silver suits you. Good contrast with your dark hair. I never could wear it. I always looked better in browns, golds—you know, those fall colors. Sure you don't mind driving?"

"Not at all, if you're sure you don't mind me driving your car."

Seated at their table in the Red Pump Restaurant, Isabelle explained, "I thought you might enjoy Italian since that's never on Clara's menus. She's pretty much a Southern cook, as you've noticed."

"You got that right, but I'd never complain. Her food's too good. But this is nice. I haven't had a pizza since I left home. Would you split one?"

"Sure, I don't usually eat pizza, but why not? Ballet is new for you, so why not pizza for me? Right?"

"Right," said AJ, as the waiter approached. AJ ordered a Budweiser and Isabelle chose wine, merlot as it turned out; then they collaborated on the pizza toppings.

"Speaking of merlot, I went riding today."

"Not on Merlot, I hope. He's a handful."

"No, Santos let me ride Topper. He's a sweetie. We took a two-hour trail ride. God, it was awesome. I hope to make it a regular Saturday thing as long as the weather holds. Maybe even in the snow would be fun if it's not icy."

"I'm glad you found something to do besides work. It's good to have a diversion. Speaking of a diversion, what did you think of all those letters, diaries, and journals? Quite a family history, isn't it? I told you they all felt it necessary to write down what they did. It's like they thought if they didn't, it hadn't happened." Isabelle laughed.

"Glad you asked. I've finished reading them all. Fascinating! Moses, poor guy. He got the short end of the stick, that's for sure. And Molly, her diary just stopped. I understand why the war journal did; he was freed. Thank God. But hers, geezy peezy. She just stopped. So how *do* you know the rest of the story?"

As they ate, Isabelle explained. "I knew her. She was still alive when I came to work for Jack. He knew Ben and what happened to him, too. Molly said he used to think he was still marching, and he'd wander the house at night, but it sounded like he was marching again. Jack said he was always angry, withdrawn, and often drunk. Not the guy he was before the war at all. He told me that he saw Ben berate Molly more than once."

"Damn, that's terrible. I read about some of that in Molly's diary right after he came back. Did he physically abuse her, too?"

"Hard to say. She went to work and was out of his way much of the time, so maybe not. But according to Jack, he wasn't pleasant to be around because he was drinking. Then about a year after Ben came home, she had another affair with a guy from work. Poor thing. I think she was just so lonely, and in reality, she didn't have a husband. I don't condone what she did, but she certainly didn't use good judgement. Thank goodness it didn't last long, and this time, she didn't get pregnant. But I think Ben found out. Jack said he seemed to get worse about that time. Sadly for Molly, she did the noble thing; she didn't leave Ben. Instead, she ended the affair, although I think she was really in love with the guy. He was an accountant at the hospital. In the office where she worked. If she'd only met him later, maybe things would have been different."

AJ sipped her beer. "Different how?"

"Well, she might have married him after Ben committed suicide. One night about five years after he came home, Ben went up to the attic where his journal and other war mementos were stored, took out his service revolver, and shot himself. Molly found him when she got home from work."

"Oh my God. I wondered how he did it. How awful. I can't even imagine. Even if she didn't love him anymore, that would still be horrible. Poor thing. So, was there a specific reason you wanted me to read about them?" AJ asked.

Isabelle set down her wineglass. "Well, she was just one more Morgan who did what she had to do to hold her life together. If you think about it, all the Morgans were tough; they persevered no matter what. You're from that same stock, AJ. I can see that in you from the stories you've told me about your life."

"I guess I am like them."

"You are. As for Molly, she held up pretty well despite Ben's suicide and being a widow so young. I don't know if she felt like it was partly her fault or not, but she never dated after he died and was pretty lonely by the end of her life. No husband, no kids. Sad. But she kept on keeping on, as they say." Isabelle folded her napkin and placed it on the table.

"Being a widow is tough. I know. We all need someone, don't we? I agree; it is sad." AJ looked into the distance as if she were seeing Jeff.

"Okay, enough sad. Let's go see something beautiful. Finish your beer and we'll just walk to the ballet. It's not far." Isabelle paid the bill, and the pair left the restaurant to walk the few blocks to the performance hall.

"What's the name of the ballet?" asked AJ as she wrapped an oversized scarf around her shoulders.

"It's *Sleeping Beauty*. Remember the fairy tale? Where an evil fairy puts a curse on a princess at her christening? She'll prick her finger and fall asleep forever . . . unless?" Isabelle asked.

AJ finished the story. "A handsome prince wakes her with a kiss, right? I do remember. So, this ballet shows all that?"

"Yes, and the music is beautiful. I think you'll love it. It was written by the Russian composer Tchaikovsky. I'm a real fan of his music."

"Classical music ain't exactly my bag, but I'll give it a try." AJ smiled at her host.

Minutes later they were sitting comfortably in Isabelle's third-row seats. "How'd you get these seats, Isabelle? I'll be able to see them sweat."

Isabelle laughed. "I doubt they'll sweat, AJ, but these were Jack's seats, and I just continued to get them after he died."

"I'm impressed already. It's a beautiful theater."

"Just wait," said Isabelle as the curtain rose.

As the first costumed dancers floated on stage, AJ gasped. Isabelle looked at her and smiled. AJ smiled back, then turned back to the stage, mesmerized.

At intermission, AJ said, "This is magical. I've never seen anything like it. How those girls stay on their toes like that is beyond me. And the costumes! Wow!"

"As they say, practice, practice, practice. Years of it. They did do a great job with the costumes, didn't they?"

"Tell me again who wrote the music? I nearly jumped out of my seat at the beginning, but then it was so beautiful, I got goosebumps. And it's a real live band."

"*Orchestra*, dear. It's an orchestra when it has strings, like the violins. Bands don't have them. And it's Tchaikovsky. He wrote several other ballets and lots of other pieces. We've got a whole collection at the house if you are interested."

"Hmm, maybe. Why are the lights flashing? Is there a problem?"

"No, it means we should return to our seats. Intermission is over."

Back in their seats, AJ grinned like a child watching her favorite cartoons as the ballet resumed. "Who's the guy, Isabelle?" she asked as a handsome young man joined a group of others on stage.

"That's the prince. Watch. The lilac fairy will be back. She'll tell him about Aurora and ask him to go save her."

Again, AJ was captivated by the dancers and the illusion they created. She didn't say another word until it was over. As the curtain fell, Isabelle said, "Well, what did you think? The prince saved the day, didn't he?"

"Well, he saved Aurora, but that lilac fairy, she was Wonder Woman. She got rid of that evil witch, first. Without her, the prince wouldn't have had a snowball's chance in hell. Looks to me like she saved the day for sure. But the dancers were beautiful. I loved it."

"Hmm, I'd never thought of it that way. I think the composer would have said that every girl needs a prince, but he lived in a completely different time, didn't he?"

"I guess. You've done fine without a prince, haven't you, Isabelle? And I've been without one for a long time. Don't look like it's stopped either of us none." They reached the car, and AJ unlocked the doors.

"Well, I had one, but he died. You see, Jack was my prince." Isabelle blushed as she ducked into the passenger's seat.

"I thought so," AJ said in a triumphant tone. "I've thought you and Jack were, you know, more than whatever. Just little things you've said. I think that's so sweet."

On the way home, Isabelle told AJ how the two had met during a tour she was giving at Monticello. Jack had asked her out, and they quickly fell in love. Then he hired her so they could be together all the time. AJ asked why they never married.

"Jack thought his family would never accept me since I was working for him. Dumb, I know, but I went along with it. He was sort of old school like that. We might as well have been married, though. He provided generously for me, except for one thing—he didn't include me in his will. I never will understand that, unless he thought someone in Reeves's family might contest it down the road. That's why this job is so important, and why I hope you'll stay. This house feels like home to me. I'd hate to see it leave the family or to have to leave it myself."

AJ was quiet in the face of Isabelle's honesty. Finally, she managed, "I'm sorry he didn't leave you the place. Seems like it should have been yours, not mine."

"Well, it's not, dear, and there's nothing to do about it. I don't resent it, mind you. I know you are family. I just hope . . . you know."

"I know, Isabelle," AJ said as they left the car. "Thanks for a wonderful evening. I'll never forget it. See you Monday."

Isabelle rounded the car to reach AJ's side, and without hesitation pulled AJ toward her and kissed her on the cheek.

"Night, AJ. I had a wonderful time too," Isabelle said as she pulled back, retrieved her keys from AJ and got in the car, her high heels crunching in the gravel.

ᴄ CHAPTER THIRTEEN ᴄ

On Monday morning, AJ spotted Tom Beckett's car in the driveway when she came down to breakfast. "Morning, Clara," she said, pouring a cup of coffee as she dashed for the manager's office. Clara still made AJ breakfast, but she'd relented on the matter of the coffee.

"Where you off to in such a tear?" Clara said.

"I'll be back in a few minutes. I see Tom's back and I want to see if he can meet with me this morning. Is French toast out of the question? I love the way you make it," she said over her shoulder.

"No problem, Miss AJ," Clara said as the door latch snapped shut.

AJ knew Tom was due back at work today, so she'd been watching for his car. Since she didn't want a repeat of what happened last week, she thought she might catch him off guard before he could come up with another excuse to avoid their inevitable meeting. She'd forsaken her new leggings, and instead wore a long skirt and top that tied on one hip. She hoped the outfit said, *I can handle whatever you can dish out.* Now, as she stood there in front of his imposing door, she started to lose her nerve. Recalling their initial encounter, her stomach turned queasy. Nevertheless, she took a deep breath and knocked.

"Come on in, Isabelle," he yelled. *Well, apparently, she don't need an appointment.*

AJ poked her head in the door and caught his anticipatory smile. "It's me, not Isabelle," she said as she crossed the threshold. "Got a minute?"

"Not really," he said. Once Tom saw it was AJ, his expression had changed faster than a chameleon's color. Glowering, he turned to his desk and began shuffling papers. "I'm really behind from being gone all last week."

"Yeah," she said, following it with a pause. "About that. Didn't we have an appointment, like, ten days ago? I came. You weren't here." She didn't want to sound pissed, although she wanted him to realize that she knew he had stood her up.

"I had business in Richmond." He finally swiveled his chair around to face her, with his arms on his chest. Below, his belly rolled over his belt, hiding it from view. "So, you thought you'd just come now? Without an appointment? I mean, can't you see I'm working?" He waved a hand across his paper-strewn desk.

"Okay, I get that, Tom. When *will* you have time? I need to get started here. You know I'm on a deadline. I hoped since it was so stinking early, we could chat before you, you know, got real busy. I need to see the farm's financial records if I'm ever going to manage it. I know you said you'd take care of everything, but I want to be able to do it without you, if you ever, you know . . . if you want to change jobs, or something." *Damn. Sounds like I'm trying to get rid of him.*

"Not likely, but I get your drift. Give me until tomorrow morning. There are the income and expense statements, the general ledger reports, and the sales reports. It's a lot for a newbie to process. What would you want first?" Resigned to the situation, his tone modified. She was going to look over the books whether or not he liked it.

"The income and expense statements. For the last five years. Got those?" She'd been talking with Isabelle about what she should look for, so she was prepared. She felt smugly satisfied when she saw Tom's surprised look. *He didn't think I'd have a clue.*

He sighed. "I'll have to find them," Tom said, as if it were going to be an arduous task.

"Ten o'clock tomorrow then?" she said, without acknowledging his implied complaint.

"Yea, I'll see you then. Close the door when you leave."

AJ left without responding, but she let the door close heavily. Once outside, she leaned against the door, her palms sweating. Despite her bluster, her stomach had been in such a knot the whole time that she was glad to be out of there. She felt like she'd just told off her daddy, something she'd never have had the nerve to do. Despite the satisfaction that gave her, Tom's disrespect infuriated her. *Didn't even have the manners to stand up. Or to say goodbye. Asshole. I need another cup of coffee . . . or a beer.*

The next morning, as AJ doubled back to her desk for a legal pad to take to Tom's office, she spotted a large manila envelope placed on its center. Her name was on a yellow sticky note on the front. On the back were two red cardboard circles wound with a thin red cord, which she undid. Wondering whose handwriting the note carried, she pulled out five manila file folders, each marked with the years from 2009 to 2014—the reports she had requested. *Shithead. He don't even have the freakin' courtesy or the balls to meet with me. What the hell is his problem?* She replaced the thin files, put the envelope in a drawer, and went to find Isabelle.

Seated at Jack's old desk with her schedule book in front of her, hat firmly in place, Isabelle was on the phone. She signaled with her index finger that she'd be off in a moment. AJ stood firmly in front of the desk, her arms crossed on her chest, her lips pursed, foot tapping on the thick Persian rug.

"What?" Isabelle said, as she replaced the receiver.

AJ exploded. "What the hell is wrong with Tom Beckett? I was supposed to meet with him this morning, again. Instead, he just put the file folders on my desk. Is he afraid of me? Or does he hate women? Or is it just me he hates? Jesus."

"I have no idea." She frowned. "He should have honored the meeting, both of them actually. I'll talk to him." She leaned back smiling. "At least you finally got the files. Why don't you just ignore it, and by the time you're ready to talk about them, I'll make sure he sits still and listens. I'll make the appointment and go with you to be sure he shows you the respect you deserve. How's that sound?"

AJ took a deep breath. "You're right. I really wouldn't have had anything to talk about today, anyway. It just makes me so mad that he treats me like . . . like I'm just not important. Or that I'm not really worth talking to. Maybe he thinks I'm a dumb hillbilly too, or that I'm not serious about learning about the farm." She sighed. "I let him have it yesterday, though; I demanded he give me what I needed. Maybe I made matters worse." She was beginning to see how hard this was going to be unless she came to some sort of understanding with Tom. For now, he held the financial strings.

"That's possible," Isabelle said with regret. "He's a tough one, like I said. But he's done a good job for Mr. Jack." Isabelle grinned. "You know the old saying 'You catch more files with honey than you do with vinegar'? Maybe, after you see how well he's managed things, you'll have a different attitude and can at least compliment him for that. It might soothe his ego." She laughed. "You know how men are."

"I sure do," AJ grimaced. "I had to deal with my husband, and my drunk of a daddy. I'll get some more coffee and start reading. If I have any questions, will you be here the rest of the day? I'm sure not going to go ask him."

"I've got to run into town in a few, but I'll be back by lunchtime. Make notes if you need to and we'll sort out your questions then."

AJ smiled, thanked Isabelle, and headed to the kitchen.

AJ started with the oldest year-end financial statement. Although she'd never prepared such a detailed report for her farm, she remembered analyzing them in college. *Thank God I took accounting before I had to drop out.* As she looked at each statement, side by side, she was reminded again that Langford Hall was a significant agricultural concern, not merely a successful farm. Net income each year was in the high six-figure range, although it had declined somewhat each year. *Mulgrew wasn't kidding when he said "substantial." That's a wad of profit, but what's causing the decline?* She also noticed that the amount of bad debt charges had increased from year to year. Considering the farm's overall revenue, it wasn't a high percentage, but it was still in the thousands of dollars. A variance in *gross* revenue over the five-year period could maybe be attributed to crop yield, but she didn't think so. Besides, the drop was in the *net* income, not the gross revenue.

The numbers didn't make sense. The crop reports looked solid. *Was Mr. Jack becoming senile and making bad decisions about who he dealt with? Suppose the books were ever audited? Surely he would have had that done periodically.* AJ rubbed her eyes, closed the folders, and locked them in the drawer until she could talk to Isabelle about them. Meanwhile, she made a list of the questions she wanted to discuss, and then headed to the barn hoping to watch Santos put Merlot through his paces.

The beautiful gelding was on a long lead in the middle of the exercise ring, his blond mane flowing in the Indian-summer breeze as he moved. Several jumps had been arranged to provide a simulated course the horse might face in competition. Some were higher than others and of different construction: planks, logs, hay bales; yet he took them all effortlessly. *What a beauty. Looks like he's flying.* As AJ watched, her mind was elsewhere, however. *Wish I'd known great-uncle Jack. That way I'd know if the bad debt and falling profit were his fault or something else. If it's still going on, that sure ain't good. Ole Tom ain't gonna like me questioning him, that's for sure.*

AJ jumped at the ring of her cell phone. Her ringtone was the Rolling Stones' "Can't Get No Satisfaction." Santos laughed when he recognized the tune. Merlot never flinched.

"Hello?"

AJ began walking away, heading toward the house as she listened to Isabelle.

"By the exercise ring. I'll be right in. I'm getting hungry anyway. Have you had lunch? Great. I wonder if Clara has any chicken salad left? See you in a few."

AJ knew better than to discuss business in front of Clara. So after lunch she brought the reports to Isabelle's desk and spread them out, pages turned to the revenue sheets, and pointed to the net income line on each so Isabelle could easily see the incrementally decreasing profit.

"How long do you think this has been happening? And what about the bad debt? Do you think this is common? Every year?"

"I can't explain the income drop, but I'm sure some bad debt is to be expected. Not all customers are as diligent about paying their bills as one would like. But I wouldn't think they would increase this much. Jack would have been persistent about collecting any bad debts he could. And I'd think Tom, bulldog that he is, would have been as well after Jack sort of let Tom handle things."

"I hate to ask this, but was Jack slipping in his later years?"

"Mercy no! He was sharp as a tack. He could recite poetry he'd read years earlier. He used to do it all the time. 'How do I love thee—'" She stopped, blushed, then continued. "He read the *New York Times* and the *Wall Street Journal* every day. Nothing wrong with that man's mind." AJ smiled knowingly. Isabelle sounded both adamant and defensive.

"Okay, then what?" AJ scratched her head. "What do you think the problem is?"

"I truly have no idea. I'm not the person to ask," Isabelle said as she began to shuffle the reports back into chronological order. "Tom is. I think you'll have to ask him at your meeting. Get this cleared up, then move on to the crop reports and the full ledgers. Maybe compare them to the reports Hank gave you." She handed AJ the thick envelope.

"Oh, one more thing, Isabelle. Did Mr. Jack ever have the books audited?"

Isabelle sat quietly for a moment. "You know, I don't ever recall seeing or hearing about one. Maybe you should ask Tom that, too. Sorry, I haven't been much help."

"That's okay. I got the questions I needed answered. Now to check with Tom. Will you set the appointment? In the next few days, if you can."

"Done." Isabelle picked up her phone to call Tom. AJ watched her face as she talked. She could both hear the smile in her voice and see it in her eyes. *Damn, that Southern charm works every time. I need to learn some of that.* Soon Isabelle gave AJ a thumbs-up. "Tomorrow, at one," she mouthed. AJ nodded and returned to her office, entering the appointment on her iPhone calendar as she walked.

After dinner, AJ made her nightly calls home and to Dew. Annie's strep throat had cleared up and she was back in school. She asked her mother again about coming home for Halloween, but before she committed, AJ reminded her to find out if that would be around report card time. Annie also told her she'd made a new friend.

"His name's Albert, but he likes *Bertie* better. He thinks Albert sounds sissy, but he isn't one. He's cute. He's got a Mohawk and a chain tattoo around his wrist," Annie said.

"That's nice, Annie. I'm glad you're making new friends." *God, I hope they're only friends. She's way too young for a crush. At their age guys thought girls were gross. And a tattoo? Lord. Who gets tattoos for their kids?*

When Annie turned the phone over to her mother, the conversation grew more serious, at least on Alice's part. "I heard what Annie was telling you. She oughten take up with a boy like that.

A Mohawk? Ain't that one of them ugly haircuts where their hair sticks up in the middle and is shaved ever where else?"

"Yeah, but if you make a big stomping deal of it, Alice, she'll only hang out with him more. Don't say nothin', hear me? I don't like it neither, but it ain't hurting nothin'. . . No, I don't like the tattoo neither. Dew's got them, though, so I can't say much about that. Besides, a haircut and a tattoo don't tell what a person is like inside, Alice. How's the harvesting coming along?"

"Pretty good," Alice replied. "Jimmy's doing good business at the farmer's market. The squash, green beans, and corn are selling good."

"Good. He knows to use anything overripe for the cows, don't he? Okay, I was just checking." As they continued to talk, AJ wanted to tell her mother about the huge operation she had been plunged into but feared it would upset her to compare their meager farm to Langford Hall. Finally, Alice said it was Annie's bedtime, and called a halt to the conversation. They said their goodbyes, then AJ punched in Dew's number.

"Hey, babe, how was your day?" she said instead of hello.

"Not bad; yours?"

"Shitty. Can I tell you what happened? You've got to keep it to yourself though. Promise? I don't want Alice to think things are going badly here, but they are, so far." She spent the next five minutes detailing all her encounters with Tom Beckett over the past few weeks. "I've been here damn near six weeks and I don't know much more about this place than I did before I came. What should I do? Isabelle says stay cool, but that's not getting me far."

"I agree with her. I'm sorry he's a pain in the ass, but, honey, right now you need him. You got to find a way to make him cooperate. Maybe if you play dumb, you know, the sweet Southern gal, he'll love that shit. Make him feel macho to have to teach this poor little hillbilly."

"No fucking way am I going to play dumb for that son of a bitch. He already thinks I am a hillbilly, for God's sake. I want him to teach me because he's supposed to. Damn it, who's in charge here?"

"Right now, he is," Dew said. "Only when you learn all you can from him will you be able to take over—assuming you want to."

"Don't go there tonight, Dew. Shit. I've got enough to stew about right now. And I can't make a decision about that until I *am* in charge."

"Sorry, I shouldn't have said that. I'm on your side, no matter what, remember?"

"I know." She sighed. "You may have a point now that I think about it. I'll give some thought to polishing up my hillbilly accent. Hey, any chance of you coming over this weekend? It's been too long. We need a long visit, if you know what I mean."

"Yeah, I think I can. Actually, I was hoping you'd say something. I've kept the weekend open just in case. We'll talk later in the week. I could drive over on Friday after work and not have to leave until Sunday evening. How's that sound?"

"Just perfect," she said, a smile in her voice that matched the one on her face. "Night, babe. Sleep tight."

⁓ Chapter Fourteen ⁓

"Ready?" asked Isabelle as she approached AJ's desk. It was close to one o'clock and AJ was nervous.

"Ready as I'll ever be." She rose and gathered the files from the desk and placed them in the envelope. "I've spent the morning reading them again and comparing them to Hank's crop reports. It looks like our output was just about the same all five years, maybe a tad bit higher last year. So, I gotta ask him why the net income is lower and the expenses is higher."

The two walked out the back door and headed down the path to Tom's office. Leaves crunched underfoot, and the maple tree in the front yard glowed orange in the afternoon sunlight.

"Ask away. It's your business, and you've got a right and a fiduciary duty to know."

"*Fiduciary*? What's that mean?"

"It means you have the responsibility to hold the farm's interest first and that you bear the duty of protecting its money. It means, too, that in willing the farm to you, Jack felt a family member could be trusted to do that and be loyal."

"Wow. That's a big responsibility, ain't it? I hope I'm up to it."

"Once you learn it all, you'll be fine," said Isabelle as she knocked on Tom's door.

"Come in, AJ," came Tom's voice from the other side.

"Oh, that's funny. He don't know you're with me." AJ laughed as Isabelle opened the door.

"Hey, Tom, I thought I'd join AJ for this meeting. I hope you don't mind." Isabelle made herself comfortable in one of the office chairs to the side and motioned for AJ to sit across from Tom, who hadn't bothered to stand for his guests. Isabelle had taken charge, and Tom looked like a chastised child. His face flushed red. As AJ settled into the chair, she wondered whether he was embarrassed or angry, or both.

"Sure, Isabelle. Whatever you want," Tom said flatly as AJ pulled the files from the envelope.

"So, Tom, can you just go through how you put together them financial statements?" AJ asked. "In other words, what do you do each month? And are all the finances computerized?"

Tom picked up a gold pen and began clicking it open and shut. Over and over.

"Like anyone would prepare a financial. It's simply a report of all the income and expenses. I make the deposits from sales as they come in; I pay the bills twice a month, and I prepare the payroll each week. We've been fully computerized for at least five years." Tom's tone hinted condescension. He answered without elaboration, leaning back in his chair as if he were through with the discussion. It sounded to AJ as if he wasn't going to be any more forthcoming than necessary.

"Was Uncle Jack computer savvy?" AJ used the familial appellation on purpose. She wanted Tom to be fully aware that her relationship to his late employer was by blood.

"No. I offered to teach him, but he was almost ninety and he said, 'This dog is too old to learn that new trick.'" He'd begun to rock in his chair.

"Okay, so you handled everything—deposits, payments, and reports?" AJ asked. "And I'd be expected to do the same?"

"Right. I didn't always, but once Mr. Jack decided to let me computerize, he quit handling anything. He resisted that for some time, but I finally convinced him to let me make the switch."

"Before that, who did what?" AJ wanted to see how and when things had been put fully in Tom's hands.

"Jack made the deposits. I did the rest. Jack would look over the financial reports, and if he had questions, I answered them."

"Okay. I think I understand. So, could we go over some of the expense categories, so I can learn what items go in each? I mean, postage and shipping are obvious; but what about these—outside contractors, or maintenance? And supplies? That could cover a lot of things."

Tom sighed and brought his chair upright; then he began explaining each category to AJ. When he finished, he said, "I'm sure you won't remember all of that. It may take you a while to get a handle on doing all this. Are you sure you even want to?"

"Oh, I most certainly do, and the sooner the better. As my accounting teacher used to say, 'You can't manage it if you can't measure it.' I've got a couple of specific questions about some numbers. Do you mind?"

"What numbers?" Tom said, again fidgeting with the pen. As AJ turned the two latest statements toward him, he continued clicking it.

"Well, for instance, the net income. What accounts for the decrease there? It's happened every year for the last five, but these two years are the most dramatic."

"Soybean crops weren't as good and sales were down."

AJ knew this wasn't true, but she kept silent.

"And those three expense categories I asked you to explain. Each was a bunch higher than five years ago. What caused that?"

"Damn, are you going to nitpick every little thing before you even know what the . . . what you're doing?" Tom's voice increased a decibel.

"Tom, answer her questions," Isabelle said in measured tone. "She needs to know, and she has a right to ask any question she feels necessary." It was the first time she'd said a word since arriving.

He flushed again. "Okay, which ones? The outside contractors painted one of the barns last year; the year before we had to do something to the stable. I don't remember what. And before that, I'd have to look back at the files. What else? Maintenance and repair? Just what it says; we've got some old equipment that keeps breaking down."

AJ knew this wasn't true, either. Farm equipment was one area she knew something about. She'd gone over Hank's reports like an investigative reporter for *The New York Times*.

"What was the other one?" Tom sounded exasperated by AJ's probing.

"Supplies," answered AJ with a poker face. By now, she thought he was going to break the pen with his constant clicking.

"Oh God, that can cover lots of things. Gloves, uniforms, disposable paper products, grease for the equipment, trash cans . . . geez. I'd have to look at the checkbook to see what all we've been buying, but you know, prices have climbed from year to year. You can't expect these expenses to stay static."

"Of course not," AJ admitted, unconvinced that was the full story. The two talked a bit longer as AJ asked the questions she'd jotted down on her legal pad. They were mostly about procedures instead of specific information in the reports.

"Well, I think I got everything I wanted to know, Tom. We won't keep you any longer. I'm sure, though, if I have more questions, you'll be happy to answer them." She flashed a disingenuous smile. "By the way, could I have the check registers for last year so I can see who some of our vendors are?"

Tom's eyes narrowed. "Couldn't I just give you a list?" He glanced over at Isabelle, who shook her head slightly.

"Give me a minute," he groaned as he shoved his chair back and lumbered over to the file cabinet. He leaned over, pulled out a leather-bound checkbook, and handed it to AJ without taking his hands off of it. AJ fixed him with a stare for an awkward moment, and he released the large book.

"I'll get it back to you soon," AJ assured him. "I appreciate your time today, Tom. Thank you." She turned toward Isabelle. "Ready?"

"Ready," she replied. Isabelle opened the door then turned toward Tom. "Thanks for your cooperation, Tom. Much appreciated."

As the two women crossed the walkway, Isabelle was smiling. "I must say, for someone who was afraid of Tom a few weeks ago, you sure held your own today. You are one smart cookie. Jack would have loved seeing that meeting."

AJ didn't respond until they reached the porch. Then she said, "He's lying, Isabelle. And I think he's hiding something."

Isabelle stopped in her tracks. "Seriously? Jack had the utmost confidence in him. What did he lie about?"

In a stage whisper that forced Isabelle to lean in toward her, AJ said, "First off, the soybean crop being smaller than before. Remember? I read Hank's reports. It was bigger, not smaller. And that the equipment is old and needed lots of repair? Hank's reports show a lot of fairly new equipment. He's been upgrading over the past five years. I saw that on the financials too, but those purchases were listed in another category. I didn't ask about it because I knew why that one was up."

"So, what are you going to do?" Isabelle had stepped inside in case Tom had come outside his office, and she gestured for AJ to follow her.

"I'm going to go see Mr. Mulgrew if you are sure I can trust him."

"Lord, I thought *Tom* was trustworthy, so my judgment may be off. But Morton was Jack's friend, attorney, and confidant. I'd say he can be trusted. Hard to believe Tom's lying. You think it's just because he doesn't want you to succeed? I suppose he's devious enough to do that. Confuse you; make you make mistakes. Who knows?"

"Who knows, indeed. Please, don't breathe a word. I've got to get Mr. Mulgrew's opinion on this, and I don't want Tom to know I'm going behind his back, or that I know he lied."

"No, I won't. I would never do anything that might jeopardize Langford Hall's well-being."

⌣

That afternoon AJ called Mr. Mulgrew but couldn't get an appointment until Thursday morning. In the meantime, she studied the check stubs for 2014, making notes of what she thought were questionable expenditures. She was alarmed to see that Tom had written many sizeable checks to himself. They ranged from $900 to $1,200 each.

What in the hell are all these for? I'm no accountant, but this ain't good at all. The notations on the checks were vague, but they put each one in the categories she had questioned Tom about. She made a list of the check numbers so she could easily show them to the attorney.

If Tom is screwing around with things, I can't let on that I suspect anything about it.

She decided to see if Santos could go riding. That would take her mind elsewhere. She buzzed Isabelle and told her where she was going, then changed into jeans and headed to the stables.

"Santos? You out here?" she called as she approached the open sliding door.

"Sure am," said the disembodied voice of the stable master. "What's up, Miss AJ?"

"Could we give a pass to the Miss? How about just plain AJ?" She smiled broadly.

"It's a term of respect, but if you prefer, I'll drop it," Santos said, looking chagrined.

"Thanks. It's no problem really, but it just sounds like I should be dressing like an old maid. Anyway, I've got some time on my hands and wondered if you could go riding. I know it's a workday, but maybe just for a short one?" AJ kicked at the thick shavings in the center aisle. The sweet smell of cedar rose around them as she smiled at Santos like a little girl asking her father to come play with her.

"I don't think so. I've got to exercise Merlot." He smiled back. "Wish I could."

"Damn, I was really hoping—"

Santos looked at AJ appraisingly. "Do you think you know the trail well enough to go alone? I could let you give it a try. I know you can handle Topper; he's a piece of cake to ride. Remember the way?"

"Oh, I think I will once I get on the path. I'll stick to the trail through the woods."

"Okay," Santos said. "If you don't take that second loop through the fields, the woods trail should take you about an hour. If you aren't back by then, I'm coming after you." He laughed and AJ realized he was just kidding.

Santos brought Topper out of his stall and let AJ saddle him while he went to get Merlot. "Have fun, AJ," he said as she mounted the large horse and wheeled him toward the doors.

"I will," she yelled back.

Although it was a sunny day, as AJ entered the woods, the skies darkened under the canopy of multicolored leaves. Underfoot the dappled leaves crunched. AJ smiled. It was just like riding at home. Gunner was easier to handle, but this old boy was a sweetie. She gave him a pat on the neck. Home seemed so far away, today. Here she was in charge of this beautiful farm, riding a thoroughbred horse through acres and acres that would be hers if she just said yes.

Is home where you come from or where your people come from? I'm not sure anymore. I really felt in charge today. But damn that man. *He's such an ass. Okay, AJ, you came out here to ride and to forget him. Now do it.*

With that she gave Topper a swift kick and he jumped into a smooth canter. Soon, AJ wasn't thinking about anything but the ride. *What a smooth gait he's got. Never misses a beat.* She was breathing hard and loving every moment of the exhilarating ride when Topper rushed into a turn and under a low-hanging branch. AJ didn't see it coming.

⌒

When she awoke, she was on the ground looking up at the trees. She had no sense of how long she'd been there. When she turned her head, she saw Topper standing nearby. She felt dampness on her forehead and cheek. She stirred and an excruciating pain ripped through her left arm. *Oh damn, what have I done?* She raised her right hand to her temple and came away with blood. *Shit. What the hell did I hit that knocked me off? I need to get back on. I can't stay out here all night. Wonder how long I been here?* She struggled to sit up and immediately was dizzy. She lay back on her right elbow. *Give it a minute, girl. You've got to get up from here.* She tried again, her left arm dangling awkwardly, and sat upright.

With her right hand, she pulled her left arm across her body, hoping to protect it. When she did, her low scream split the silence. After waiting a moment for the pain to lessen, she pushed herself onto one hip, turned over so she was on her knees, and eventually managed to stand. She walked haltingly toward the horse and leaned against his warm body. "Good boy, you didn't leave me, did you?"

Thank God. I ain't never gonna be able to get back on you, though. I'd need both hands to do that, and this left one ain't working for shit.

She glanced at her watch, but her sight was clouded by blood. *Shit. I hate to use my brand-new shirt, but I ain't got a scarf nor nothing.* She used her good arm to wipe away as much of the blood as possible and looked again at her watch. *Damn, I've been out here over an hour, closer to two. I hope Santos makes good on his threat to come find me.* She reached for Topper's reins and began walking in the direction from which she'd come. *God, I hope I'm going the right way. Maybe Topper knows how to get home.*

It was after four when Santos found her walking slowly, crying, and leading Topper by the reins. As soon as he spotted her, he jumped off Chia and ran toward her.

"*Dios mio*, what happened?" he said as he reached her.

"I guess I lost a battle with a tree branch. At least my head says I did. And I think my arm is broken. I must have landed on it when I hit the ground. I don't really know. I just woke up on the ground, bleeding and hurting like hell." She leaned into Santos shoulder, crying. Santos put his arms around her and let her cry. He pulled a bandana out of his pocket, and handed it to her. She blew her nose and wiped her eyes.

"We've got to get you to the hospital. You look pretty beat up. Can you ride? That would be lots faster than walking. I can lead Topper if you can get back on."

"I don't see how with only one hand."

"If we can find a stump, I'll help you get up on it; then you maybe you can. Let's make a sling out of the bandana. That will steady your arm. Okay?"

She sniffed, glad to have someone else in charge. "Okay. I'll try. Thanks." AJ handed the damp and slightly bloody blue cloth back to him. Santos tied it into a sling, then helped AJ ease her arm into it. She winced but didn't cry out. They walked several yards more while Santos looked for something for AJ to use as a mounting block.

"Here, how about this?" Santos asked, pointing to a large downed tree. "Stand on it, and you can easily get in the saddle," he said, holding out his hand to help her up. She climbed up, threw her leg over the saddle, and Santos boosted her into position as he would have a child, his hands cupping her butt.

"Owww, that hurt," she yelled. "Sorry, Santos, I know you're doing your best. Thanks." She took a deep breath, clenched her teeth, and said, "Okay, I'm ready." Santos mounted Chia and they started back toward home.

⟿ CHAPTER FIFTEEN ⟿

When AJ entered Mr. Mulgrew's office on Thursday, his secretary looked at her with the practiced eye of one who often encountered battered women or accident victims.

"I'm sorry, you must have the wrong office. Mr. Mulgrew doesn't do personal injury cases. Mr. Bergin down the hall handles those."

AJ laughed. "I'm not surprised you didn't recognize me. I'm AJ Porter, the, um . . . heir to Langford Hall. I have an appointment with Mr. Mulgrew. I caught the wrong side of a low-hanging tree limb while I was riding the other day. Did a number on myself, huh?"

The secretary blushed. "Oh, Mrs. Porter, I'm so sorry. I'll let him know you're here."

Within minutes, Mulgrew threw open his door and his arms to welcome AJ. He stopped short of a big Southern bear hug when he saw her arm cast.

"Whoa, what happened to you?" Before she could answer, he ushered her into his inner office and closed the door.

AJ explained what had happened as she put the canvas bag in which she'd carried the reports and check register on the floor and settled into the chair across from Mulgrew's desk.

"Bless your heart," Mulgrew said. "Thank the Lord it wasn't worse and that it wasn't your right arm. Hard to do much without that right arm. I broke mine once and was laid up for weeks."

"Oh, I'm doing okay, just can't ride for a while. Finding something easy to put on is a challenge, though." She laughed, then turned serious again. "Anyway, I think I've got a problem out at the farm and I need your help."

"If you're looking to me for help in running the place, you've come to the wrong man. Tom Beckett is the man you need." *Still thinks of me as a hill girl without enough brains to handle the job.*

"No," AJ said shortly. "Actually, I think Tom Beckett *is* the problem. I think he's stealing, but I can't accuse him or fire him without proof."

"Whoa! That's a mighty serious accusation, young lady. He's been with Langford Hall forever. All those years, I never saw any reason to suspect him of financial hanky-panky. Nor did Jack, for that matter."

AJ pulled out the financial reports. "I don't think he *was* doing anything wrong until Uncle Jack turned over all the farm's financial dealings to him, like five years ago? Do you know if Jack ever had the books audited?"

Mulgrew sat back in his chair, tapped his fingers on the desk rhythmically. "Hmm, not that I ever recall. He had a mind like a steel trap most of his life. Thought he could handle it all himself and saw no reason to let outsiders handle anything. Except me, of course. I did all his investing." He tucked his thumbs in his suspender straps in a manner that said, "*And I did it right well.*" The scene where Prissy in *Gone with the Wind* told Rhett Butler she'd delivered Melanie's baby all by herself popped into AJ's mind.

"Would you look at some of the reports and the check register and tell me if you don't think an audit now would be a good idea?" AJ pulled out the reports and laid them on Mulgrew's desk. "First of all, Tom tried to avoid meeting with me, several times, and he delayed giving me these reports. Isabelle had to pull rank to get him to finally do it. Meet with me, I mean. I think he's hiding something."

She rose and went behind him, careful not to hit him in the head with her cast, then pointed to the figures she'd highlighted and began to explain her concerns.

"Hmm," Mulgrew said, over and over, as she voiced the questions she wanted answered. He turned to look at her. "These *don't* look good, I'll admit, but maybe there are reasonable explanations. Did you ask Tom?"

"Yes, and he lied through his teeth about them. He didn't know I knew he was lying, though. That's why I think someone else needs to look at all the records. And look at this." She walked back to her chair and retrieved the check register. She flipped through the book pointing to each check stub she had listed. "What's he doing writing all these checks to himself?"

"Great Scott! That *does* look suspicious."

Mulgrew frowned deeply and pushed his chair back from the desk as if the books were a sack of ripe horse manure he wanted to avoid.

"Alright, here's what I think. You should put him on paid leave immediately. Take his keys when you do and escort him off the farm. Continue to pay him but tell him it's only temporary until an audit is done. Then, based on the results, tell him he will be allowed to return if all is satisfactory. I'll find a good accounting firm to do the audit and handle the books in the meantime. They'll move in, handle it all right there, from his office."

She gulped. "Geez, that's gonna be tough. Could you be there when I do—you know, to back me up? He's gonna throw a ring-tailed hissy fit. I just know. He already doesn't like me one bit. I think he resents me trying to take over. Course, maybe that's 'cause he knows I'll find out what he's done, what's he *is* doing."

Mulgrew hesitated. "Very well, I'll bring someone from the accounting firm with me, too. That should help keep him in line. I'd suggest Isabelle accompany you, too. He knows better than to cross her. I've seen her put him in his place more than once. I guess her relationship with Jack wasn't much of a secret all those years. Paid off, though. She's still respected out there. Even though Jack's gone, it's like he's still in charge through her."

"Yeah, I saw Tom fold into a blue funk the other day when she gave him the stink eye," AJ said, then chuckled. "It was cool."

Mulgrew stood. "Alright then, I'll call you once I've secured a firm to handle it all. Meanwhile, just act as if everything is fine. Don't confront him. He should think you are satisfied with his explanations. Tell Isabelle, if you want, but no one else. This all needs to be handled with care. Understand?"

"Of course." AJ rose as well and put out her right hand. Mulgrew clasped it in both of his.

"I think you've done a fine thing, here, Miss AJ. Jack would be proud of you. You've definitely got his spunk, and it looks like you've got his brains, too. I'll support you all the way." He let her hand go, then said with a toothy smile, "You take care of that arm and your head, my dear. Can't have the mistress of Langford Hall going around looking like a battered wife."

⌐

Back at Langford Hall, AJ found Isabelle conducting a tour for a senior citizen group. She signaled to her that she was back and mouthed, "We need to talk." Isabelle nodded. An hour later, she was at AJ's desk.

"What did Morton say? I've been dying to know."

AJ relayed the conversation with Mulgrew as accurately as she could. When she repeated Mulgrew's recommendation to put Tom on leave, Isabelle looked worried.

"Oh my, that's not going to set well," she said. "Tom, bless his heart, will have a real conniption fit, don't you think?"

"Oh, I'm sure. That's why Mr. Mulgrew and someone from the accounting firm are going to be here when we do it. Until then, we are the only ones here who can know."

"My lips are sealed. How's your arm? You still on your pain meds?"

"No, I'm doing fine without them. I didn't tell anyone back home, and my boyfriend is coming this weekend. That should be interesting. Speaking of fits, I'll bet he throws a mini one for not telling him," AJ said. "This pump knot on my head will scare him worst, I'm guessing. He'll think I should've been resting instead of running around. And maybe I should've."

Isabelle nodded, as if she would agree with Dew.

"I know, but I needed to see Mr. Mulgrew and didn't want to postpone it. I think I will go lie down until dinner, though. I am sort of tired. Tomorrow I'm going to take it easy, too. Dew won't be here until after dinner, so maybe I'll be good as new by then."

"I agree; taking it easy is a good idea. Thank goodness you didn't have a concussion. If you tell him that, maybe it will ease his mind. Go rest. I'm eating out tonight, so you can just relax and have your dinner in peace and quiet. I'll leave you alone tomorrow too. If reading doesn't hurt your eyes, take a book from the library and read it in bed. Do you good," Isabelle said, patting AJ's good arm. "I'll even ask Clara to bring your breakfast and lunch up to you, if you want."

"Now you're pampering me. You sound like my mom fussing over Annie. Not necessary though. If I spend that much time in bed, I'll get bed sores. Thanks, though. See you tomorrow."

Isabelle gave a tiny wave as she walked away. When she was out of sight, AJ put her head on her arm, which was resting on the desk. She winced and whispered, "Shit, that hurts." She'd returned *Mockingbird* to its shelf, having devoured it in one day, and went to find another book. However, she wasn't at all sure she would actually read. Napping sounded much more appealing.

⌒

Early Friday afternoon, AJ's phone vibrated on her bedside table. She reached for it, hoping it was Dew, but it had already gone to voicemail. She played it back. "Hey, babe, on my way. Got off earlier than I thought, so I'll be there before dinner. Love you."

Shit. I didn't think he'd be here that soon. She picked up the house phone and punched in the kitchen number.

"Clara, it's AJ. I know it's late notice and that I said I'd just have soup and a grilled cheese sandwich in my room, but can you fix dinner for two tonight? My boyfriend will be here earlier than I thought."

"Of course I can, Miss AJ. Want scallops or shrimp? I can do either on the spur of the moment," Clara said.

"Oooh, I love your scallops. Let's have those. I know he hates broccoli. How about some of that yellow rice and grilled veggies but no broccoli? What can you do for dessert? Something chocolate?"

"I made a mousse today. I thought you might like it since it's not heavy," Clara responded.

"You know me pretty well, don't you? All that sounds wonderful. Thanks. About seven?"

"Seven gives me plenty of time," Clara said.

AJ hung up and went to pick out what to wear. She wanted to make a good impression on Dew since they hadn't been together for nearly two months. Excited that she had a whole new wardrobe to pick from, she chose a turquoise silk top that she hadn't worn since she bought it, black leggings, and a long chain with a shard of abalone shell on it, also new. *This ought to do the job.*

In her plush robe, after her shower, AJ brushed out her hair and let it flow, added some Obsession perfume, and looked around her room. She began picking up things, made sure a drawer for Dew's essentials was empty, and pushed her clothes to one end of the closet.

Around six AJ's phone chirped again. She was dressed and downstairs in the rarely used living room reading *A Slave in the White House*. Knowing it was about President Madison, who had been a friend of the Morgans, had hooked her. She grabbed the phone.

"Hey, babe, I'm almost there. You said there are gates. Are they open?"

"No, I'll have to open them. Text me when you're in front. Did you have any trouble finding Hadleigh?"

"Nope, GPS on my phone worked just fine. I'll text when I get there." He kissed the phone as his goodbye.

Fifteen minutes later, AJ's phone lit up. *OUT FRONT. OPEN UP.* She dashed to the control box and punched in the code, then grabbed a sweater and stepped out onto the porch. Her heart beat faster as she watched Dew's SUV pull into a parking space.

"I'm so glad to see you, babe," she yelled as he bounded up the steps.

He started to throw his arms around her but stopped when he saw the cast. "What the fuck, AJ?" He kissed her, but from an arm's length. Then, he held her by both arms and stared at her face. "God, your head! Someone sucker punch you? What the hell happened there?" He pointed to her forehead.

"When I was riding last week, I got knocked off. Didn't see a damn limb. But I'm fine." She stepped closer and half embraced him with her good arm. He returned the hug, but to AJ it seemed forced. "I won't break, I promise." He relaxed somewhat and gave her a more intimate hug, then kissed her again.

"Welcome to Langford Hall," she said ceremoniously as they stepped inside to the front hall. Dew put his backpack down and looked around like a child in a toy store at Christmas.

"Holy shit," he said. "Is this a fucking museum?"

"Well, sort of, but I've gotten used to it. Actually, it's pretty comfortable," AJ said as she led him into the library. "Have a seat," she said, gesturing to the deep leather sofa. "I'll show you around, then we can eat. Hungry?"

Dew nodded, still appearing overwhelmed by his surroundings. "God, look at all the books . . . and those rugs. I'll bet those things cost a freaking fortune. And look at you!" His last comment was mixed with admiration and shock. "I never seen you so dressed up. Do you wear that kind of thing all the time? What happened to jeans and sweatshirts?"

"I sort of ditched them unless I'm riding. They don't seem to fit in here, especially since I'm in charge of the place now. And I kind of like dressing up. Don't you like it?"

"Take some gittin' used to. I liked the old AJ—braids, jeans— comfortable, you know? I didn't think you'd change like this." He fidgeted in his seat. "Got any beer? I could use one."

"Sure, I'll ask Clara to bring some."

"Who the hell is Clara? Can't you just go get it?"

"She's our cook and . . . I don't know. She brings out food for guests. Yeah, I can go. Whatever." She stopped short of calling Clara and went for the beer herself. "I'll be right back," she called over her shoulder.

Dew rose after she'd left and began pacing the room. He pulled out a book or two from the shelves, then shoved them back. As AJ returned she saw Dew staring at his reflection in the large gilt framed mirror on the end wall. He was turning from side to side, looking at his worn jeans, stained from work, and his scuffed steel-toed boots. He looked dejected.

"What's wrong?" she asked.

AJ handed him the beer as he said, "I guess I should have gotten some new clothes. I look like a bum and I feel out of place."

"Don't worry about it. You ain't gonna see nobody but me and Clara. Maybe Santos, if you want to ride."

Dew sneered. "And who in the hell is Santos?"

"He's the stable master. He's from Guatemala, but he's been here for years. You'll like him."

"Goddamn." He let out a long slow whistle. "Cooks, maids, stable masters. You've got yourself quite a little bunch of servants here, don't you, princess? Ain't you gotten a bit above your raising?"

"Oh, don't start that shit again, Dew. I thought you were cool with me being here. It's just part of the deal. I can't dress like I used to. No one would respect me or see me as being in charge. Come on. Chill out. I missed you and want you to have a good time." Her tone brightened again. "Let me show you the rest of the house."

He acquiesced, albeit somewhat grudgingly, and the two took their beers as AJ walked him through the downstairs repeating some of the stories she'd heard Isabelle tell during her tours. Until they were back in the hall, Dew hadn't said a word. He grabbed his backpack. "Wanna show me where to put this? Or do we need to have Clara do it?"

"Dew, what's with the 'tude? You sounded like you were excited to be coming over, but now you act like you'd rather be in hell. I was looking forward to this to be a fun, relaxing weekend. Just the two of us. Quit being such a . . . I don't know . . . a snob. Yeah, it's different from back home, but I'm not. I'm still AJ. Come on."

Dew slung the backpack on his arm and started up the stairs. "Whatever. Which way, Miz Porter?" AJ ignored his petulant tone. When they reached her room, she said, "I cleared some drawers and a space in the closet for you." She opened an empty drawer, then walked to the closet and opened the double doors revealing a wide empty space.

"A drawer will do," he mumbled. "I ain't brought that much."

AJ sat on the chaise as he unpacked, the room full of their silence. When he finished, he turned to her. "Now what?"

"Dinner, if you're hungry. Clara has fixed us a really nice one. Okay?" She took his hand, drew close to his face, and kissed him. He softened and returned the kiss.

"Do we have to? That bed looks like where I'd like to take you." His face now wore an invitingly sly smile.

"Later," she promised. "I told Clara we'd eat about seven."

Dew frowned. "Shit." But he smiled, too.

In the dining room, AJ could see that Clara had used the best linens, china, crystal, and silver. It made her wince. The candles glowed softly, but she felt uneasy. *Maybe a burger in the kitchen would have been better—more Dew's style.*

"Holy shit," Dew said as they took seats at the long table. "Who the fuck did you think you were inviting? The president?"

"No, it's Clara's way of putting our best foot forward. I know it's not what you're—we're used to, but you have to admit, it's pretty. And kinda romantic with the candlelight? Huh?" She winked and smiled what she hoped looked like a come-hither smile.

"Looks silly, all this silverware and shit. Simple knife, fork, and spoon'd suited me. Might be hard to see what the hell I'm eating, too."

Before AJ could reply, Clara came in with two bowls of soup, acorn squash garnished with cinnamon. "Dew, this is Clara."

Dew mumbled, "Hey." As she left, he leaned toward AJ, pointing to his bowl. "What the hell is this?"

"Acorn squash soup. It's good. Try it, please." It was as if she were trying to convince Annie to eat spinach.

Dew took a spoonful and admitted it wasn't bad. As he cleaned his bowl, AJ tried to muffle a giggle, but Dew caught her. "What? What's so funny? Okay, so I liked it. Don't laugh at me."

AJ went silent and they didn't speak while they ate their salad, but when Clara brought the scallops, rice, and vegetables, Dew stared at his plate. "What the fuck are those? They look like fried marshmallows. Is that what we're eating?"

AJ couldn't hold back and busted out laughing. "No, silly, they're scallops—you know, seafood? I know it's something we don't eat at home. But that's why I asked her to fix them. Geez, we can't eat pizza all our lives."

Dew poked one with his fork, then took a bite. "Damn this thing is as chewy as a, uh, as fucking bubble gum." He threw down his napkin. "I can't eat this shit. Wish I had me a bologna sandwich." AJ started to respond, but he yelled, "And don't go asking that damn Clara to fix one."

AJ put down her fork. "Dewey, don't yell. She'll hear you."

"I don't give a fucking rat's ass," he yelled again.

AJ put her hand on his arm. "Look, I'm sorry you don't like them. I love them and thought you would, too. After Clara leaves, we'll go back in the kitchen and I'll find you something else. At least try the rice and veggies, so Clara won't have her feelings hurt. And you'll love the dessert."

"Fuck dessert. And fuck you! This place ain't for me. I don't fit in here. You seem to love it. Just like I thought you would. You've obviously made your choice. You'll never come back home. And if you do, you'll hate it. It won't be fancy enough for you. Look at you. Fancy jewelry, fancy schmancy shoes, whatever. 'I don't wear jeans unless I'm riding with fucking Carlos,' or whatever his name is." He'd jumped up when he began to yell. Now he was glowering over her. "Just show me a fucking bed for the night and I'm gone tomorrow. This ain't no place for me." He fled and took the stairs two at a time.

At the top landing he turned and yelled, "You know what? Fuck it. I'm leaving. Now." He rushed toward AJ's room. Stunned, she stood at the foot of the stairs, listening to him slamming drawers and stuffing clothes into his backpack.

To hell with him. I'm not begging anymore. He's been a butt all along. If he can't accept me like I am, then good riddance.

Within minutes he ran back down the stairs, backpack in hand.

"Fine! Go then! If you can't accept the way I live now, then maybe you *should* go," she yelled as he brushed past her.

As Dew slung open the door, he yelled, "Fucking bitch princess!" then ran off the porch to his SUV. AJ followed him out onto the porch into a swirl of wind and leaves. She watched dry eyed as he spun gravel pulling away from the house and into the dark.

∽ CHAPTER SIXTEEN ∼

On Saturday afternoon fall was in its full glory. The trees sparkled with crimson, gold, and orange. One was so brilliant, it looked like a fireball when the sunlight hit it. Curled up on the library sofa intending to finish the book about Madison's slave, AJ found she couldn't concentrate. She glanced up when the skittering leaves began to dance against the windows.

What a beautiful day. Dew and I could have gone walking in the woods if he'd stayed. But he was such a butt last night, I'm sorta glad he left.

AJ invited him because she didn't want to wait until Halloween to see him. She now realized it was a mistake.

Maybe dinner was too fancy. I should have had Clara fix something simple. But if he's going to keep up that tantrum shit, I'm better off without him. Who needs it? I know he didn't want me to come here, but I thought finally he'd gotten used to the idea. After the way he acted last night, though, I don't think he ever will. I do miss him, though. Back home, we had some good times, lots of them.

In her pocket, her phone began to vibrate. *Maybe it's Dew. If it is, he'd better be apologizing.* When she looked down, she saw her mother's face.

"Hey, Alice, what's up? Is Annie okay?"

AJ sat bolt upright as Alice began to talk. "She's fine, but I'm calling to . . . I need to tell you . . . I don't know how. . . I'm sorry, honey. Dew was killed last night."

"WHAT? NO!"

"They found his car overturned on I-64, just inside the West Virginia line. He'd crashed into a tree. I guess he was speeding. I thought he was with you this weekend."

AJ broke into sobs that shook her entire frame. "We . . . he got mad . . . we fought . . . I told him . . . he just left." She struggled through her cries to explain. "I gotta go . . . can't talk . . . call me later." She hung up, wrapped herself in the plaid blanket on the sofa, and, rocking back and forth, she wept.

Later, she called Alice back and learned the details of Dew's wreck. They'd found both full and empty beer cans in the car, and the tire tracks indicated he'd been way over the speed limit.

"He musta just lost control," Alice said. AJ guessed she was remembering her husband's similar wreck.

In bed that night, AJ again second-guessed her actions. She replayed the good times with Dew, and their arguments after she decided to come to Virginia. Her sadness turned almost immediately to guilt. In her mind this was all on her. She questioned the changes in her since arriving and her relationship with Dew. Her thoughts ran from *I should never have come here* to *Did I flaunt the house in his face? Maybe he was right; maybe I* have *gotten above my raising. But what's wrong with trying to improve your life? Was I supposed to turn this down and stay on the farm just because he wanted me to? That don't make sense, not to me anyways.* She fell asleep crying.

⌣

When Isabelle asked her Monday morning how her weekend had been, AJ burst into tears again. "Oh, Isabelle, Dew's dead."

"Oh my God! What happened?" Isabelle moved closer, putting her hand on AJ's arm.

"We had a fight, and he left. On the way home, he was killed in a car accident, and it's all my fault." She sobbed so hard Isabelle folded her into her arms like a small child. AJ bawled for a few moments, then snuffled. Isabelle released her, reached for the box of tissues on her desk, and handed them to AJ. Once AJ had composed herself, Isabelle said, "Okay, tell me."

She led AJ to the sofa, pushed her to sit, and sat down beside her. AJ took a deep breath and gave Isabelle the details of their fight and Dew's accident. Isabelle countered her every guilty remark.

"First of all, if he was drinking, and possibly speeding, it certainly wasn't your fault. I know you think telling him to leave puts the blame on you, but you're wrong. You might not want to hear this, especially now, but maybe you and Dew were good for each other back home, but now that you're here, you've changed and he hasn't. That had to have put a strain on your relationship. Maybe he just couldn't accept that you've outgrown him. It's sad, but it happens sometimes. I'm sorry for you and extremely sorry he died; but it wasn't your fault."

AJ sniffed, "That's what my mother said, too. Thanks, Isabelle. I needed someone here to talk to. Sorry for the crying jag."

"Sometimes that's just what the doctor ordered." Isabelle smiled and patted her hand, then went to her office, leaving AJ to think about what she'd heard.

Isabelle's probably right. Dew never accepted my moving here. Maybe he was jealous. It's not my fault. And I can't let it consume me. I've got to get it together.

Later in the day, Mr. Mulgrew called to tell AJ he'd learned that two firms would be needed to handle the audit and the ongoing bookkeeping. He said having only one would violate accounting standards. He had secured a firm to do the audit, but he still had to contact another for the bookkeeping duties. AJ said she'd wait until he had both under contract before dealing with Tom Beckett. She had enough on her mind without that. Mr. Mulgrew said he hoped to have both ready to go by midweek.

Isabelle approached her the next day, asking if she was going home for Dew's funeral. AJ managed her short answer without tears. "No, I don't plan to," she said.

"Are you sure? Until Mulgrew gets the contracts signed, you really don't have that much to handle. I'll keep things organized."

"I'll think on it," she replied, more to stop the conversation than with any real conviction. She did think about it, wavered, almost decided to go, then changed her mind.

In the end, AJ did not attend Dew's funeral. As she told her mother when she called to give AJ the funeral arrangements, "Alice, the whole town will be blaming me. Especially his family. And maybe they should. Yeah, we argued, and I told him to leave knowing he was angry. I probably should have tried to calm him down and get him to stay, but I didn't. I can't change that now."

Alice had to admit that AJ was probably right. The locals would be talking; they always did. She tried again to tell AJ that the accident was Dew's fault, tried to tell her not to blame herself. But it hadn't helped. At the end of the conversation, AJ remained firm, but told her mother to tell Annie that she'd still be there for Halloween.

⌣⌐

Mulgrew called on Wednesday to say he'd secured the two firms to handle the audit and take over the bookkeeping duties. AJ asked, "When will you be able to come out to help me tell Tom?"

"They can't come for a week or so. Is that a problem?"

"Well, the sooner the better. Every day he's here, the more he can steal."

"Let's aim for next Friday. That way, they can move in on the following Monday."

"Suits me," said AJ. "I was planning to go home the end of the month to celebrate Halloween with my daughter. They will have had a week to get familiar with the systems by then. Thank you. I really appreciate your help. I'm not looking forward to this, but it's got to be done."

"Yes, it does. That's what the auditor I spoke to said. We'll be there to protect your back. Take care."

Ten days later, Mulgrew and three men in expensive-looking suits arrived at Langford Hall promptly at four o'clock, as arranged with AJ and Isabelle. The day was cold and gray. AJ thought that was appropriate for what was about to happen. She met them at the front door.

"Welcome to Langford Hall," she said. "Please come in. Good to see you again, Mr. Mulgrew."

"Thank you, AJ. Let me introduce these gentlemen. This is Leon Alexander," he said of a balding and pudgy forty-something fellow. AJ smiled and stifled a giggle. *He reminds me of the Pillsbury Doughboy.* "He's one of the leading auditors at Alexander and Burnett. He won't be working alone, of course, but he'll act as the lead on the audit. And this is Barry Peterson with Peterson, Vass, and Billups. Their firm also comes highly recommended." Peterson reached to shake AJ's hand, smiling broadly. His hand warmed hers during the brief time he held it.

"Mrs. Porter," he said.

"And over here," Mulgrew said as he turned to his left, "is Arnold Chelyan. He and Barry will be on property day to day doing all the accounting duties." AJ shook hands with Chelyan, but Barry Peterson's smile continued to hold her attention. Chelyan was obviously the older of the pair. His gray hair, slicked back from a deep widow's peak, looked to AJ as if he had used too much Brylcreem, a product she associated with her grandfather. His hand was damp and cold. AJ surreptitiously wiped her palm on her pants.

"I'm so glad you're here. And thank you for making time for us so quickly. I'm sure Mr. Mulgrew has briefed you on what we—what I—suspect." She hesitated, glancing at each. They nodded in unison like a bunch of bobblehead dolls. "So, if you need anything from me, I'll be right here. And I'll get you keys to the office, as well. Would you like some coffee or anything else before we go see Mr. Beckett?" All four declined.

Mulgrew said, "Let's do this before he has a chance to leave on his own. Ready, AJ?"

"Let me call Isabelle, and then I'm as ready as I'll ever be," she replied pulling on a Polar Fleece jacket. She picked up the house phone and called Isabelle.

"They're here; can you join us?" she asked. "Good, we'll come through your office."

AJ ushered the men to Isabelle's office where the introductions were repeated. Then the cadre walked through the covered passage to Tom's office. Isabelle knocked and then called out, "Tom, can I see you a moment?"

"Sure," came Tom's voice from inside. AJ could hear his chair snap back from its reclining position.

Isabelle opened the door and held it while AJ and the group of men walked in. The room was stuffy from the heat of an oil heater. Tom looked up, puzzled, but he didn't rise. AJ stepped forward. "Tom, you know Mr. Mulgrew. These other men are from two accounting firms in Charlottesville. Mr. Alexander is an auditor with Alexander and Burnett." At the word *auditor*, Tom's face turned ashen and folded into a frown. AJ continued. "Since Langford Hall has changed hands, so to speak, I thought an audit would be a good idea. There's never been one, so it's time. Mr. Alexander is here to do that. While it's in progress, I'm placing you on leave, with pay, of course. I'd like you to pack your things and give me your keys." Tom's face became as red as if he'd suddenly developed a high fever.

"What? That's stupid. They'll need to talk to me if they're going to conduct an audit. Besides, you can't do that."

Isabelle chimed in, "As a matter of fact, she can, Tom. She is in charge now. I suggest you gather up your personal things and leave without a fuss."

Tom jumped to his feet and stared at her uncomprehendingly, yet his eyes held a wild look. "You turning on me, too? After all these years? I thought you and I were a team." Pointing to AJ, he said, "She doesn't know a damn thing about how to run this farm. Who in the hell is going to do the bookkeeping if I'm not here?" His eyes narrowed as he looked Isabelle straight in her pleading blue eyes. Suddenly, he crossed his arms belligerently. "I'm not going anywhere," he said through gritted teeth. Then he turned and waved toward Peterson and Chelyan. "And who are those assholes?" he yelled, addressing no one in particular.

AJ calmly said, "They're from another firm, the one that will be doing the accounting during the audit. If everything checks out, you'll be back, maybe around the first of the year, depending on how long the audit takes and what they find. Can I have your keys, please?"

He glared at AJ with pure venom. "Hell no! I said I'm not leaving. This is my office, has been for twenty years. You all can just turn around and go back to your own fancy offices. Get out!" Tom yelled, waving his arms at all of them as if he were shooing away a flock of pesky geese. When they didn't move, he smacked his coffee cup with the back of his hand and sent it flying off the desk. "I said leave," he screamed. As the cup flew, then crashed against the file cabinet, AJ jumped, then looked to Isabelle and Mulgrew for help.

The two approached Tom. Mulgrew placed his hands firmly on Tom's shoulders. "Tom, you don't want to make a scene. I can call the sheriff if I have to, but I really don't want to. I don't think you want that either. Just give her the keys and leave," he said in a firm monotone.

"Come on, Tom," Isabelle added. "It's no good. Fighting this won't help. It just makes matters worse." She placed her hand on Tom's arm, but he shrugged it off as if she had leprosy.

Around the edges of the office the three visitors stood agape, unsure of what to do. Chelyan was looking down to be sure coffee hadn't landed on his suit pants. When AJ stepped back, Peterson had moved protectively toward her. Mr. Alexander looked around nervously.

"We can go," he offered.

"No, stay. Tom's going to leave, aren't you?" Mulgrew said, looking directly at him. Tom still stood stiffly behind his desk, but it was obvious the fight had left him. Without answering, he rustled in a bottom drawer, withdrew a small shopping bag, and began filling it with a few personal items: a lighter, the gold pen, a Rotary paperweight, and the photograph of a woman with a young girl that had been sitting on his desk. He fumbled in his pants pocket for his keys and handed them to Isabelle, rather than to AJ. "I trust you to give them back, after—but I don't trust that bitch as far as I can throw her," he snarled, jerking his head to indicate the younger woman.

With that, he curled the top of the bag inward, grabbed a peacoat off the tree stand, and stomped out the door, slamming it behind him. AJ let out the deep breath she hadn't realized she was holding and slid into a chair.

"God, I'm glad that's over. I knew he'd be upset, but I didn't think it would be that bad," she said to no one in particular.

Isabelle had walked to the window to be sure Tom had driven away; then she returned to AJ's side. "I'm sorry you gentlemen had to witness that. AJ, you did a fantastic job of staying calm, but I suspect we could all use a drink. Shall we?"

She motioned toward the door, and without hesitation, Mulgrew opened it. "Hell yes, it's five o'clock somewhere. Fellas?"

Their faces broke into smiles as they followed him into the house.

⌐ Chapter Seventeen ⌐

Driving back to West Virginia for the first time since Labor Day, AJ brimmed with mixed emotions. She assumed someone would have put a cross at the place where Dew ran off the road. It would have been typical of the folks back home. And she knew she didn't want to see it. It would resurrect guilt and sadness, so she assiduously kept her eyes on the road instead of enjoying the lingering fall foliage. Nevertheless, she thought she caught a glimpse, out of the corner of her eye, of what might have been the very thing she was trying to avoid. But when the hills began to rise, her spirits rose with them. Suddenly she felt better, protected, and warmed by the closeness of her West Virginia mountains. It was the feeling she always got from them.

Home. She was going home. The mere word filled her with joy and exuberance. She couldn't wait to see her little farm, her family, and Gunner, even if she couldn't ride him. Yes, she enjoyed the comfortable life Langford Hall provided. She'd luxuriated in no longer having to do the farm chores and not having to worry about money. But, at the same time, she hadn't realized how much she missed Annie and, surprisingly, the ever-sharp tongue of her mother. In Virginia, life presented different challenges, ones she'd felt somewhat ill equipped to handle. At home, the familiar problems were just that, *familiar,* and therefore within her ability to cope.

Yet, as she climbed the familiar highway, she noticed, as if they hadn't been there before, the small, dilapidated homes barely hanging onto the sides of the mountains. She began to count more than a few closed gas stations, grocery stores, bait shops.

How come I never realized how poor this area is before now? Guess it was so familiar I didn't pay attention to it. Maybe it's the contrast to Langford Hall and Hadleigh, but this is pitiful.

She looked down at her outfit: tailored slacks, a ruby cable-knit sweater, and the abalone necklace that had become a favorite, and realized how out of place it was going to look on Turkey Knob where she'd been raised.

Maybe it's me that's changed. Geez, am I really gettin' above my raising like Dew said? Hope I've got some old jeans at home. Alice won't recognize me dressed like this.

As she continued driving, her thoughts, unbidden, drifted back to Virginia.

Wonder what it's gonna be like to have all those accountants milling around when I get back. Suppose we'll all eat together? Wouldn't mind eating with Barry . . . Barry Peterson. He's got one hell of a smile. Unconsciously, she smiled, remembering his warm handshake and his move to protect her when Tom got so angry. *I'd like to know him better. Seems like a good guy.*

⌒

Turkey Knob, West Virginia, was a rural town, so rural that trick-or-treaters, if they went from house to house, would have to hike up and down rugged hollows to get even a few pieces of candy. In light of this,

Halloween was celebrated in town instead. Children of all ages, as well as some adults, came in costume and prowled the downtown's main street to gather treats from the shopkeepers. Cornstalks decorated all the lampposts and telephone poles. The smell of hot cider wafted from shop doors as the treat-seekers came and went. A local band, the Wormwood Fiddlers, played in the town square, and senior citizens brought lawn chairs to enjoy the festivities. On the courthouse lawn, the annual costume contest ended the evening, although by then several families had usually gone home. Worn-out mothers often ended the evening by dragging their children in their Walmart costumes to the car crying because they weren't allowed to enter.

On Saturday, Annie, delighted because her mother had come home for the holiday, had dressed excitedly. She'd chosen to go as Wonder Woman in a costume her grandmother had worked on for weeks. Dressed in a skirt of starry gauze, a sequined, cardboard headband, and blue tights, AJ thought Annie looked adorable. All she lacked were thigh-high boots, and maybe boobs. Since AJ was still wearing her cast and a small bandage on her head, Annie convinced her to dress up as well and to complete the mummy look by wrapping gauze on the rest of her body and making a big turban to match. She felt silly, but at least she knew she'd be warm.

Once costumed, they asked Alice to come with them, but she declined just as AJ knew she would. It was hard to get Alice off the home place except to go to church. So, mother and daughter set off. It reminded AJ of their last adventure before she'd left for Virginia—the day at the Labor Day carnival.

"Annie, you got to promise me there won't be another roller-coaster ride today. Remember what happened last time?"

Annie giggled. "I do. And I promise. But if you eat too much candy, you might puke again, anyway." When AJ laughed out loud, Annie said, "Well, that's what you always tell me. But I think you just say it so you can steal some." Her giggles both delighted and saddened AJ, realizing how long it had been since she'd heard them.

"I do not," AJ said in feigned shock at Annie's accusation. "I always keep a private stash for myself, so there." She joined in the laughter. "By the way, how's your friend, what's his name? The one with the Mohawk and the tattoos?"

"Oh, we aren't friends anymore. He says bad words and I don't want to hear them."

AJ made no reply to this, but inside she was thinking, *Yes!*

They parked behind the bank and walked toward the decorated main street. The air was crisp but not so uncomfortable that heavy coats were necessary. Annie carried a sizeable white-oak basket for her loot, but AJ planned to have cider instead of candy, so she had eschewed a basket. As they entered the hardware store, one of AJ's distant neighbors, Betsy Anderson, stopped her. She wore a black pointed hat and black lipstick in what AJ assumed was her idea of a witch's costume.

"Hey, AJ, I thought you'd moved to Virginia. Whatcha doing back home? Back to see what us country folk are up to?" she said derisively. *Costume suits her.*

AJ didn't rise to the bait. Instead, she said, "Hey, Betsy. No, I didn't move; I'm just staying there for a year. I still have a home here, remember. I thought you knew that. How's your family?"

"Oh, we're all hanging in there. Bobby had a spell with his back, so we didn't get all the harvest in we'd hoped to. Couldn't get nary soul to help. They was all getting in their own crops."

"Sorry to hear that. And sorry I wasn't here to help. I would have; you know that."

"You hear about Sally Dawson's boy? He done overdosed. Died last week right there in his room. She found him the next morning. Nearly put her in her grave. I heard his older brother Delmer's dealing, too. Eustis always was bad to do drugs. Bad lot, both of 'em. I could have bet he'd end up dead like that."

"Oh no, poor Sally. I knew he had some problems, but I thought he'd gone to rehab. I'm sorry to hear that. Addiction is a terrible thing."

Betsy snorted as if she thought he'd deserved to die. "Uh-huh," she said as she left the store with her son in tow.

Annie grabbed her mother's hand. "Come on. Let's go to the drugstore. Someone said they're having an apple-bobbing contest. Please?"

At the drugstore, several non-costumed mothers were sitting at the counter while their children bobbed for apples in an old metal soft drink chest. AJ remembered pulling icy Cokes from it as a child. Now, a tall, gleaming red machine had replaced it.

"Hey, AJ, good to see you," called a woman from the end of the counter. A plump older lady, she wore a sheepskin-lined jacket. Her graying hair hung below her collar. "Sorry to hear about Dewey. You two was real close, wasn't you? I'd always thought you made a good couple."

Each stool's occupant swiveled to look at AJ. She wished she could melt into the woodwork. Having her love life bounce off the tile floor so everyone could hear it was just what she needed. She moved to the end of the counter before the woman could say more. With tight lips she said, "Thanks. It was a tragedy. But he knew better than to drink and drive." The other woman nodded. AJ added, "I do miss him, though."

"What happened to your arm?" the woman asked. She'd read AJ's tone and knew not to pursue the topic further.

"I got knocked off a horse by a low-hanging limb."

"On Gunner? I thought you knew all them paths."

"No, this happened in Virginia. Heard anymore blasting lately?" AJ changed the subject.

"Yeah, I heard 'em over the hill the other day. I ain't gone to look, but they must be close by. Them fracking folks been coming around, too. I heard they been offering good money. And I heard the Dunlaps done signed to let them drill on their land."

Before AJ could learn more, Annie ran up to her yelling, "Look,

Momma. I won a prize. I bited one of the apples." She was carrying a huge bag of jelly beans.

"*Bit*, Annie, not *bited*. I call dibs on the licorice ones," she told Annie as she dug in the bag for the black ones. "Later," she called to the woman, whose name she couldn't recall, as she and Annie headed out the door and down the street.

In store after store, she encountered folks she'd known since she was young, and they all seemed to know the details of her life. More than one person mentioned Dew, but most wanted to know what she was doing over there in Virginia. By the end of the evening she felt as if she'd been through the Spanish Inquisition.

When they returned home, Alice was waiting to hear all about their night. AJ was tired and ready for sleep, but after Annie calmed down and went to bed, her mother said, "Audrey Jane, hold up a minute. I want to talk to you."

AJ took a seat at the kitchen table, began unwrapping her costume, and wondered what on earth her mother wanted as Alice got a cup of coffee and sat back down.

"You liking it down there?"

"Well, it's different, but yes, it's a pretty nice life. Course, it's sorta fakey in a way. I'm living on somebody else's money and ain't got to worry what nothing costs. Why?"

"Just wondering is all. You never said. It is nice to have them paying all our bills, too, I gotta admit. But it ain't gonna last. Then what? You coming back home?"

"Gosh, Mom, I've only been gone a couple of months. I can't say for sure now. Why?" AJ was stunned that her mother thought she could make that decision so quickly.

"Well, I been doing okay up here, with Jimmy helping out and all, but I worry about them fracking men. What if they come here? What do I tell them? And I hear some folks been signing on to let them drill. I been reading stuff in the papers saying fracking's bad.

Ain't that gonna affect us? What if all them chemicals poison our well? How's a body supposed to know what's true?"

"As far as I can see, if they're trying to sell something to make them money, they'll say anything. I'd believe what I read, if I was you. If they come around, tell them the owner ain't here and won't be for a long time. And don't never tell them where I am. Hear?"

"I promise." Alice smiled.

AJ laid her hand on her mother's bony arm and smiled back. "It'll be okay. Don't let 'em rent space in your head."

That night, tucked in her old familiar bed, she replayed the conversations she'd had that evening. Other than the enquiries into her own life, most had revolved around who'd done what to whom, who had died or divorced, who'd lost their farm or sold out to the mining companies, or who was on drugs. Stories were peppered with lots of "Bless his heart," or "Ain't it a sight." And they told stories about the salesmen who'd come around for the fracking company. Yes, there *was* news, but mostly it was gossip.

This town's amazin'. Ain't no secrets here. Everybody knows everybody else's business. I used to think that was cool, that people just cared, but now that it's my business they know, I ain't so fond of it. Do I want to come back to that? Course, maybe it ain't so different in Virginia. Isabelle talked about gossip there about her and Jack. I'll bet Molly stirred up the gossips for sure even before Ben killed hisself. Maybe people are the same everywhere. But if mountaintop mining gets any closer, what do I do? And then there's them damn frackers. Lots of folks don't got a choice, but we do, now. I could sell out and move Mom and Annie to Virginia. Would Alice ever adjust to life at Langford Hall? Hell no, she'd be in the kitchen fighting with Clara. Maybe she'd get over it, but, damn it, it's my land. I grew up here. My roots are in these mountains, and I don't want to see them ruined.

She was tired but tossed until the blankets were a tangle, finally falling asleep from exhaustion with a frown.

⌐

On Monday, AJ returned to Virginia, leaving Annie in a puddle of tears before she left for school, and Alice looking more tired than usual. Tears loomed behind AJ's eyes, as well, but once she descended the rocky lane from Gimlet Hollow, she began to focus on Virginia. She looked forward to working with the accountants—especially Barry Peterson—to learn how the farm's financial business was handled.

I'm sure they'll be more helpful than that damn Tom.

⌒ Chapter Eighteen ⌒

Instead of luxuriating in bed, AJ rose early Tuesday morning. She had two things she wanted to do—see the horses, and be in Tom's office when Barry Peterson and his partner, Mr. Chelyan, arrived. It was foggy when, armed with coffee, she scampered to the barn like a kid drawn to a new toy. Bundled in a white fleece jacket, her left arm barely covered, she knocked on the barn door. No answer. *Maybe it's too early.* When she knocked again, she heard the nickering of the horses. She didn't want to spook them, so when a third timid knock went unanswered, AJ returned to the house.

She pushed through the kitchen's swinging door and saw that Clara was moving slowly as she made breakfast. To AJ it looked as if she were in pain.

"You okay, Clara?" she asked as she plopped down at the island counter.

"Great Scott, you scared me to death, Miss AJ. What you doing sneaking in like that?" She put her hand to her breast, as if her heart were beating out of it. After a few recuperative breaths, she eyed AJ and laughed. "You look like a snowman in that jacket. Why'd you ask if I was okay?"

"You looked like you were limping when I came in, is all."

"Oh, that. On cold mornings, my joints don't feel like they've got the juice in them that they need to move. I'll be fine once I warm up." She walked to the oven and turned it on.

AJ noticed a pan of biscuits ready for the oven sitting on the counter.

"I was going to skip breakfast to spend some time with the horses this morning, but I couldn't rouse Santos. Now I'm glad. I'm going to wait right here for those," she said, pointing to the pan. "Yum."

Before she could ask Clara what else she was planning to fix, Isabelle appeared in the doorway. "Welcome home, AJ. How'd Halloween go? I hope you and Annie had fun."

"We did, thanks. It was good to spend time with her."

"Have you seen Hank this morning? He wants to talk to you," Isabelle said as she poured a cup of coffee.

AJ looked at her watch. "It's so early. I'm surprised he's here. I couldn't even find Santos, and he's usually up with the chickens. Have you heard from him?"

"Yes, he called in. Said he'd be late today, but he didn't say why." Isabelle stirred her coffee.

"Thanks, I was a bit worried. You know why Hank wants to see me?"

"Not really, but he said something about the year-end crop report. Maybe you should call him."

"I will as soon as I eat. Want a biscuit? They'll be ready soon, according to Clara. I saw them go into the oven, and I'm waiting. Honey and biscuits—nothin' better."

Isabelle declined, then said, "Come see me after you talk to Hank," as she left the kitchen. Isabelle's hat was bright red with a wide grosgrain ribbon around the crown. AJ imagined ornaments pinned to the hatband. *She looks like she's already decorated herself for Christmas.*

Clara grinned at AJ's remark. "Ever try sorghum? Now that's some fine eating."

"Oh, God, yes. Back home, we used to buy sorghum every fall at the farmer's market. Sometimes we even watched the women making it. If you've got any, I'd rather have it than honey any day."

As soon as she returned to her office, AJ called Hank. "I hear you want to see me. Can you come to my office? I need to go out to meet with the bookkeepers pretty soon, so I'd rather you came here."

"On my way."

AJ returned to the kitchen for more coffee, then paced until he arrived. She scratched at her hand under her cast with a pencil. Her arm itched, and the cast's limitations were really annoying her. She was ready to have the thing off. *I have to admit, though, that it could have been worse. It could have been my right just as easily.*

Hank burst through the door in a rush of cold air. He was breathing heavily as if he'd walked rather than driven from his office across the fields. The cold seemed to radiate from his heavy jacket. In his meaty fist, he had several pieces of paper. AJ shivered as he stood in front of her.

"See these reports?" he said, waving them in her face like semaphore flags. His face was flushed, his voice raspy. When he started speaking, she thought maybe he had a cold, but the longer he talked, she realized he was just angry.

"They aren't good. This year's yield of soybeans and wheat were both way down. You know why? Cause of the drought this summer. And you know what? It could have been avoided if that lazy bastard Tom Beckett had approved my request. No, it was a demand, a demand to extend the irrigation system." He finally ran out of angry steam and quit, collapsing in a chair like a deflated helium balloon. "'Scuse me for cussing, Miss AJ."

"Good to see you, too, Hank," said AJ, chuckling as she put out her hand to take the papers.

"I'm sorry, ma'am. Good morning. I'm just so gol-durned mad, I could spit nails. We did all we could to keep the fields from going completely dry, but you can't water that many acres with only a water truck. Mr. Jack had the pipes put in some fields with plans to expand later, but after he died, Tom never did it. Always said it was too expensive; he thought Jack had wasted money putting in the first section. Well, now look where we are. Our income is going to suffer more than it would have cost to extend the damn system."

"Are we in financial trouble?" she asked, panicked.

"No, nothing that bad, but it's not good. We sold all we could harvest, but lots of the plants just had to be plowed under. I think we should put that system in now before we have another bad summer. I think global warming is real; and I don't want to take a chance, do you?"

"Not really. I'll look for Jack's information about the system in Tom's papers, then I'll get back to you. Okay?"

The room seemed to warm after Hank left, but AJ couldn't enjoy it. She retrieved the last two years' crop reports and began comparing them to the one Hank had just given her. She could see that what he'd said was right—a substantial decline in output. With the papers in hand, she went to see Isabelle.

"Got a minute?" she asked as she entered the room. She noticed that it was much warmer than her office. *Maybe I shouldn't have been so quick to dismiss working in here. There's a fireplace here for when it gets really cold.* She shivered at the thought.

"Well, Hank could have had better news." She scowled as she laid the papers in front of Isabelle, then slumped in the chair in front of the desk. "We had some bad crop yields this year. Look at the decline. Hank says it's because of the drought."

Isabelle looked over the reports for a few minutes, then said, "I see."

"Hank blames Tom for not putting an irrigation system in all the fields. He says Jack wanted to extend it, but after he died, Tom dropped the ball, either on purpose or . . . I don't know, but Hank is furious." She sighed. "So far this hasn't been a good fall. First, we find out Tom's probably been stealing us blind, now this. Keeping this place going is tough, isn't it?"

Isabelle looked up, studying AJ's obvious consternation. "Yes, it's always been one struggle or another, but they all persevered. When I was doing Jack's family history, I remember reading about how the Confederates commandeered the house as a hospital, then used all the food grown to feed the patients and the army officers. The family nearly starved, even though they were Southern sympathizers. After World War I, another Morgan, actually his widow—Mildred, I think her name was—had to take in boarders to survive, but it turned out to be a disaster. Some were drunks and one stole a family heirloom. Later, another boarder tried to rape her. She had a gun and held him off, but it scared her so badly, she closed the boarding house and moved into town in a tiny rented apartment. Once her son was grown, he moved back and managed to make Langford Hall flourish again.

"And Reeves, remember him from Molly's diary? He was a lousy manager. He almost lost the farm. I think he might have had a gambling problem, but Jack never said so. He just hinted that Reeves got into terrible debt. I can't imagine what else would have caused it. He finally sold off some land that wasn't being farmed, and things were good again. Struggle is part of life, AJ. These are small problems, comparatively. Think you can handle it?"

"Yeah, I'll manage. I've dealt with worse back home. Besides, Hank says we'll be fine, so I'll stop worrying. Okay, I'm off to get my first accounting refresher. Just wanted you to know. Later," she said as she retrieved the papers from Isabelle and headed back to her office for a jacket. She stopped in the doorway and turned back toward Isabelle. AJ's usual smile returned. "Thanks for telling me Mildred's story. I skipped those letters. It's good to see how another woman coped when she was in charge."

"You're welcome," Isabelle said as AJ waggled her fingers goodbye on her way through the doorway.

For the next few weeks, AJ's routine was predictable. She rose early, took coffee out to the stables to visit the horses, then met Barry and Mr. Chelyan. Unlike Barry, Chelyan never asked to be called by his first name, and largely ignored AJ unless she asked him a direct question. Barry, on the other hand, invited her to shadow him as the two managed the accounting of the farm. He explained his every move and anticipated the questions she might ask. Even though she sometimes felt as if she were an intern at her own firm, she was enjoying every moment.

While Chelyan was all business, she and Barry did as much chatting about other things as they did about the work. Whenever one of them laughed, AJ could see Chelyan's jaw tighten, his lips draw into a straight, disapproving line, but she didn't care. She was delighted to have someone close to her own age to talk to.

Over the course of the month she learned that Barry was divorced, had never had children, and was born on a Monroe County, West Virginia, farm. She'd laughed when he answered her "Where ya from?" question.

"West Virginians," she had told him, "at least rural ones, always say the county. They know the person who asked wouldn't know any of the small-town names even if they were told. That's how I knew you were a real West Virginia hillbilly." Barry laughingly agreed.

By Thanksgiving week, the two had become close. Some nights Barry didn't leave work with Mr. Chelyan. He stayed, telling Chelyan he had a few more things he wanted to show AJ. Then, when they were through working, the two would go into the house, have a beer and relax. One night, AJ asked Clara to fix dinner for two, and Barry stayed.

"I'm so glad you didn't have to go back into town early," she said, smiling as Barry pulled AJ's chair out for her.

"Me too," he replied. "I can cook, but I'm sure Clara's a lot better at it than I am."

AJ grinned as Barry brushed back the dark shock of hair that seemed determined to consistently cover his brow, then began on his salad. To her the habit seemed endearing.

"What's your favorite thing to cook?" she asked.

"Fried chicken. I know it's not very healthy, but my mom taught me to make it, and I still love it. It reminds me of her, and of my dad, who loved it better than anything." His face fell. "They've been gone ten years this year and I still miss them."

AJ took a bite of her salad. "My dad's gone, too. Car accident. He was drunk and missed a curve. I can't say I miss him much, though. He was mean to my mother."

"I'm sorry. My dad was wonderful. Kind, generous, sweet to Mom, and to us kids. He became a lawyer when I was in elementary school, so we had a good life. He bought a plane, a Cherokee 140, and he loved to fly. One day we were all supposed to go to Washington, DC, for the weekend. I didn't want to go, some school thing, I think. Might have been finals week at WVU. Anyway, Mom, Dad, and Susie, my little sister, went without me. His plane crashed and they were all killed. Never knew what happened. Wasn't weather; it was beautiful that weekend. Maybe engine trouble, I don't know. Susie was only sixteen. I felt guilty about it for years. I thought I should have been with them, you know?"

AJ placed her hand on his. "No, there's a reason you were spared. You shouldn't feel guilty. Maybe you were left to carry on the family name, and the family memories. I wish I could have felt sad about my dad. But actually, I was furious at him. His death stopped my college career. Later, I was just relieved that he wouldn't be there to beat my mom anymore." As Clara pushed through the swinging door with a platter of roast beef and Yorkshire pudding, AJ quickly removed her hand from Barry's.

"Thank you, this looks delicious," Barry said, reddening slightly. When she'd gone, he said, "I hope she didn't see that—your hand on mine, I mean. If she did—"

"She'd never breathe a word. And besides, what's it matter? Can't we be friends?"

"Of course we can, but I'll bet Chelyan would prefer I keep my distance. Appearances, you know."

AJ snorted. "Oh yeah, we must look proper. Don't worry about it. He's an old stick in the mud. I don't feel guilty at all."

Barry laughed, then AJ continued. "What I *do* feel guilty about is the recent death of my former, uh, friend, Dewey. He was here for the weekend, but we argued and he left in a huff. I heard he got himself liquored up and accidentally drove off the road. He died when he hit a tree." Her eyes teared, and she dabbed at them with her napkin.

Barry reached for her, touched her shoulder. "That wasn't your fault any more than my dad's crash was mine. I went through a lot of counseling to come around to believing that, but it's true. We can't control what happens to anyone, sometimes not even to ourselves. So, let's just enjoy the day, the evening, the moment. Okay?"

AJ smiled weakly. "Okay. It's a deal."

Barry left around nine, and AJ went upstairs smiling. She couldn't get her mind off him. It was the first time she'd spent an evening with a man who could laugh at himself, was knowledgeable about current events, was committed to protecting the environment, wasn't afraid of talking about feelings, and enjoyed all kinds of music. In the shower, she began thinking of the contrast between Barry and Dew. It couldn't have been sharper.

On reflection, she realized her relationship with Dew hadn't started out with friendship. He'd put the moves on her from the first, and she'd acquiesced after only a few dates. Soon, it was mostly about the sex. She now realized they'd had little in common, other than where they lived, and the sex. He was content to spend his life working eight to five, drinking beer, and having sex. She'd always wanted more, had wanted to become a vet. Granted they'd never argued, until she decided to come to Virginia, but otherwise, they'd rarely talked about anything substantial or intimate. She was sorry he was dead, but she now knew that the relationship probably wouldn't have lasted, even if he hadn't been killed. On the other hand, she and Barry had become friends. He was easy to talk to even if he sometimes made AJ stretch her mind to consider how she felt or thought about the topic under discussion. She liked that, and returned from the shower happier than she'd been in a long time. AJ climbed into bed, flipped off the light, and curled up under her granny's quilt. She was asleep in minutes.

⏤ Chapter Nineteen ⏤

AJ fumbled for her chirping phone in the half-dark bedroom. *Damn, I should have put that sucker on silent.* She heard papers flutter to the floor just before she found the light and her phone. "Hello," she mumbled without looking to see who called.

"Audrey Jane? You don't sound like yourself. Did I wake you?"

She sat up in bed and pulled the quilt around her shoulders. "It's okay, Alice. I needed to get up anyway. What's wrong?"

"Well, the vet was out here last night. Something's wrong with Flossie. She got loose the other day, and we found her down by the creek. I don't know if she drank from it or not, but she's got blisters in her mouth and won't eat. Doc Watson said maybe something in the water caused them blisters or that she might be poisoned. You think that creek could poison a cow?"

AJ was wide awake now. "I don't know, but I sure as hell wouldn't drink any of her milk, at least not until she's better. And if you get a good day, don't you dare let Annie go near that place, you hear?"

"Don't worry. I wouldn't never. I hope she gets better, poor thing. We need that milk. When you coming for Thanksgiving? Wednesday?"

"Yeah, I reckon so. It might be later in the day, though. I'm working with these accountants, you know, and if they're going to be here, well, so am I. We'll see. I might could leave right after lunch, though. That work?"

Alice said it would, then disconnected. AJ sat there with the silent phone in her hand. *I'll bet that stream is poisoned. I've thought so ever since Annie found those two dead frogs. That damn mining company. If I could figure out how to stop them, I would. They're ruining ever stream in seven counties. What if that shit gets in people's wells? Then we're all screwed.*

When she stepped out of bed, she saw what she'd knocked off the nightstand as she fumbled for the phone. Hank's crop reports that she'd brought up to study further. She gathered them up carefully, resorted them, and replaced them on the bedside table. She looked at the time on her phone. *Oh crap, it's eight thirty. I got to get moving.* She quickly showered, dressed, and went downstairs to eat before heading to Tom's office.

A few minutes before eleven, as she was entering payments into the computer under Barry's watchful eye, Tom's phone rang. AJ picked up the receiver. "Langford Hall Farms, may I help you?"

"Tom Beckett there?" came a deep voice.

"I'm sorry. He's on leave right now. This is AJ Porter; can I help you?"

"When will he be back? And begging your pardon, ma'am, but who are you?" His voice had become hesitant.

"I'm not sure when he'll return, but I'm the owner of the farm now." AJ glanced over at Barry with a look of skepticism and shrugged as if she wasn't sure where this conversation was going.

"Oh," the caller responded. She heard the surprise in his voice. He paused, then after a moment brightened. "Well, maybe you're the person I should be talking to anyway. My name is Curt Michaelson. Tom and I been talking about what was going to become of the farm ever since old man Morgan died. I've been interested for some time in buying the property. I didn't know there was a new owner. Would you be interested in selling? The old geezer never was, but now . . ." He trailed off.

"Absolutely not," AJ huffed. "And don't call him an old geezer. What made you think I might be? Did Tom suggest that?"

"Well, he told me someone was staying here, but he didn't make it sound as if you were actually the owner. He said something about it just being temporary."

"Oh, he did, did he? Well, I'm afraid you've been misled, Mr. Michaelson. I'm Jack Morgan's great-niece and I have no notion of selling Langford Hall. You've been wasting your time talking to that . . . to Mr. Beckett. Actually, you and I are done talking about it, too." She banged the phone down on the receiver. "Damn, can you believe that man?"

"What? Who was it?" asked Barry. "I'm sorry; it's really not my business, but you look so upset."

AJ looked over at Chelyan, who was staring at both of them. "Let's go get some fresh coffee and I'll tell you." Chelyan snorted derisively.

As they walked, AJ repeated the telephone conversation. "I need to tell Isabelle about this. Let's see if she's got a minute," AJ said as they entered the house. They found her coming out of the kitchen with a coffee mug in hand. "Isabelle, are you real busy? I need to talk to you," AJ said as they continued toward Isabelle's office.

Isabelle looked first at AJ and then stared at Barry. "I've got time; what's going on?" Her eyes narrowed and then lingered on Barry, who got the hint.

"AJ, if you'd prefer to talk in private, I'll grab my coffee and go back to the office," he said.

"Might be a good idea, Mr. Peterson. We won't be long. Right, AJ?"

"No, we won't, " AJ said, feeling admonished. She turned back to Barry and smiled, "I'll be back in a second."

Barry nodded and walked back toward the kitchen while AJ went on with Isabelle to her office.

"What's he doing coming in with you? I thought he was only here to do the accounting."

"We were going to get coffee. He'd overheard what I wanted to tell you, so I didn't see that it made any difference to bring him. Besides, we've become good friends. I've shared a lot with him. I wouldn't have minded. Do you?"

"Well, frankly, yes, I would have. I don't know what you needed to talk about, but any business of the farm not related to the audit should be ours alone . . . and I don't think it's a good idea for you to get so chummy with a hired accountant."

"Frankly, I don't see the problem. He's only going to be here a few months. Besides, it's not much different from you and Jack, now is it? Except we aren't having an affair." She looked at Isabelle hesitantly. It was the first time she'd challenged Isabelle on anything, and now she was worried that she'd gone too far.

After a pause, Isabelle sat back in her chair and chuckled. "No, I guess it isn't. You got me there, girl. I apologize." Isabelle smiled. "So, now, what was it you wanted to tell me?"

AJ repeated the phone conversation from Mr. Michaelson. "Is he the same guy Mr. Mulgrew mentioned way back when? The one who wanted to turn this place into a housing development?"

"The very same. I thought he'd given up, but apparently he simply turned to Tom to press his case. As I recall, I think the two are related somehow. I'll check on it, but I'm pretty sure someone told me that." Isabelle hesitated a moment. "You wouldn't sell, would you? That would break my heart."

AJ started to respond, but she saw that Isabelle had tears in her eyes. She paused as Isabelle shook her head, and then sighed.

"I feel like Langford Hall is part of me, too. But you need to know why . . . why I'm so desperate for you to keep the property. You see, there was more than an affair between me and Jack. There's a child . . . a son. Jack really did have an heir, but he wouldn't legally claim him because he was born out of wedlock."

AJ sank slowly into the chair across from Isabelle's desk, shaken from the bombshell. She started to comment, but Isabelle held up her hand.

"I went to my sister's in Richmond to have him. After he was born, I stayed there until he was weaned. She raised him as her own until he was about twelve, then Jack sent him to boarding school at Randolph Macon Academy outside of Washington. My biggest regret is that Jack never formally or legally acknowledged him. He met him, and I'm sure he loved him. But he insisted that it was best not to allow him to come to Langford Hall. We had several *discussions* on the subject, but I always *acquiesced* to Jack. Now our son lives in California." Isabelle's face melted into that of a grieving mother.

"Oh, Isabelle, I had no idea. You should have told me sooner. Bless your heart," AJ said, putting her hand on Isabelle's arm. "What's his name? Do you ever see him? What does he do?"

"I named him Jack Morgan Collins. I haven't seen him this year, but I usually do at least once a year," she replied, then snickered. "You asked what he does? He's a very successful commercial real estate developer. Isn't that a coincidence?"

AJ chuckled too. "That is funny. Do you have a picture of him? I'd love to see it."

"I do," Isabelle said, reaching for her purse. She pulled out a billfold and opened it to a photograph of a dark-haired young man dressed in hiking gear and standing in front of a reddish stone monolith. "He loves the outdoors. That's him in Sedona, Arizona. I think that was in 2014 when he traveled the Southwest."

"Wow, he's very handsome, Isabelle. And I can see Morgan features in his face. I think it's the eyes. Does he have a family?"

"Just a wife. He married a lovely gal about five years ago. She's got Indian blood and has these piercing dark eyes. Smart as a whip, too. She's a radiological technician. No children, though, at least not yet. I think she's pretty career oriented, at least for now. Clock's ticking, though, right?"

"How old is she?"

"In her late twenties. She's younger than Jack. She got her radiology training after they married."

"Aww, she's got plenty of time," AJ said with a dismissive wave of her hand. "I'd better get back to work. Thanks for sharing your story with me."

"I've wanted to for a long time, but it never seemed to be the right time. Now, you've got to promise that it goes no further. Promise? Not even to Barry," she said with a knowing grin.

"Scout's honor." AJ crossed her heart.

⌣

"Look at all the movie posters," said AJ as she and Barry entered Bizou in downtown Charlottesville. "And the jukeboxes; it looks like an old-fashioned diner all dressed up to go somewhere fancy." She took a deep breath. "God, it smells wonderful, too." She tried not to gawk, but the surroundings almost overwhelmed her. The high ceilings. The deeply padded red booths. The gleaming wall sconces.

As Barry took her coat and laid it over one of the chairs, he caught AJ looking longingly at the booths. "Would you rather sit in a booth so we can play the jukebox?"

"Yeah, let's do," AJ responded eagerly.

The waitress seemed unruffled as she moved them from the table to a nearby booth. "Here you go," she said as they settled into the cozy space. "I'm Ainslie and I'll be back to take your order soon." She handed them menus.

"This place is so cool. I guess you've eaten here before," AJ said as they looked over their menus.

"A few times. They're famous for their locally sourced foods, so anything that says that on the menu should be great. I especially like the catfish. It's local, I know."

"Yew. Back home, I'd be afraid to eat anything caught in our streams. I think they're all being poisoned by mine runoff or by fracking chemicals."

"I think you're safe here," he laughed. "But in case you're nervous about any of the fish items, the meatloaf is also wonderful." They studied the menus for a minute longer; then AJ began flipping through the selections on the booth-side jukebox.

"Got any quarters? I want to play Patsy Cline. How about you? Want to hear Jefferson Airplane or Ike and Tina Turner?"

"Jefferson Airplane sounds good," he said as he fished several quarters from his pocket. "But play whatever you want." The waiter returned and they ordered as Patsy Cline's "Crazy" floated from the speaker system.

Once the waitress left, AJ turned to Barry. "Barry, what do you know about fracking? When I was home for Halloween, my mother told me folks around us are being pressured to let a gas company drill on their land. The representatives swear it won't bother them, but—"

"From what I've read about it, I wouldn't let them drill if I owned property there. There've been too many stories about the ground around the wells being so toxic that nothing will grow. The drilling is also very noisy. And some environmentalists suggest that in places where earthquakes never happened before, fracking is the cause. Did you know they had earthquakes in Pennsylvania and the Midwest last year?" AJ shook her head as he continued. "They weren't that strong, but neither of those areas had ever had an earthquake before. One article said that a well, *one well*, could affect thirty acres of a forest. And I know water *is* being contaminated. I've read several studies on it. You ought to Google it."

"I will. If the neighbors give in, it'll affect us even if we don't sign, won't it? I'm really worried about it. Our cow had blisters in her mouth that Alice thinks were caused by our creek water. And last summer, Annie found two dead frogs in it. I thought it was from mining runoff, but now I'm not sure. Maybe it's from fracking." She gave Barry a warm smile. "Let's talk about something else, okay?"

"Sure. Tell me more about you and your life in West Virginia. I want to know everything." Barry reached for AJ's hand.

AJ blushed, an unusual reaction for her, but she'd wanted him to make a move for the last month. As she ate, she told him more about her background. About Jeff's death, about Annie, about the ongoing disagreements with her mother, and about the farm. He listened intently, nearly forgetting his own meal.

"You miss it, don't you? The hills, your home place, I mean."

"Yeah, but I sure don't miss arguing with Alice. I like it here, too. I like it a lot; but it's not home. You understand? I've got a tough decision to make and I'm still not sure what I'll do. But now it's your turn. You tell me about your life."

Throughout the meal they shared stories with each other. They lingered after dinner for coffee and dessert as if neither wanted the evening to end. As they finished, Barry noticed that the restaurant had nearly emptied. "I guess we'd better go. Looks like they want to close. Want to go somewhere else for a drink? It's still early."

AJ nodded. "Yeah, I'm not ready for this to be over." She hooked her arm in his as they turned toward a nearby bar.

He smiled down at her and placed his warm hand over hers. "Neither am I," he said.

It was nearing midnight when they pulled down Langford Hall's lane. A stiff wind whipped the dead leaves around their feet as Barry and AJ mounted the few steps to the porch. AJ clung to Barry's arm, more out of a desire to be as close to him as possible than in search of warmth. As she dug in her purse for her keys, Barry took her shoulders, turned her toward him, and gazed into her face. She smiled up at him. Without hesitation, he cradled AJ's face in his warm hands, leaned over, and kissed her.

AJ leaned back, looked at Barry, and said, "God, I hoped you'd do that."

"I hoped you'd let me." They laughed and kissed again.

"See you in the morning," they said almost in unison.

Inside the house, AJ leaned against the big door and hugged herself. Her face glowed like a lantern, and her smile, like the Cheshire cat's, remained.

⌒ CHAPTER TWENTY ⌒

The following morning, AJ told Isabelle she was going out to the office. "I need to do some research on fracking. According to my mother, the drilling company's sales reps are trying to talk our neighbors into letting them drill on land near us. Actually, right next to our property. I need to find a way to fight them. We can say no to our land, but we could still have our water poisoned if they sign on. It's crazy. It's like they have no respect for personal property."

"That's not a problem we have over here, but I think everyone who ever lived here has had some sort of struggles. I guess it goes with the territory."

"Well, right now, my struggles are in West Virginia. I don't want our property or ground water ruined. I've got to find a way to stop them."

By lunchtime, she'd learned through Google searches enough to know she wanted no part of fracking and was determined to do whatever she could to stop the practice, at least in her own backyard.

Now she needed to find out how. She said as much to Barry as they ate lunch.

"I've got to start some sort of anti-fracking campaign, but it's hard to do that from here. Do you think doing something on social media would help? I could post stories about it."

"Maybe. It certainly can't hurt. It would at least draw attention to the problem. But it seems to me that the only way to truly stop them is to own the land under siege and then just say no."

"Well, that's certainly a pipe dream. I only own our few acres. If I owned as much land as we've got here, that would certainly keep them at a distance, but I don't."

"You could if you sold Langford Hall and used the money to buy up some of the land around you."

AJ's mouth and eyes were as wide open as a ventriloquist's doll, but she remained silent.

"What?" he said, surprised by her expression.

She fired back, "Sell it? To that asshole? No way. I don't want Langford Hall to go out of the family, period. Wait. What if . . . never mind. I was just thinking . . . never mind. It's a crazy idea. Maybe I'll tell you about it another time."

Barry looked puzzled. "Okay. If that's what you want." He could see she was clearly hatching a plan, but apparently didn't want to share it.

Even if I don't sell, I'll still have Uncle Jack's money. Twelve million dollars. That could buy up a lot of land.

She thought about leaving Langford Hall and never seeing Barry again *Why does this have to be so hard? Jack shoulda just given the place to his own damn son.*

"I wonder how the audit is coming," AJ asked.

"Non-sequitur alert," Barry said, then laughed.

"What's a *non-sequitur*?" AJ reddened.

"It's when someone abruptly talks about something that doesn't follow what had been said previously." He chuckled again, "Anyway, in answer to your question, I don't know, but you could call them and ask. Now it's my turn. Would you like to have dinner with me tonight? We can just grab a burger in town if you like?"

"I'd love to."

⌣

For the next few weeks, AJ lived in a whirlwind as she continued to learn the business's accounting systems, Christmas shopped, and dated Barry. They had dinner together at least three times a week, and on Saturday night as well. They ate either at Langford Hall or in the Charlottesville boutique restaurants Barry seemed to have a knack for finding. The week before Christmas, he invited AJ to his home for dinner for a change. He said he wanted to cook for her and she accepted gladly. He promised the evening would be special.

Barry met her at the door wearing a Santa hat and a bright-red sweater. "Welcome to Peterson Hall," he said just before he wrapped her in an embrace and kissed her. "It's not quite as grand as Langford Hall, but I like it." Barry took her coat to the hall closet.

"Love the hat," AJ called as she looked around the living room with its well-worn leather couch and two comfortable-looking upholstered chairs. Underfoot, a beautiful oriental rug of deep burgundy, green, and white covered much of the dark hardwood floor. A fire burned in the stone fireplace between the chairs while the couch faced it. On the other side of the room, a magnificent fir tree, filled with traditional red, green, and silver glass balls, nearly touched the high ceiling.

"Did you do all this yourself? It's beautiful and so cozy," AJ said.

"I sure did, gal. I've got skills you have yet to discover." He waved his hand toward the fireplace where a swag of greenery held ornaments that matched those on the tree. "I did all the Christmas decorating, too. I love this time of year. See the nutcrackers? I collect them." Three tall wooden figures in various uniforms stood at attention on the fireplace hearth, and several more flanked the tree.

Under it, presents that looked professionally wrapped were stacked two and three high.

She wondered who they were for since Barry had no family.

Pointing to the presents, he offered, "Those are yours," as if he'd read her mind.

"No. Really? All of them? Barry, you shouldn't have. I wish I could wrap presents like that. Mine always look like Annie did them," AJ laughed as she pulled one out of her purse and added it to the pile. "See?"

"Aww, that's not so bad. At least it has a bow." Then in mock surprise he added, "For me?" Barry leaned over and acted as if he were picking it up.

"No, it's for Santa." AJ laughed. "Of course it's for you, but you can't open it until after dinner."

"Okay, that's fine. Want a drink? Or a beer?"

"Beer, thanks. Something sure smells good. What are we having?" She settled onto the sofa, kicked off her shoes, and curled up into one corner. Barry stood in front of the fire, his hands clasped behind him as if he were warming them and his back. He gazed at AJ for a moment, taking in her red silk blouse designed to slip provocatively off one shoulder.

"I fixed a pot roast. I thought with this cold weather, we could use some comfort food. That's my go-to for a home-cooked meal. And, I must say, you look stunning." He moved toward the kitchen, motioning for AJ to join him. "Come on. I've got to check on something and get your beer."

"Thank you. You look pretty good yourself, mister," she said as she rose and padded to the kitchen in her stocking feet.

As Barry checked the oven temperature, AJ looked around. Spotting the dishes in the glass-front cabinets, she said, "Oh my gosh. You've got Fiesta dishes. My mom had them when I was a kid, but over the years I guess they broke. We've only got one yellow pitcher left."

"I bought those in Charleston a long time ago. I just love them. I understand they are very popular again. Want to help? If you'll get out the salad and toss it, we'll be ready when the rolls come out of the oven. I've put the dressings on the table."

"Sure. It will be the first time I've done anything in the kitchen since maybe Halloween. Alice wouldn't let me do a thing at Thanksgiving. Said it was my vacation. I laughed. Even though she's always been the main cook, I always helped with dishes, even as a kid. We used to sing while we washed. Of course, with her, it was always hymns. Thank goodness we finally got a dishwasher. I got tired of hearing 'The Old Rugged Cross.'"

Barry laughed. "Do you go to church now?"

"I would if people weren't so judgmental. I get frowned at for wearing my hair down. It's a really fundamentalist church. Not my cup of tea. You?"

"I did growing up, but I was so angry with God when my family died that I quit. I know now it wasn't His doing exactly, but I guess I just got out of the habit." As he pulled the rolls from the oven, he motioned toward the table set with gleaming candles and a small vase of red carnations.

"Dinner is served, madam."

After dinner, the two cleaned up the kitchen. As AJ cleared the plates and Barry loaded the dishwasher, she suggested they sing—not the old hymns, but Christmas carols. His rich baritone harmonized perfectly with her clear soprano. As they ended "I'll Be Home for Christmas," Barry said, "I know you're excited to be going home, but selfishly I wish you were staying here. In my dreams, you *are* home here in Virginia." He dried his hands, caressed her face, and kissed her.

She returned the kiss. "I know. I'll miss you terribly, too. I wish you could come with me, but—"

"Me too, and I understand. But as Kenny Rogers says, 'We've got tonight.'" He grinned, and with his arm around her, they walked back into the living room. Barry sat in one corner of the long sofa and patted the cushion beside him. "Come here."

She sat close to him. "Dinner was delicious. You could easily make Clara jealous if you challenged her to a cookoff."

He laughed. "I don't know about that, but I'll never starve." He pulled her close. "I'm so glad that cast is gone. It made hugging you very difficult. And I like hugging you . . . a lot." He kissed her nose, her cheeks, her forehead, and finally her lips. As she responded, his hand caressed the small of her back and then moved up inside her silk blouse, exploring her soft skin. She ran her fingers through his thick hair while her breathing quickened. AJ did not resist as he brought his right hand back to her waist, then reached up, deftly unsnapped her bra's front closure, and gently cupped one breast. AJ brought her leg over Barry's thighs, and as she did, she felt him rising. "Shall we continue this in my bedroom?" he asked in a throaty whisper.

"Only if you'll fix me breakfast in the morning."

As the two walked toward the bedroom, AJ gasped. "Oh, you didn't open your present."

"In the morning, You're the only present I want right now."

⌒

Early morning sunlight filtered through the slats of the plantation shutters as AJ stirred, then stretched her arms above her head. At the sight of Barry's tousled hair, she grinned, then leaned over and kissed him before burrowing back under the covers. He turned on his side and pulled her toward him so they nested like two spoons in a drawer. The down comforter and Barry's warm arms would have been enough to keep her in bed until noon. Finally, she rose on one elbow. "I've got to go to the bathroom, but I'll be right back. Don't you dare go anywhere. You don't happen to have a fresh toothbrush, do you?"

"In the top left-hand drawer. I started to get you a stocking and put it in there like my mother always did on Christmas, but I thought that might have been presumptuous." He grinned sleepily. "I also got you a—"

AJ stopped him in mid-sentence. "Don't tell me. I love surprises." As she rose from the bed, she said, "Don't look."

Barry burst out laughing. "Last night, I explored every inch of your body, and made love to you, several times. And now you don't want me to watch you walk away naked?"

"I know, it's silly, but don't. Maybe I'll get used to it later. Cover your eyes."

Barry pulled the sheet over his head and AJ dashed to the en-suite bathroom. A few moments later she returned wrapped in a thick bath towel. "Did you drink the glass of water that was by the sink?" she asked.

"Yeah. I was thirsty in the middle of the night, why?"

She began giggling. "My contact lens was in it. I didn't have my case with me, so I used the glass. I just wear one mono-vision lens, and you drank it."

"Oh, God. I'm so sorry. I had no idea." He laughed. "Well, at least now I can tell people that I've got inner vision."

AJ ran to the bed, jumped in, and kissed him, hard.

⌐ CHAPTER TWENTY-ONE ⌐

A J inched her truck down Turkey Knob on her way back to Virginia after Christmas. It had snowed, delighting Annie, whose main wish had been for a white Christmas. AJ wasn't nearly as thrilled; she hated driving in the snow. In fact, she'd delayed her return a day just so she wouldn't have to battle any untreated local roads. Fortunately, the snow had mostly cleared, but patches of ice still clung to the dark pavement where shadows hovered in the December light. As the miles melted away along with the ice, she replayed an argument she and Alice had the day she arrived.

She'd told her mother about her new relationship with Barry, thinking Alice would be happy for her. She was wrong, dead wrong; and even now, she wasn't sure what had set her mother off. Arguing often seemed to be their default mode of conversation. First Alice said AJ should slow down, that she was rebounding from her relationship with Dewey. AJ told her she'd figured out Dew was the wrong kind of man for her, and that it wouldn't have lasted anyway. Then Alice complained that if she got serious with Barry, she'd stay in Virginia.

"I'd never let Barry keep me away from you or Annie."

At Alice's humph, AJ realized Alice didn't believe her.

"And another thing . . . you shouldn't poop where you eat."

AJ was shocked to hear such a vulgar reference to sex come from her mother and wondered if there were something deeper in her mother's objection. *Is she afraid I'll take Annie but leave her? She should know better. If she thinks that, she sure doesn't know me very well.*

⸻

While AJ was home, she'd had an unexpected visit from Alpha Coal. A really pushy twenty-something man had appeared two days after Christmas suggesting that if they didn't sell some of their acreage to them, they'd take it through eminent domain. AJ furiously told him that wasn't legal, although she really didn't know if she was right, and that if they tried, she'd get a lawyer and sue them. He must have been new to his job because her threat caused him to back off and leave. She was pleased with her bluff until he said he'd be back. As she drove, she played that conversation over and over as well.

Seems no matter where I am there's always a problem. Pushy assholes and poisoned creeks here; droughts and an embezzler over there. At least I'm better set to fight Alpha now than I was before I ever heard of Jack Morgan. With all that money there's bound to be a way to stop them. Gotta figure out what it is. Same with the damn frackers. I'll stop them all if it takes every cent.

By the time she hit I-64, she'd put Alpha and the argument with her mother out of her mind and was pleasantly reliving the night with Barry before she left for the holidays. The engraved ID bracelet she'd given him seemed insignificant to the cache of gifts he lavished on her: a cashmere sweater, a Burberry scarf, a thick terrycloth robe and slippers, and a heart-shaped diamond necklace. She'd felt it was wrong to spend Langford Hall's money on personal gifts, so the bracelet was what she could afford. Barry, of course, said it was just what he wanted. She'd had his monogram put on the front and *From AJ, with love* engraved on the back along with the date. But as Barry had said that night, having each other was the best gift of all. It had taken all the willpower she could muster to leave the next day, but she still had to pack and wrap a few presents for Annie before she could leave for West Virginia.

AJ was head over heels in love, and it appeared the feeling was mutual. While she was giddy about the relationship, she realized it did add a layer of complication to her pending decision.

If she decided to go back home, would he come with her? Could he work from home? Would he want to? Or, if she stayed in Virginia, would Alice agree to come to Langford Hall? She might not. *I can't leave her by herself even if it would make my life easier. Sooner or later Barry and I are gonna have to talk about the future if he feels the same way I do. I know one thing, I sure as shit don't want to leave him behind.*

All the way back AJ mulled her dilemma. She knew she had to choose soon, but today that answer eluded her. Too many unknowns. She could dream, but that didn't get her any closer to the decision she knew she would have to make in the spring.

⁓

On New Year's Eve, Barry took AJ to a dinner dance at the country club, the same one where she'd had the run-in with the snobby girls. She told him that story, but he assured her it wouldn't happen again. He said he would stop any such nonsense before it began.

"I know how you must have felt. Remember, I'm a hillbilly, too," he said.

There she met several of his friends, some of his associates in the firm, and one of the partners in the firm doing Langford Hall's audit. All of them seemed very pleasant, and there wasn't a single hillbilly joke. She wanted to ask the partner how the audit was coming, but she knew this wasn't the right setting for such a conversation.

As the evening of dancing drew to a close, the lights dimmed just before midnight to reveal a crystal ball in the ceiling that threw shafts of light over the crowd as it spun. AJ and Barry joined everyone else in the countdown: ". . . five, four, three, two, one. Happy New Year!" Barry pulled AJ close, whispered, "I love you," in her ear and gave her a lingering kiss. As they broke apart, she replied, "I love you too, Barry."

Two weeks later, AJ received a phone call from Mr. Alexander, the lead auditor. It was late Friday afternoon, and she'd been watching the snow settle outside. As long as she didn't have to drive, she liked seeing it pile up. She especially loved the way everything was quieter as if the silence had arrived on the backs of the snowflakes. When she heard who was calling, her total attention was on the call.

"Mrs. Porter, it's Leon Alexander. We've finished your farm's audit and would like to come discuss it with you. When would be convenient?"

"Monday is fine with me, but can you give me any idea what you found?"

"We'd rather discuss it in person if you don't mind. There are some things we really need to point out to you. Unfortunately, Monday is Martin Luther King Day and we're closed. How about Tuesday at, say, two?"

"That's fine," answered AJ, but inside she wished she could see it right then. Waiting over the long weekend, she knew, would be agony. Barry had left early that day, and they weren't having dinner together until the next night, so when she thought he'd arrived home, she called him.

"Hey, did you have any trouble driving? I was worried about you," she said when he answered his cell.

"It was slick in patches, but I was fine. What's up? Miss me already?"

"Of course, but I called to tell you that the audit is done. Mr. Alexander is coming out on Tuesday to discuss it. I want you to be there, okay? You understand these things better than me."

"I'll be there unless Isabelle runs me off. I don't think she likes me much."

"Don't worry about her; I'll be sure she understands that I only want your professional expertise." She laughed, knowing that wasn't the whole truth.

Barry laughed, too. "Okay. See you tomorrow night. Where do you want to go?"

"If it's really snowy, we could just stay here. Isabelle's gone for the weekend and Clara wouldn't dare say a word. I think she's kinda sweet on you anyway because of the way you praise her food."

"Okay, we'll decide when we see what the weather does. I love you, AJ."

"I love you too, sweet Barry."

⌒

Tuesday afternoon AJ, Isabelle, and Barry were in Isabelle's office when Mr. Alexander arrived. After offering him a seat on the leather sofa, she took the chair beside the sofa. Barry stood behind her, and Isabelle remained behind her desk. Before sitting, Alexander distributed copies of the audit to each of them. He'd brought an extra thinking Mr. Mulgrew might be there as well.

Alexander cleared his throat and began. "In matters of auditing, the purpose is to examine the financial statements and issue an opinion on them. Finding no issues gives us what we call a clean audit. If there are unresolved issues, we issue our findings on them. In the case of our audit of the statements presented, we could not declare it a clean audit. Unfortunately, your suspicion seems to have been correct; we found some evidence of fraud."

"Damn, I knew it," interrupted AJ. "I'm sorry; please go on."

Alexander gave her a tight smile, then said, "What we found, as did you, were many reimbursement checks written by Mr. Tom Beckett made out to himself. However, we were unable to match them with actual invoices for such expenses. In other words, he doctored the statements to reflect that the amounts he paid himself fell under certain expense categories—the exact categories that you pointed out that had risen dramatically. Additionally, we looked at the company's credit card statements and found many charges that bear no relationship to anything used by the farm, like, for instance, a Coleman stove and a tent. I'm afraid he's been doing this since your uncle stopped monitoring his work."

AJ sighed as if she wasn't surprised by the report. "How much do you think he's taken? Should we prosecute him?"

"It's very hard to say. Maybe in the neighborhood of fifty thousand dollars? I think he probably started small, but when he realized no one else was looking over his shoulder, he increased the amounts and the ways in which he embezzled them. That's pretty typical, especially if he'd been a longtime trusted employee."

"That he had," said Isabelle. "He's been with us a long time. And I always thought he was a trustworthy fellow. I guess I was wrong."

AJ looked at Isabelle, then at Barry. "What do you think we should do, besides fire him, I mean?"

"From a professional standpoint, I think proving your case might be hard since the evidence is so sketchy. He could always claim the invoices were lost, or that they didn't provide one. It could get messy," Barry said.

"I agree," said Isabelle. "And it's not a fortune in the grand scheme of things. He had a good salary. I wonder why he felt he had to steal on top of it. Anyway, you'll probably never get it back even if you were to win. You know he's surely spent it over the years; and I'll bet he doesn't have the wherewithal to repay it. I say be glad he's gone; change the systems so it can't happen again and be done with it."

"It's a pot-load of money to me, but I think you're both right," said AJ. "We don't need the heartache of a trial. The less I see of Tom Beckett, the happier I'll be."

She turned and extended her hand. "Mr. Alexander, thank you for your excellent work. I really appreciate it."

"My pleasure. I'm glad we were able to help. In the back of the report are our recommendations on how to prevent this ever happening again. I hope they will be helpful as well." He rose, took his coat from the couch arm, and started to leave.

"I'll walk you to the door," said AJ. "I'll be right back," she called to Isabelle and Barry.

When she returned, AJ said, "Well, I guess I'll be writing Tom a letter."

"Why don't you let Mulgrew do it?" Isabelle asked.

"Because it's my job as the manager and owner of Langford Hall."

"Right," Isabelle said with a satisfied smile and a glance at Barry, wearing a matching grin.

∽ CHAPTER TWENTY-TWO ∽

Isabelle came into the accounting office with a newspaper in hand and looking grim. "Have you seen this week's *Hadleigh Bugle*?"

"No, I rarely read it. Why?" AJ replied as she looked up from the computer.

Isabelle handed the paper, folded to reveal the obituary page, to AJ. AJ's face blanched as she read the headline: *Thomas K. Beckett, local accountant, struck and killed by train.*

"Oh my God," AJ said as she continued to read.

A man died after being struck by a train Monday morning outside of Hadleigh. He was walking along the tracks around 4:30 a.m. when a CSX freight train struck and killed him. The engineer, Jay Miller, said he was going only about forty-five miles an hour.

"I sounded the horn and tried to stop, but I couldn't. The guy was on the track staggering toward the train, and as we got closer, he turned his back to it," Miller said. The victim, Thomas K. Beckett, was identified Tuesday through dental records by the Virginia Medical Examiner's office in Richmond. Beckett, 52, is survived by his wife, Helen, and a daughter, Marianna. The family had no comment on the accident.

"Oh my God, Isabelle, that sounds like he meant to do it. I mean, he turned his back on the train after the guy blew the horn to warn him? Geez. Why would he commit suicide? Because I fired him?" Her voice choked and tears flowed. "I didn't like the guy, but damn, I didn't want to see him dead. This is awful."

"I knew it would upset you. I doubt your letter did it, though. According to the article, the engineer said he was staggering. Maybe he didn't mean to kill himself, just wandered there drunk. It could have been an accident. In any case, you weren't going to prosecute, so it wouldn't have been a matter of public record that he embezzled from us. I mean, he could have found another job, surely."

AJ ignored Isabelle's suggestion that it might have been an accident. "Yeah, but he didn't know that. I never mentioned not prosecuting in the letter; I just told him the audit had found some irregularities and that his services were no longer needed. You think I should call his wife to offer my condolences?"

"Maybe I should do it, instead. You might be a *persona non-grata*, I don't know. But I've known her for a long time. I even remember when Marianna was born. I'll order flowers and a food tray and make the call. I'll let you know what she says. Then you can decide whether or not to go to his funeral."

AJ had stopped crying and blew her nose. "Dental records. God. I guess that's all they could go by." She sniffed again. "I want to call Barry and tell him. Let me know what Mrs. Beckett says."

The next afternoon, Isabelle caught AJ at lunch. "I got hold of Helen Beckett this morning. She was devastated by Tom's death, of course, but she did say he'd been a gambler throughout their marriage. Apparently, a few years ago, he got in with a high stakes crowd and was losing larger and larger sums of money. She thinks they began pressuring him. He left a note stating how desperate he was, that he owed big money to some pretty shady characters, and that now he realized he couldn't possibly pay them. I guess he didn't see any other way out. Sad, really. But it probably explains why he started embezzling from us, from the farm."

AJ sighed. "Well, that's sort of a relief, but still, if I hadn't fired him—"

"I doubt it would have made a difference. If the stakes were high enough, the amount he stole wouldn't have been enough to pay back any loans he'd gotten from mobsters—that is, if that's what they were. I guess we'll never really know, but don't blame yourself. You've got enough on your plate without that worry."

AJ sighed again. "I guess you're right. Now that Barry's not here every day, I'm the new Tom. It's a lot, I'll admit it. I'm just glad I've got you and Barry to help me blow off steam. Hank and Santos are a huge help, too. I couldn't do this without any of you. Back home, it was only me, Alice and Annie, but the responsibilities were a lot less. I'm not sure which is harder: the scope of operations at Langford Hall or being poor in West Virginia."

"That's a question only you can answer, dear. And decision day is closer than you think."

"I know. It's tough."

⌒

On Valentine's Day, Barry planned a special dinner for AJ at his home. Winter had taken a much-longed-for breather, and AJ was delighted to be wearing a new pair of pale-yellow slacks and a lemon-yellow cotton pullover. The sunshine and the lighter clothing made AJ feel as if a weight had been lifted from her shoulders. Since Tom Beckett's suicide and funeral the previous month, things had improved for her and for Langford Hall. She'd mastered the bookkeeping duties she'd assumed after putting Tom on leave, thanks to Barry, of course. Plans were in the works for the spring planting. Some crops were already underway. She had always loved spring—the fresh green of the tender new leaves on the trees, the softness of the air, the faint scent of early spring flowers. Here in Virginia, she was enjoying them long before they usually arrived in her West Virginia mountains, and she was grateful. It had been a tough winter, and she was glad it was over.

Laden with a bag of presents for Barry, she rang his doorbell. It had taken her days to decide what to get him. After all, he had nearly everything he needed and could buy anything he wanted. Finally, she had settled on books about West Virginia. From the looks of the bookcases that flanked his fireplace, he loved to read, and she was sure these would be ones he hadn't read. She smiled, thinking this was another thing they had in common.

"Hey, babe, happy Valentine's Day," Barry said as he opened the door and pulled her into an embrace and kiss. "I've missed you."

"It's only been a day since you saw me," AJ said, laughing.

"I know, but I missed you anyway. Can I take that?" he said, pointing to the bag she was carrying.

"No, thanks. I'll just put it by the couch. It's for later."

"Can't I peek now?"

"No," she said, smacking at his hand. "Later, I said. Got a beer?"

"Sure, help yourself." She followed him into the kitchen. "I fixed a cheesecake with strawberries for dessert. Strawberries at the market smelled like they should. I couldn't resist."

"Oooh, let's just skip dinner and have dessert," AJ said, as she opened her Budweiser.

"No way. It's chicken divan. You won't want to miss that either."

"I'll admit it. You *are* a really good cook. I love your meals."

They chatted as they ate. Barry had a new client whose books were a mess, and AJ was full of news about spring plans at Langford Hall.

"Can I ask your advice on something?"

"Of course, you can."

AJ took a deep breath. "Okay, first you have to promise not to let anyone know what I'm about to say."

Barry nodded.

"My great-uncle Jack and Isabelle had a long-standing affair."

"I wondered why she still worked there, and that sort of explains it," Barry said.

"Right. Besides, I needed her. But there's more. They had a son, a son Jack never acknowledged, legally, that is. If I decided to—"

"Stop! Not another word. I don't want . . . I've got something to ask you, too; but let's finish dinner first, please?"

Puzzled, AJ agreed. The two cleaned up the dinner table in relative silence; both were alone in their own thoughts. *Why didn't he let me finish? Maybe he knew what I was about to say and didn't want to hear it. I guess I didn't handle it very well. I know he doesn't want me to leave, and I don't want to leave him, but—*

When they finished, Barry grabbed AJ's hand and began walking toward the living room. "Come with me. I've got something to say." His tone was soft, sweet. "Sit here, beside me." He patted the couch cushion. He leaned over, pulled a sizeable box from under the table and handed it to AJ. "Open it."

AJ took the bright-red box, pulled the huge bow and ribbon off, and lifted the lid. Inside was another wrapped box, a pink one. She laughed and repeated the unwrapping process only to discover a small silver box with a red bow on top. "Are you screwing around with me, Barry Peterson?"

He laughed. "No, I promise I'm not. Open it."

AJ took off the bow and removed the lid. Inside was a ring box. She lifted the top to reveal a diamond and sapphire ring. Her jaw dropped. When she looked up, she found Barry on one knee in front of her.

"AJ Porter, I love you. Will you do me the honor of marrying me?" He took the box from AJ and lifted out the ring.

"Oh, Barry, I love you too, but—"

"But *what?* If we love each other, we can work out the rest. That's why I didn't want you to finish talking earlier. Now, just say yes . . . please."

"Yes," she said and flung herself into his arms. The two fell to the floor laughing, kissing, and hugging.

After a few minutes, Barry said, "Hold on, I don't want to lose your ring. Here," he said as he placed it on AJ's finger. He kissed her again.

"Barry, it's so beautiful. I love it. I'd be so honored to be Mrs. Barry Peterson." She kissed him again, then asked, "Now can I finish what I was going to say? Oh, wait, your presents." She scrambled up from the floor and retrieved the bag from the floor near the other end of the couch.

"No multiple boxes here—well, at least, not inside each other." She pulled out a pyramid of multicolored wrapped packages, tied with one red satin ribbon and topped with an oversized bow.

Barry removed the ribbon and the stack tumbled down. One by one, he unwrapped the seven books, exclaiming his delight each time. She had given him two books by Denise Giardina, *Storming Heaven* and *The Unquiet Earth*, and *The Beulah Quintet* by Mary Lee Settle. "I thought since you're a West Virginia native, you might enjoy these. I know you haven't lived there for years, but—"

"I love them. You know, I've always wanted to read Settle's books, but never took the time. Now I will. Thank you, honey. Okay, now you can finish talking about . . . you know."

AJ settled into the corner of the couch and took a deep breath. "Okay, what I was saying was this; if I decide to go back home, what would you think of me selling Langford Hall to Uncle Jack's real son? He's the rightful heir and Isabelle says he's been very successful in California, so I think he can afford it. Besides, Uncle Jack should have left it to him in the first place."

"Well, I would have said I think it's an interesting idea, but it makes me wonder if Isabelle has had that in mind since you came. You know, maybe she hoped you'd consider that, especially after feeding you all those stories about the past." Barry gave her a skeptical look.

AJ shook her head. "I don't know. If that's the case, she or Jack could have protested or contested, whatever it's called, the will when Jack died. And if that's what she really wanted, why'd she try to convince me to stay?"

"Good point. I guess I'm being too cynical. You know, I wish you'd keep it since I don't really want you to leave. I know West Virginia's home, but . . . wait a minute, are you trying to lure me back with those books?" He grinned as if he now got the joke.

"Well, it crossed my mind, especially with the Giardina books. They're both about coal mining and how it has destroyed communities and families. A little like what I'm fighting back home. I don't want our land destroyed, honey; it's been in our family a long time. Not as long as Langford Hall, but it's home, you know? I think I need to fight for it just like the other Morgans fought for Langford Hall. What if we went back together? Would you ever consider it?"

"Well, as I said, I want you. The rest we can work out." He kissed her, again. "Let's talk about it in the morning."

"Good plan," AJ said as they rose, holding hands, and headed toward Barry's bedroom.

━ CHAPTER TWENTY-THREE ━

AJ had always done her best thinking while driving. Maybe it was the monotony of the roads she now knew so well; maybe it was the silence. But today, it wasn't working.

As she drove back to Langford Hall from Barry's, she glanced often at the beautiful ring now resting on her left hand. Each time, she thought about the reaction the two older women in her life would have to her engagement. She predicted that Isabelle would be thrilled, thinking it signaled that AJ would stay at Langford Hall. She also suspected Alice would repeat the complaints about Barry she'd voiced at Christmas even though she had never met him. She'd warn that AJ's acceptance was too hasty, and that AJ was merely on the rebound from Dewey. Mostly, Alice would be worried that AJ wouldn't be coming home, that she would decide to stay in Hadleigh because it was Barry's home.

And then there was Annie. How would she feel about having a father figure in her life for the first time? AJ still had to decide about

Langford Hall, but today the related questions were her worries. The big decision wasn't coming easily. Should she call Alice to tell her, or take Barry home and surprise her?

If I do that and she has a hissy fit, he'll be so uncomfortable. We all will be.

What if Annie doesn't like him? Should I go home alone to tell them? Or should Alice and Annie come to Langford Hall to meet Barry?

If they took the train, it would be an adventure for both of them. They've never been here, and Annie's never ridden a train. Who knows? Maybe Alice will love it. I know Annie will. She's been dying to come see the horses anyway.

As for Isabelle, AJ felt sure she'd be happy as a pig in slop if her son, Jack, decided to live at Langford Hall. *But how do I ask her about him? If I ask her to tell me how to get hold of him, she'll want to know why. And what if my plan doesn't work out?*

Isabelle would be doubly disappointed if AJ decided to sell Langford Hall to someone else and go back to West Virginia.

But is that really what I want? Life here with Barry would be all she'd ever dreamed of. But she feared he wouldn't be happy in West Virginia. He had a good practice in Virginia. How long would it take him to get re-established?

Yesterday, I thought I knew what I wanted; now, my mind is back in a muddle. Maybe I did jump too fast. Alice always said I was too quick to hook my life to some man's. But this time, she's wrong. We were friends first and then lovers. I've known him since October. Alice just needs to get to know him, and she'll see he's right for me.

By the time she drove up the familiar shaded lane to Langford Hall, she *had* decided two things: she needed to arrange a trip to Virginia for Alice and Annie, and she needed to call Isabelle's son to float her idea past him. She parked, climbed the steps to the front porch, and paused. She turned to look at the landscape. Spring wasn't quite here yet, but she could see the pinkish glow that trees and shrubs got just before their new leaves appeared, the shimmer of new life in the grass, and the lilies of the valley bobbing in the sunlight. A perfect day for new beginnings.

AJ found Isabelle in her office, a new fuchsia hat firmly in place. "Nice hat, Isabelle," she said as she plopped down in the chair in front of her desk.

"Good Lord, you startled me, girl. I didn't hear you come in. How was dinner at Barry's, as if I couldn't tell from the big grin plastered all over your face?"

"It was just lovely," AJ replied, waggling the fingers of her left hand over Isabelle's desk. "See anything new?"

"Oh my God, you're engaged! That's wonderful, but I must say, it's not much of a surprise, at least not to me. The ring's gorgeous. You set a date? And does this mean you're staying in Virginia?"

"I don't know. It depends on several things. Barry says we can work it out, whatever I decide. But I need to talk to Alice, and to you. I don't want you to get your hopes up, but do you think your son would ever want to come back here? To own Langford Hall, I mean? It seems to me if Jack had just acknowledged him, he'd have inherited it instead of me. So, I thought maybe he'd want to buy it from me, at a favorable price, of course." She watched Isabelle's face change from shock to a look of tenderness.

"Oh, AJ, that would be the best thing I could ever hope for, but he's been out West so long, I don't know if he'd even consider it. And his wife's family is there, too."

"Why don't you give me his phone number and let me talk to him? Can't know unless I ask, right? He might surprise you."

Isabelle scribbled Jack's number on a sticky note and handed it to AJ. "I'll keep my fingers and toes crossed. Let me know what he says."

"I will. Next, I want to get my mother and daughter over here for a visit. See how they like living the good life. Who knows? They might surprise me too. I'm checking train schedules. I thought about waiting until Annie's Easter break, but that's too far off. I need to tell Alice about Barry now, and that seems the best way to do it."

"You sound like a girl on a mission. Good luck."

"Thanks, I'll need it."

AJ walked toward her own office. First, she called Amtrak and booked two seats from Montgomery to Charlottesville on Friday, February 20, and return seats for Sunday. She knew it was a risky move. Alice could easily refuse to come, but she thought if Annie got excited about riding on a train, Alice would eventually give in. Granted, it would be a short trip, but she didn't want Annie to miss any more school than necessary. Then she called Alice. True to form, at first her mother said it was impossible, that she couldn't leave. But after AJ said she was sure Jimmy could handle the farm for a few days without her, would drive them to the station in Montgomery, and that their tickets were already paid for, she relented. Then she began worrying about what to wear. AJ assured her that she didn't need anything special, but that she should be sure Annie had something she could wear to the barn, and maybe riding, if the weather allowed.

Next, she picked up the phone to call Jack Morgan, but then she hesitated, unsure of exactly how to approach him. She stared out the window, watching the breeze wave the tender new tree branches. Several minutes later, she returned to Isabelle's office.

"Isabelle, I'm not sure what to say to Jack. I mean, he doesn't know me from Adam's house cat. What if you call first and tell him who I am and that you've told me his story? I just can't see myself calling to say, 'Hi, I'm your cousin, or whatever I am, and I want to sell you Langford Hall?'"

The two women laughed.

"Yeah, I can see how that might be a tad awkward, especially since no one else here even knows he exists. I'll give him a call and then I'll let you know how it goes. Might be tomorrow, though. I can't always catch him on the first try."

AJ said that would be fine and left to go back to the accounting office. She wanted to call Barry but knew better than to bother him at the office. He was coming for dinner that night, and she could talk to him then.

After dinner, over coffee and apple cobbler, AJ asked, "Can we talk seriously about what happens after May? I'm still trying to figure out what to do."

"Sure. What's bothering you about it? I told you we could work out the details whatever you decide." He took a bite of cobbler. "God, this is delicious. Tell Clara for me."

"I will. I know you said that, and I love you for it. So, here's a few questions for you. If I decide to go back to West Virginia, could you work there? Maybe from home with the same clients you have now? And would you be happy on a rural farm?" She paused, fork in midair.

"Well, I have to admit, I've been a big-city guy for a long time. I'm not sure how I'd adjust to milking cows." He laughed as AJ started to protest. "I'm just kidding. For one thing, you wouldn't let me since I'd probably pull the wrong thing and hurt the poor cow."

AJ laughed, her mouth full of cobbler.

Barry continued, "As for working at home, that might be possible. I've known guys who did it. Kept their same clients. Firm wasn't too happy, but the clients were. That's pretty easy with computers these days. I guess I might have to travel some, but that could be worked out." He took another bite, swallowed, then asked, "But are you hell-bent on living in your old home place? Why couldn't we build a new house, maybe nearby, so your mom would . . . so we would have some privacy? I mean, if I sell my house, we could easily do that."

"Maybe you wouldn't have to. We could keep it as a vacation place. See, I'll inherit a pretty good nest egg from Uncle Jack, even if I don't keep the estate. But a new house would be wonderful. Alice would be happier where she's been all these years, anyway, but we could fix it up, too, couldn't we? It could sure use some work."

"Certainly. But I want to provide you and Annie with a home, a nice one. I mean, look what you've gotten used to. You should keep your inheritance to pass on to Annie. I'll help you invest it, if you like. But I'm curious; do you mind telling me what a pretty good nest egg is?"

"Mr. Mulgrew said it's around twelve million."

Barry nearly choked. "Good Lord, AJ! Did you say twelve million? That's a bit more than pretty good, honey. Geezy peezy! That's an incredible amount of money. Listen, if you want to save the land around your home, you could sure do it with that kind of cash, and still have what you called *a pretty good nest egg* left to pass on to Annie."

"Yeah, that crossed my mind, but those mining companies would still be after me. And the frackers, for that matter. What else could I do?" She rose to take the plates off the table. "Be right back. I let Clara go early."

As she returned from the kitchen, Barry said, "Ever heard of the West Virginia Land Trust? I have a friend I went to school with. He's real active in raising money for them. As I understand it, you can give them your land outright, or will it to them so it can never be developed. If that's something you'd want to do, I'll contact him for you to see if I'm right about how it works."

She retook her chair and poured them both more coffee. "Really? That's a great idea. We can explore that, later. Now, here's another scenario. Suppose I decide to stay. Would you be comfortable living here, with Alice and Annie?"

Barry hesitated. "Hmm, now that's a different kettle of fish. I don't want to sound harsh, but Annie alone will be an adjustment. Don't get me wrong; it's one I'm eager to make. But living with my mother-in-law? Dunno about that. Let me ask you a couple of questions. What do you want to do with the rest of your life, assuming you don't stay here as the mistress of the manor. And if you decide to go home, what's your plan for Langford Hall? I know you don't want it developed, either. Got any other options?"

"Remember sometime back when I said I had an idea but I wasn't ready to share it?"

Barry nodded.

"Okay, here's the deal. Remember I told you Uncle Jack had a son with Isabelle, but because they never married, he wouldn't acknowledge him."

Barry nodded.

"Stupid, I think, but he must have been a pretty old-fashioned guy. At least that's the way she described him. Anyway, if I could get young Jack to come back here to run Langford Hall, not develop it, just manage it and live here, that would be perfect. Like I told Isabelle, it should have been his anyway. And it would have been if Jack hadn't been so damn proper.

"Man, you are just full of surprises tonight, aren't you? Have you talked to him?"

"No, Isabelle was going to call him first, since he doesn't know that I know he exists. And I have no idea if he'd ever leave the West. His wife is from out there. But if he would, that would sure make my decision easier. About your other question, I never got to finish college. I think I told you I wanted to be a vet, but now, maybe not. If I became a lawyer, I could fight those SOB mine companies. I don't know. It's just a thought."

"You'd make a hell of a lawyer. I'm all for that. You're right; it would give you a good platform for fighting. Think about it," Barry grinned.

"I will, but back to right now. Alice and Annie are coming here next weekend on the train. I want you to come for dinner on Saturday to meet them, okay?"

"Sure, I'm looking forward to it. I hope I pass inspection," he said, pushing his hair off his forehead like he was primping for a formal photograph.

AJ laughed. "How could you not, you handsome devil?" She leaned across the table and kissed him. "Can you stay? I'll let you if you promise not to drink my contact again."

"I thought you'd never ask."

He pulled her from her chair and into his lap and kissed her again.

⌐ CHAPTER TWENTY-FOUR ⌐

When Alice and Annie arrived in the late afternoon, AJ awaited them at the station in Charlottesville. Annie couldn't stop chattering about the wonders of the train ride while Alice wouldn't stop complaining that the train bounced along the tracks like it was on a potholed road. But once they started the drive back to Hadleigh, she was quiet. AJ thought her mother had fallen asleep until they pulled through the stone gates of Langford Hall and passed through the arch of tree branches.

As the house came into view, Alice said, "Are you kidding me? This is where you live now? My word, it's *huge*. Just look at that house. I ain't never seen a place so fine."

"I hope you like it, Alice. I've got a special bedroom picked out for each of you. Unless you want to sleep in my bed, Annie. That might be fun."

"No, thanks. I want my very own room, Mama, if you don't care. I'm not a baby anymore, you know."

AJ rolled her eyes and grinned. "I sort of knew that, darling. I was there when you were born, remember?"

Annie giggled.

Upon seeing the car, Eddie, who had been pruning the boxwoods, came forward and offered to carry in the bags. At first, Alice gave him what AJ called her "stink eye," but after she frowned at her mother, Alice released the handle and let Eddie carry both hers and Annie's.

Inside the front hall, Alice's jaw dropped. "I ain't never seen ceilings this high. And look at that staircase. Bet it costs a fortune to heat." AJ ignored her. Annie dashed up the stairs before AJ could stop her.

"Is my room up here? Where's yours? Where's Granny's? Can we see the horses today?" This last question was nearly out of AJ's earshot. She called, "Slow down, missy, so I can show you where to go." AJ topped the stairs and showed Alice to one guest room and Annie to another. Alice's had a burgundy-and-gold tapestry spread that matched the drapery, and Annie's featured a thick down-filled white duvet and crisp yellow curtains topped with a white-and-yellow plaid cornice. Both looked delighted at their lavish accommodations.

"You can share the bathroom between your rooms. If you want to rest a minute, go ahead, or you can come back down with me and I'll show you the rest of the house. Dinner won't be ready until about six thirty. Annie, you hungry?"

"No, I had ice cream on the train. It was so cool, Mama. We saw a big river. People were in boats with long paddles. And lots of little towns. Granny let me have a ham salad sandwich and chips for lunch. Then I had ice cream later. I love riding the train."

"I thought you'd like it. Wanna see the rest of the house? I'll take you to the barn in the morning."

"Okay. Then can I read until dinner? I brought *The Red Pony*. It looks like an old book. I found it at home. Was it yours?"

"Sure was. It was one of my favorites when I was your age. I always had my nose in a book just like you do." Annie giggled when AJ tweaked her nose. "And I always wanted a red horse, but I ended up with Gunner instead. We've got a horse here that's sort of red, but I don't ride him. The one I fell off of was brown."

Alice decided to rest in her room while AJ gave Annie the five-cent tour. As they walked, Annie seemed bored, but held onto her mother's hand, something she hadn't done since she was five. AJ had the feeling Annie agreed just to be with her. The only thing she got excited about were Dolley Madison's shoes. She wanted to try them on, but of course, AJ refused.

That night, after the simple meatloaf dinner AJ had asked Clara to fix, Annie disappeared to her room, which she boasted must have belonged to a princess. She said she wanted to read, not listen to her grandmother and mother talk. That was fine with AJ because she needed to tell Alice about her engagement. She had decided to do that first, then tell Annie the next morning.

"Aren't you glad you didn't have to do dishes, Mom? Having Clara is really nice, ya know?" The two women were still sitting at the empty table.

"Yeah, it's a treat, but I don't think I'd ever get used to it. Have you?" She searched her daughter's face. "Is this the life you want from now on?"

"That's something I wanted to talk to you about. You remember I told you about Barry? The accountant I've been dating?"

Alice looked uncomfortable, as if she didn't think she'd like where the conversation was going. "Yeah, and you remember what I told you?"

"Don't interrupt, Mom. Let me finish."

"Okay then, go on."

"Barry has asked me to marry him, and I said yes."

Alice opened her mouth to comment again, but AJ stopped her. "Wait. Before you panic, he said he's willing to move back to West Virginia if that's what I decide to do. While he's been in Virginia most of his life, he's from there. But if we decide to stay here, would you be comfortable living here?" She gestured around the room. "Maybe not *here* exactly, but in a new house on the farm where you could have your privacy. What do you think?"

What she didn't say was that it would also give her and Barry their privacy.

Alice didn't respond right away.

"Mom, he's a terrific guy. I think you'll like him."

Alice took a deep breath. "Audrey Jane, you're a grown woman and I love you, but since you was a young girl you always thought you needed a man to take care of you. You didn't because, you know, I learned a long time ago I could do it on my own. I had to after your daddy. You need to believe that, too. Now with your own money, a man sure ain't necessary for you to get along. I thought all you was doing was living here temporary to get the house; then you was gonna sell it and come home. Now you're talking like you might not, and if you do, you're gonna bring some man with you. Honestly, I wish you'd never got that letter. It's changed you. It's changed everything."

Alice stopped talking as her head drooped until her chin nearly touched her chest. AJ watched her mother twist her napkin in her hand as if she were wringing out a dishrag.

AJ came around the edge of the table and sat beside her mother, then reached for Alice's fidgeting hands, stilling them in her own.

"Mom, look at me. I ain't changed. I'm still AJ, in nicer clothes, maybe, but I know what I'm doin'—with Barry, I mean." Alice looked up briefly, then lowered her chin again as AJ continued. "Being in charge of Langford Hall has made me realize that I'm even stronger than I knew. Look, I had to fire a guy who later killed himself, maybe 'cause of me. I've learned how to manage this huge place. And I'm not marrying Barry so he can take care of me. I *can* take care of myself. I love him. It's that simple. We'll work out what's best for everyone. Remember when I had to drop out of college?"

Alice nodded, but she still wasn't looking at AJ.

"Well, now I want to go back and finish. But instead of becoming a vet, I want to learn how to stop the mining companies from destroying our land. I probably can't do that from here. But I've got to figure out what to do with Langford Hall first. It's part of my family history, too. I've read about lots of my ancestors, folks I never knew about. They worked hard to keep it in the family all these years. I've got to honor that. Understand?"

Alice raised her head. "I do. That's an honorable thing to do and I respect you for it. I just hope you don't feel like you have to live here to do it. And having Barry don't make it easier for you to come home. I'm sure he'd rather be here."

"Don't judge until you meet him, promise? I told you. He'll do whatever I decide. Just wait and see."

⌒

The next morning, Annie burst into AJ's room, jumped on her bed fully dressed, yelling, "Can we go to the barn now? Huh? Please, pleeeeze?" AJ grabbed her daughter, hugged her tightly, and tickled her until she gasped, "Stop, Mama, I can't breathe."

AJ stopped and brushed Annie's hair off her face. "Could we eat breakfast first? How about pancakes? I'll ask Clara to fix some bacon, too. Sound good?"

"Yes, but will they be as good as Granny's?"

"Better, but don't tell Granny." AJ laughed and put her finger to her lips.

Later, as AJ and Annie headed to the barn, Annie asked if she could ride.

"You'll have to ask Santos."

"Who's he?" Annie asked as she skipped along the path.

"He's the guy in charge of the horses. You'll like him. He came out and found me when I broke my arm. But before we go in, I want to talk to you."

Annie stopped and looked up at her mother. "What? Did I do something wrong?"

"No, sweetie, not at all. Sit up here on the fence like a cowboy."

Annie climbed up and hooked her feet on the middle rail. She looked puzzled. AJ put both hands on Annie's knees.

"All your life, it's just been you, me, and Granny, right?" Annie nodded as AJ continued. "Well, that's about to change. I met a really nice man. His name is Barry and we're going to get married. You'll have a daddy and a mommy for the first time in your life. What do you think of that?"

Annie jumped down and started toward the barn, stomping her feet like a miniature soldier. "I don't like it. Not one bit. Why? Why do things have to change? We're fine just like we are." She flipped her pigtails over her shoulders.

Surprised by her outburst, AJ followed. "Annie, wait, let me finish."

Annie stopped, but kept her back to her mother, her arms crossed defiantly on her chest. AJ circled around to face her scowl.

"Remember when you liked that boy with the Mohawk? It's sorta like that."

"He cussed. I *don't* like him."

"Well, Barry don't cuss, and I love him, like I did your daddy, but he's gone. Annie, I want you to give him a chance. Having a dad can be fun. You'll see. Some dads hike better than moms; he can help with your homework 'cause he's way smarter about that stuff than I am. He loves to read, too. And he gives great hugs. Come on, Annie. You'll meet him at dinner, and you'll see. Now, let's see about getting you on that brown horse. His name is Topper."

"Okay, Mama, I'll be nice to him. But if I don't like him, I'm staying in my room forever." She relaxed her arms but continued looking angry.

AJ laughed. "That's a deal. But I gotta warn you, you might starve to death."

⌒

Barry arrived that evening bearing a huge bouquet of daffodils, forsythia, and yellow roses for Alice and a silver charm bracelet with a tiny pair of riding boots on it for Annie. As a further Southern gesture, he kissed each of their hands as they were introduced. Despite herself, Alice blushed deeply.

"May I call you Miss Alice, ma'am? We Southern boys always refer to ladies that way. And you, Miss Annie, that okay with you?"

Alice stammered. "I ain't never been called that before, but it sounds nice. Let me go put these in some water." She rushed off, clearly flustered for what AJ believed must have been the first time in her life.

Annie smiled up at Barry and said, "I like it. Thank you for the bracelet. One of these days, Mama says I can have some real boots like those. Right, Mama?"

Her mother nodded "Let's go in the library until dinner is ready. Barry, want some wine?"

"Sounds good. Red?" As the three of them walked down the hall, AJ noticed that Annie was watching Barry's every move. In the library she took a seat on the sofa with him.

"I got to ride the horse Mama fell off of, but I stayed right on him."

"You did? Congratulations," Barry said, offering Annie a fist bump, which she returned.

AJ laughed. "Right, but there aren't any branches in the riding ring."

"Still, he's a big horse. Good for you." Barry smiled at Annie. "Do you get to ride at home?"

"Not unless Mama or Granny are with me. Or Uncle Jimmy."

Alice entered the room as Annie said her name. "What did I do?"

Barry said, "Annie says you watch over her when she rides. I'll bet she asks often."

"She does. All the time. But I only let her when she's finished her homework. Speaking of that, did you bring it with you, little miss? If you don't do it tonight, you'll have to on the train tomorrow. Or after dinner tonight. Your choice."

Just as Alice said that, Clara called them to dinner from the doorway. "May I?" said Barry, offering his arm to Alice. She reddened again but took his arm as the four went toward the dining room.

After dinner where no one broached the subject of the pending marriage, they returned to the library. After Annie excused herself to go read, Barry continued chatting amiably with Alice while AJ sat quietly smiling at the scene. *Going' better than I thought.*

Without warning, Alice blurted, "So, I hear you plan to marry my Audrey Jane. You mighta asked me first. Ain't that the proper thing? Ask the parents for the girl's hand?"

"Alice! What on earth? We're adults, for God's sake. He didn't need to ask your permission. That's ridiculous."

"It's okay, AJ. I understand. Miss Alice, I'm sorry I didn't ask your permission. So, I'll ask it now. May I have your daughter's hand in marriage?" Barry had taken both of Alice's hands in his.

Alice blushed again. "I reckon so, sees as how she's already said yes. Headstrong that one is. You might ought take notice of that."

"Alice!" AJ yelled again. "What's gotten into you?"

She shrugged. "I just figure he needs to know about you is all. Don't mean nothing bad, but it's a fact. You *are* headstrong." Her jaw was set as if she didn't see a thing wrong with warning Barry what he was getting.

Barry smiled at AJ and leaned toward her. Under his breath he said, "It's okay, really. And it's not such a bad thing, either. I actually like it." He kissed her cheek.

At that Alice excused herself. "I'll be leaving you two alone." Then with a big smile toward Barry, she said, "Barry, it was very nice meeting you. I think we'll get along just fine."

When she'd ascended the stairs, AJ said, "Well, looks like you made a hit with both of my gals. Annie said she was going to keep her eye on you, though. And if she didn't like anything you did, she'd stay in her room forever." Barry laughed as she continued. "On the other hand, it sounds like Alice plans to keep *her* eye on me—not you." She sighed and shook her head. "We've had that kind of almost fighting relationship for as long as I can remember."

"Why? What's up with that? I noticed that she seems overly critical of you sometimes."

"Well, it probably goes back to when I was a teenager. It's something from back then, long ago, that you should probably know. I'm ashamed of it. That's why I didn't tell you sooner. I hope it doesn't change things, but I want you to know." She shifted slightly away from him.

"Back then, there was a boy—from another county. We met at a football game. He swept me off my feet, I guess, and I was young, only fifteen. And naïve. Anyway, we had sex that night, and I got pregnant. I suppose nowadays you might call it date rape, but I never really fought him off. He went home, and I never saw him again. I didn't even know where he lived. One of my best friends, Delores, told me if I drank red pepper mixed in water I'd lose the baby. Said her granny told her that, just in case, you know? So, I tried it because I didn't want to have to tell my parents. All I did, though, was puke. Couldn't get it down.

"Finally, I had to confess to Mom. I remember, we were sitting in the living room. She was in her big overstuffed chair, and I was sitting on the stool in front of her. When I started crying, she did, too. But she never once reached out to comfort me. She just sat there in her own chair, crying. I begged her to tell my daddy, 'cause I just couldn't face him. I guess that night she did 'cause in the morning he wouldn't look at me. When I asked her why, she said I'd broken his heart. That hurt worse than anything, worse than her not hugging me. When she said that, I went to my room and cried for what seemed like an hour. I remember I didn't come out that night for dinner either. Looking back, I think I broke her heart, too. To make matters worse, she made me be in the Christmas pageant a month later. Probably to save face at church. I was supposed to play the Virgin Mary and she made me do it even though I was pregnant. Of course, I wasn't showing, but I was so embarrassed. It sounds funny now, but it wasn't then. Anyway, things have never been the same between us.

"It was about then that Daddy started drinking. He'd always had a beer or two when he got off work, but then he really started drinking heavy. Lots of nights out with the guys, you know, and he began beating Mom. I always thought he was taking out his anger with me on her for some reason. Maybe he thought she hadn't raised me right. He was never around to do it, that's for sure.

"The pregnancy didn't last, though. I had a miscarriage in my third month. I guess it was for the best; but losing the baby didn't change my relationship with my parents. Daddy still drank, and eventually died driving drunk. Mom, Alice, has always acted like I was about to make her life miserable again. So, I've lived with guilt, and what I guess is her leftover anger, all my life."

Barry took her in his arms and held her tightly. "Bless your heart. You shouldn't ever feel guilty. What happened wasn't your fault no matter what your mother thinks. Of course, it doesn't make a difference to me, darling. It made you the person I love. AJ, you're the strongest woman I've ever met, and I admire you. Headstrong, maybe. But frankly, I think it's kind of sexy. I'm going to be so proud to call you my wife. I love you, Audrey Jane Porter."

"I love you too, Barry Peterson, but if you ever call me Audrey Jane again, I'll smack you upside the head."

"See? Headstrong," he said. He laughed. AJ kissed him.

⌐ CHAPTER TWENTY-FIVE ⌐

Monday morning, Isabelle arrived in the accounting office just as AJ was turning on her computer. "How'd your weekend go? Did Barry pass muster with your family?"

AJ swiveled around to look at her, flipping her hand from front to back. "I think the jury's still out. He certainly charmed Alice with his Southern manners and a huge bouquet of flowers. And Annie loved the bracelet he gave her. As for becoming my husband, I'm not sure they're sold. My mother thinks I'm rushing it, and my daughter doesn't think she needs a dad at all." She sighed deeply. "Oh well, they'll just have to get used to the idea. Did you reach Jack?"

Isabelle took a seat across from AJ. "I did. That's what I came to tell you. He's interested in hearing what you have to say, *but*, and it's a big but, he doesn't know if he can abandon his development business out there to come back. You need to call him yourself. He did say he thought it would be good to be closer to me now that I'm older. Made me feel like an old crone." She guffawed. "I'm not that old, for God's sake."

"You sure don't act old, Isabelle. I hope I'm as active when I'm your age. Thanks for breaking the ice, though. I'll call him this afternoon. You'd love it if he came back, wouldn't you?"

"Well, it would be good to see him more often than once a year, but you know, and it's sad to say, but I really don't know my own child well at all. And his wife, Sonia, feels even more like a stranger. I guess it's almost impossible to have much of a parental relationship from a distance. So, if he returned, I'd be getting to know my own child for the first time." She paused, then shook her head. "I've lost so much. I'm like one of those biological mothers who reunites with their grown child after he's lived with an adoptive family all his life. Understand?"

"I do. Since Alice provides most of Annie's care, I've got sorta the same feeling about us. I've needed her to do that so I could tend the farm, but now, if my mom had her own home, it might bring me and Annie closer together. Don't you think?"

When AJ looked closely at Isabelle she saw a forlorn expression she'd never seen on her friend's face before. Isabelle said, "I do. And I hope that happens for you. Truly." The older woman rose without further comment and went toward the door. With her hand on the handle, she said, "Let me know what Jack says, please."

As the door closed behind Isabelle, the telephone rang. "Langford Hall Farms, this is AJ Porter; how may I help you?" As she answered, she pulled the Post-it note with Jack Collins's phone number off the computer edge. From the other end of the phone line, she heard a chuckle.

"Well, don't you sound official, Mrs. AJ Porter." It was Barry.

"Hi there. This is a pleasant surprise," said AJ, returning the note to its original location. "Anything wrong? You don't usually call during the day."

"Not at all, sweetheart. I just wanted to let you know I heard from my friend about the land trust thing. He says it's a bit of a process but nothing that should keep you from protecting your land if that's what you decide to do. Meet me at Bizou at six and I'll tell you all the details."

"Great. I can't wait to hear what he said. I'm getting ready to call Jack, so we'll both have something to share. At least I hope so. You know, he might not give a rat's ass about Langford Hall. And I'll bet he sure doesn't have very good feelings about Mr. Jack. That might color how he feels about living here, you know?"

"Don't project, babe. Just make the call and see what he says. You never know. He just might have wished he could be the master of the manor all his life. See you tonight. Love you."

AJ kissed the receiver. "Love you too."

After lunch, AJ retrieved the sticky note again and pasted it on the desk near the phone. She stared at it for several minutes. *How badly do I want him to come home and take over? Badly enough to just give it to him? Maybe, but I'll try the sales pitch first. Can't go up if I offer it for nothing first.* She picked up the receiver and dialed. When it began to ring, she felt queasy.

"Collins Development, may I help you?"

"May I speak to Jack Collins, please? This is AJ Porter. He's expecting my call." She took a deep breath, hoping to calm her nerves.

After what seemed like forever to AJ, she heard Jack's voice. "Mrs. Porter." His voice broadcast warmth. "This is Jack Collins. I'm glad you called. Mother told me a bit about your idea, but I'd like to hear more about it from you."

"Please call me AJ. Mrs. Porter sounds like you're talking about my mother." She laughed, then explained her situation to Jack. "So, I'd like to make you an offer. Would you be interested in buying Langford Hall if the price was right? After I found out about you, I thought you should have inherited it instead of me. It just seems right for you to live here."

"Thank you. I appreciate that. And you should call me Jack. After all, we're kissing cousins, aren't we?" He laughed, then turned serious again. "What do you consider a reasonable price?"

"I'm not sure. I'd have to have it appraised first. I probably should have done that already, but I wanted to know your interest first."

"I *am* interested, but you know, I've got a thriving business here. I'd have to decide what to do about it first."

"Could you manage it long distance or transfer your headquarters here? I mean, to Charlottesville? My friend—actually, my fiancé— says there's lots of commercial development going on there too."

"I don't know. I definitely don't know anything about East Coast development, but I could look into it. How long would it take for an appraisal?"

"I'm guessing, but maybe a week after I find someone to look at it. Mr. Mulgrew, Mr. Jack's old attorney, ought to know one." She paused. "I just had an idea. Why don't you plan a trip here over Easter? You could bring your wife, check out the farm and the opportunities in Charlottesville. Isabelle would love to see you, I'm sure."

Jack cleared his throat. "Not a bad idea. Let me see if Sonia can get off work then. Call me back next week when you have a figure." He laughed. "Of course, that may put it so far out of reach that a trip would be unnecessary. Still, I would like to see Mother. I'll let you know. Okay?"

"Sounds good. Talk to you next week. Goodbye." She lowered the receiver, then picked it up again, and dialed Mr. Mulgrew's number.

⌒

Barry was waiting just inside Bizou when AJ, damp from the rain, came through the door. "Where's your umbrella, babe? You're soaked."

AJ shook out her hair and brushed off her shirt. "It's not that bad. I forgot it, and then I had to run from the car. Sorry I'm late." She wiped off her face and leaned in to kiss him.

"No problem, I just got here myself, but I had an umbrella. When we leave, I'll take you to your car. Chivalry isn't dead; it may be wounded, but it's not dead." He chuckled, then kissed her again. "Let's eat."

Over shrimp and grits, Barry said, "After I talked to my land trust buddy, he sent me a link to their website. It explains how the process works." He pulled several pages from his jacket pocket and gave them to AJ. "As you can see, you fill out a form asking them to preserve your land. You have to be specific about what kind of preservation you want. Like, for instance, do you want to allow it to continue being a working farm, or do you want to simply give it to them. They come and look at it, discuss your goals, and see if it's worth preserving. Then, after several months, the board decides. I'm not sure why it takes so damn long, but anyway. Then there's a bunch of paperwork before the deal is completed. It sounds like it's not something you can do overnight, but I think it's worth considering. What do you think?"

AJ toyed with her shrimp with a fork. "It may take even longer than that if I want to buy some of the surrounding land first. I don't have any idea if my neighbors will be willing to sell. As a matter of fact, they may tell me to go take a hike when I go home with money and they don't have any. Money might make me a fish out of water back there. Even though I haven't been gone that long, I know I've changed. Dew said I would. That I'd get *above my raising,* and maybe I did. When I first came here, I had a bad experience at the country club and wasn't comfortable at all. I thought they looked down on me as a hillbilly. Now, I'm not all that comfortable back home. Weird, ain't it?"

"Well, as far as I can see, you're perfect. As they say, screw 'em if they can't take a joke. I mean, you are what you are, and in the long run you're trying to protect West Virginia and the land on your mountain from extractive development." Barry wiped his mouth, folded his napkin, and signaled to the waiter. "I'd think they would applaud that. Want some coffee? Dessert?"

AJ declined dessert and ordered a decaf. After the waiter left, she continued.

"I felt so sad for Isabelle today when she was talking about her son. You know, she doesn't really know him very well. Maybe this will be a good thing for both of 'em, if he comes back, I mean."

"If he does, you'll be a heroine in two states."

A week later, the appraiser delivered his estimate to AJ. Shocked at the figure, she worried that it would be too high for Jack Collins. She called her California cousin with the news, her palms sweating.

"Jack, it's AJ again. I've gotten the appraisal and wanted to share it with you. They did it in pieces: three point six million for the land, just over one million for the house, and another two million for the business itself, although I think it's worth more based on our past income streams. Is this something you could handle? Assuming you wanted to?"

Jack was quiet for a moment, causing AJ to squirm in her chair. "So, a total of around six and a half million. Is that a price you'd be willing to take?"

"Yes," she said flatly, then she waited for his reply.

"Tell you what. I'll come for Easter as you suggested, look over the property, and then we can discuss it further. That will also give me some time to think about what I'd do about my business here. I don't mind admitting that getting out of LA has some real appeal for me. And Virginia would be a much nicer place to raise children when we start a family. I'll bring Sonia as well. She's never been East. That could be a real adjustment for her. But don't tell Mother. I'd like to surprise her."

"I won't; I promise. I look forward to meeting you and to discussing this further. See you soon."

⌒

On Easter weekend the weather was as beautiful as AJ had hoped it would be—balmy, sunny, and without a trace of rain in sight. She thought it was a good omen. Jack and Sonia were arriving late on Friday afternoon, so AJ had suggested Isabelle stay for dinner. She thought about inviting Barry, too, but decided that might take away from the family reunion. Sitting in the sunroom with the French doors ajar, AJ heard car doors open and then close. As she dashed to the front door, she heard Isabelle call.

"Are we expecting someone?"

"Welcome to Langford Hall, I'm AJ," she said as she opened the door. Jack and Sonia stepped inside. "This is my wife, Sonia, AJ. Thanks for having us. Is Mother here?"

"She is," AJ said, just as Isabelle entered the hallway. Jack crossed the space between them in huge steps and took his shocked mother in a deep embrace, nearly dislodging her hat.

"Oh my God, Jack. What are you doing here?" She was near tears. "Sonia, honey, it's wonderful to see you." Isabelle reached up and kissed Sonia on the cheek. "I don't know what to say. AJ, is this your doing?"

"Sort of, but Jack is the one who wanted to surprise you."

Recovering, Isabelle said, "Well, don't just stand there. Come on in." She put her arms through those of her son and daughter-in-law and walked them to the library. AJ followed, smiling broadly.

The following morning AJ took Jack and Sonia on a tour of the property, after which she and Jack settled into her office to talk while Sonia visited with Isabelle. As AJ watched Jack, she could see the family resemblance. She and Jack had the same dark-brown, almost black hair, the same deeply recessed eyes, and the same set to their jaws. *What are we, like second cousins or something?*

"You know, I remember being here when I was about eight or nine. Mr. Jack was out of town, and Mother came to Richmond to get me for the weekend. I remember going out into the yard to play, running through that row of trees out there and coming smack dab on the cemetery. It scared me to death. From then on, I thought of ghosts whenever I talked to Mother. I was always afraid they were going to rise up and get her. I used to dream about it," he said.

AJ laughed, to which Jack replied, "No, seriously." Then he joined her laughter.

"She, your mom, took me out there too. It is a bit spooky, but the stories about the folks buried there are fascinating. Do you know any of them?"

"Hmm. No, I don't recall Mother ever telling them to me."

"Well, you need to ask her. She gave me diaries, letters, all kinds of stuff about our ancestors. They were pretty tough old birds. Determined, strong-willed. I'll bet you're just like them."

He smiled. "I'll take that as a compliment."

"I meant it as one. What else do you remember about being here?"

"I always loved going to the stable to see the horses. Of course, I never got to ride any of them. Mother said Jack, Father, wouldn't like it."

AJ laughed again. "Well, I did ride one and got a broken arm for my troubles. You were smart to stay on your own two feet. So, what else do you want to see . . . the books?" As Jack nodded, she continued. "They were just audited two or three months ago, so I'm sure of the figures. They were done by a highly respected Charlottesville firm and their report corroborates the appraiser's assessment of the value of the business."

"Good, because that would have been one of the first things I'd have done. I trust the rest of the appraisal, but due diligence would have made me skeptical of that. I would like to look over the books while I'm here, though. By the way, Sonia seems to have fallen in love with all the trees, and the rolling hills, so I don't think she's going to object. She loves that it's so green. Is there any chance you'd come down on your asking price?"

"Maybe. Like I said on the phone, it should have been left to you, not me. I'd compromise on certain conditions. First, I'd like to have my wedding here. I know that's a silly request, but I would. Second, if I stay in Charlottesville, I'd like to bring my horse here and have it boarded with Santos. He's old, but he's still a good ride. And I've never fallen off him like I did Topper. And third, I'd like you to keep all the employees on, especially Hank. He's a really good crop manager."

Jack laughed as if he'd expected much more serious requests. "Is that all? I would certainly agree to all of those. So, what's your bottom line? Assuming, I want it, of course. And if we come to terms, I'll still have to sell our home in LA and decide what to do about my business."

AJ looked at him without answering for a long moment. "How about I knock off the price of the business, the two million, and sell you the land, and house for a flat four million? I really feel bad charging you anything, but it is business, right?"

"Right. That's a number I can live with. Let me talk to Sonia again, go home and see what I can work out with my company, and I'll get back to you."

"Okay, but remember, I have to make a decision by the end of May. Think you can work things out by then?"

"I hope so. AJ, you can't imagine what you've given me. I always wanted to be back in Virginia, but I never dreamed I would ever, ever live at Langford Hall. To me, it was Jack's and always would be. As Mother told you, he really didn't want me around. I guess I was an embarrassment. Ridiculous old man." Jack shook his head. "He should have married Mother years ago. If it had happened these days, he probably would have, but geez, he was so *proper*. Everything he did was to keep up appearances, I guess. In a way, it wasn't at all fair to her. Oh well, I guess you can't change the past, but now, if it all works out, I can assure you that this grand old place stays in the family, ghosts and all. Thank you."

He put out his arms, offering a hug. AJ grinned, saying, "You're welcome, cousin," and walked into his embrace.

⌐ CHAPTER TWENTY-SIX ⌐

By mid-April, the fields of Langford Hall had lost their drab tan winter pallor in favor of tender green shoots of soybeans and wheat. On the other hand, AJ's plans still lay dormant. Frustrated by her inability to make her decision until she heard from Jack Collins, she felt like a schoolgirl waiting for a new boyfriend to call. She knew better than to call him. Still, she needed to let her mother and daughter know what their futures held. Her mother had asked about AJ's decision in their last conversation. And while Barry and Isabelle were being more patient, they deserved an answer, too. Nevertheless, here she sat, watching things on the farm move forward, day by day, while she could only envision her future in scenario after scenario, each different, depending on Jack's response. It was maddening, and she said as much to Barry.

"I know he's got a lot to work out, Barry, but I wish he'd call and give me some idea what he's thinking," she said over dinner.

"You can't rush him, honey. All we can do right now is plan our wedding. Doesn't matter where we live afterward, we still need to plan it. But no matter what, we can have the wedding at Langford Hall if you want. Jack agreed, right? Even if he's the owner by then? Right?"

"Yeah, he did. But I've been thinking, if we have it here, who would I invite? Only Isabelle, Alice and Annie? I don't have any friends here. You've got lots, but my side of the aisle would look pretty empty. And I sure don't want to have it back home. Everyone there sees me as some rich princess now. Why don't we just elope? We could sneak off, get married, and then have a party later at Langford Hall."

"Hmmm," mused Barry. "Might be a good idea. We could fly somewhere, one of the Caribbean islands. Take a long weekend, and then tell Isabelle and your family when we return." He leaned over and kissed her. "I like it. Do you have a passport?"

She frowned. "Hell, I've never even flown. Can I get one in time? If I can, doing that would sure keep Alice from objecting during the ceremony."

"Sure, we'll go to the post office and get you one. It's no problem. I think it will be fun to be married on the beach."

"It sounds wonderful."

Three weeks later, after Barry pulled a few strings to get AJ her passport quickly, Mr. and Mrs. Barry Peterson returned from St. Maarten. They'd stayed in a condo facing the lapping surf of aquamarine water at Divi Little Bay Resort on the Dutch side of the island. AJ was bursting with stories and photos of their beachfront wedding.

"Isabelle, you wouldn't believe this place. It was gorgeous. I'd never even seen the ocean until we got there, and it was beautiful. We got married on the beach with a crowd of people from the resort all around our little tent. We didn't know any of them, but it was so cool. They applauded when we kissed. A local judge—his cousin is the manager—performed the ceremony. And this parrot named Gizmo that lives there sat on his shoulder the whole time." She laughed. "I had on a sundress and flowers in my hair, like an old hippie, and

Barry wore shorts. Some of the guests were even in their bathing suits."

"I'm so happy for you two." Isabelle hugged AJ. "It sounds truly memorable. Not to rain on your parade, but you missed the call you've been waiting for. Jack. I told him you'd taken a long weekend off. He asked me to tell you to call when you returned."

"Oh my God. I hope he didn't think I was just off on a lark. Did you tell him we were off getting married? Did he tell you his answer?"

"I did, but he still wouldn't tell me his decision."

"I'll call him when it's a decent hour. I'll let you know what he says as soon as I hang up, promise." She rushed off to her own office. Because it was still too early to call Jack, AJ dialed her mother's number instead.

"Hey, Alice, how are things back in West 'by God' Virginia?"

"Fine," Alice said. "But what's wrong? You never call of a morning."

"Nothing's wrong. In fact, everything's wonderful. I called to tell you that Barry and I got married over the weekend. We went to a Caribbean island called St. Maarten and—" She stopped, and the silence on the other end dragged on. "Alice, are you there? Did you hear me?"

"I heard you, Audrey Jane. So, as usual, you didn't listen to my advice. Just went and did it. How do you think Annie's gonna feel about that?"

"Mom, she'll be fine. But you and I haven't agreed on anything much since I was fifteen. I'm sorry, but we thought it would be easier for everyone. Kept you from pretending to be happy at a wedding you didn't approve of. Believe me, I know what I'm doing. Barry is a good man. You'll learn to love him like I do, and so will Annie."

"We'll see," Alice said shortly. "Think you better call and tell her yourself. I ain't doing it. So, you staying there? Not coming back?"

"Still don't know that. I'm calling Jack Collins later this morning. Right now, it's too early in California. But let me ask; if we do stay here, would you rather stay in West Virginia or come here with Annie?"

"You thinking of leaving your own mother now? You're being very selfish, Audrey Jane."

"Come on, Alice. I'm trying to do what's best for everyone, including you. I just need to know what you want to do before I decide what I'm doing."

"Well, I ain't got no desire to come live in that museum, but if you think I can manage here on my own, you're dead wrong. Who'd take care of the farm?"

"I don't know. Maybe Uncle Jimmy would move in. We'll talk more about it when the time comes. We've still got a month to figure out things. It will all work out, I'm sure. Gotta go, Alice. Talk to you later. I *will* call Annie, but not until after dinner. Bye."

After AJ put down the phone, she sat there thinking about what her mother had said. Was she being selfish.? *I wanna protect our land. But do I want to live back on that farm? I love those hills, but some of the people . . . I don't know.*

A vision of riding Gunner through those hills flickered through her mind. As it did, a pang of homesickness hit her. She loved that smell of newly-cut hay in her fields, the jonquils that covered her hillside, the verdant summer trees she used to ride through. She recalled how her spirits always lifted when she saw West Virginia's hills rising in front of her.

Damn the gossips. It's my home. And there are good people there trying to save those mountains. I love that state and those hills.

Tears pricked her eyes, but she wiped them away.

Glancing at her watch, she realized it was probably late enough to reach Jack. She picked her phone up again and punched in his number. With the fingers of her left hand crossed, she waited.

"Collins Development, may I help you?"

"Yes, it's AJ Peterson calling for Jack Collins. Is he in?"

"This is Jack Collins. May I help you?" Jack sounded as if he had no idea who had called.

"Hi, Jack, it's AJ. I shouldn't have given her my new name. Barry and I got married last weekend."

"Mother told me. That's wonderful. I'm sorry; my secretary was used to your old name."

"That's okay. Have you decided?"

"I have. I accept your offer." AJ pumped her fist and mouthed *"Yes"* as he continued. "One of my associates is interested in buying out my business here, but until he's ready, I'll operate it from there. It will require some travel, but that's fine. Sonia's going to stay here until we sell the house."

"Oh, Jack, that's great news. I'm delighted, and your mother will be so pleased. I'll call Mr. Mulgrew to figure out what to do next. My decision is due by the end of the school year, so I'll move out in late May sometime. But I don't think it will be a problem if I tell him now. I mean, it's only a month earlier. Can I call you back after I've talked to him?"

"Absolutely. Don't tell Mother though, if you don't mind. I'll call her tonight. I'm looking forward to getting back to my roots, back to where my family has been for generations." He laughed. "Even if they didn't accept me when they were alive. Actually, it's sort of an ironic ending, don't you think? Karma, maybe."

She chuckled, "I do. Like I said, you should have gotten it instead of me in the first place. Those letters and stuff I told you about? They'll teach you your family's history real fast. One great-something was a friend of Thomas Jefferson's. Can you believe it? There were some sad stories, too. One guy died of gangrene in the Civil War. His slave brought him home. His name was Moses and he's buried out back, too. At least I think he is. If so, he's in an unmarked grave. Some incredible stories, really. Makes me think about what this old place has seen. When your mom showed them to me she was trying to convince me to stay at the farm." She chuckled. "Didn't work though, did it?"

"Doesn't sound like it," Jack said. "But they sound fascinating. I *will* read them when I come home. Home. That sounds good, doesn't it?"

"Sure does. I'll talk to you later. Goodbye, Jack." This time, when she laid the phone down, his words about returning to his roots echoed in her ears. *He's got a point. Maybe I would be happier back home, where my real roots are. Maybe not as a farm woman, but back there, I could fight the mining companies and the frackers . . . . buy up land and give it to the land trust.*

AJ picked up her phone again. When her call was answered, she said, "This is AJ Porter. Does Mr. Mulgrew have time to see me this afternoon? Around two? Thank you. I'll be there."

After lunch, AJ appeared at Mr. Mulgrew's office. The secretary greeted her with "Well, you look much better than you did last time I saw you."

Realizing her last visit was when she was still in a cast, AJ laughed. "Yeah, I'm all healed now, thank goodness."

As the two women chatted, Mr. Mulgrew appeared in the doorway of his inner office. "Mrs. Porter, to what do I owe the honor of this impromptu visit?" AJ was never sure if he was being condescending or not.

She stopped. "Actually, it's Mrs. Peterson now. Barry and I were married just a few days ago."

"Well then, I suppose congratulations are in order. Or is it best wishes you give to the woman?"

"I don't know, but thank you. Mr. Mulgrew, I'm here to give you my answer about Langford Hall."

"Well, come in, come in." He reached for AJ as if she needed to be escorted. "So, you've made your decision," he said as he closed the door.

AJ took a seat and began telling him what she wanted to do. As she talked, he flipped his lighter over and over in a somersault as he'd done in every visit she'd made to his office. "I plan to accept the inheritance," she said, "but then I want to sell it to Jack's real heir."

That stopped his lighter flipping. "Excuse me? You're the real heir. That's why you were contacted." He shook his head. "It's very clear, my dear."

"Actually, it wasn't, Mr. Mulgrew. You found me after a considerable search, while Mr. Jack actually had a son who should have got it in the first place. Your friend and Isabelle Collins had a long-standing affair, which I'll bet you knew already. But obviously, like everyone else, you didn't know they had a son. Mr. Jack never legally claimed him, but he did know he existed. Isabelle told me the whole story. So, I think he should own Langford Hall."

"Well, that comes as quite a shock. Can you prove his parentage?"

"Isabelle can," AJ said curtly. "The child was raised by Isabelle's sister to save face."

Mulgrew frowned as if she was saying he had done his job poorly. "Well, of course you can do what you want, but—"

"But what? If he's Mr. Jack's son, he should have it. And that's what I want. Can you draw up a contract? We've already agreed on a price. I'll keep the investments, and he'll have Langford Hall and the farm operations."

"Oh, my dear, I'm afraid you have badly misunderstood the terms of the inheritance. It's all or nothing. The investments go with Langford Hall."

He resumed tapping the lighter, looking smugly at AJ as if he'd suddenly won their chess match. "If you didn't understand that, I'm very sorry. Now, of course, you'll have whatever price you've accepted from Jack's son, but that's all."

AJ sat back, stunned. "Are you certain? I clearly recall you saying—"

"No, my dear, you don't. I never said any such thing. Would you like to see the will?"

"Frankly, yes. Not that I'm calling you a liar, but I do want to see it for myself."

Mulgrew groaned as he rose from the chair. It squeaked as it gave up his weight. AJ watched as he lumbered over to a row of file cabinets. A moment later, he laid the folded will on his desk in front of AJ.

"See for yourself," he said as he retook his chair, which squeaked again, and resumed fidgeting with the lighter. "I believe it's on page twelve." He leaned back and began rocking in the chair.

AJ flipped page over page until she found what she needed. She read it carefully, sighed, and lowered the document to her lap. "Doesn't matter. What in the world do I need with twelve million dollars anyway? Draw up the necessary papers. I'll accept it all, then sell it to Jack Collins. I've played princess long enough."

⟿ CHAPTER TWENTY-SEVEN ⟿

That evening, the newlyweds ate dinner at Langford Hall. They had decided that during the week, Barry would stay there; on weekends, AJ would stay at Barry's until they settled on where they would live permanently. Clara, as usual, served dinner.

As the kitchen door closed behind her, AJ said, "I'm afraid I have some bad news."

Barry started, his fork in midair, but when he saw her grin, he relaxed. "What?"

"If you married me for my money, Mr. Peterson, you got a shitty deal. Mr. Mulgrew told me this afternoon I don't get the twelve million. Jack does. It goes with the estate."

"Like that matters." Barry grinned. "You know I married you for honorable reasons, Mrs. Peterson, not for the money. I thought I should make an honest woman of you." Now he was laughing. "Seriously, does it upset you?"

"Hell no, it actually makes things a little easier. Now I won't be going back with people thinking I'm some rich bitch trying to run their lives by asking them to sell their land to me so I can give it to the land trust."

"Am I hearing you say you've finally decided you want to go back to West Virginia?"

"Yeah, but only if you're okay with it. I'm afraid you won't be happy on our old dirt farm in Gimlet Hollow. And I'm not sure I will be either. What if we leave Alice there and buy property in Fayetteville?"

"Would she go for that?"

"We talked about it some. I think she would. Her brother might move in with her so she's not alone. And we wouldn't be that far away. Besides, Annie would probably get a better education there. It's a cool little town with lots of hikers, whitewater rafters—you know, outdoorsy types. They're young too. And it overlooks the New River. Some of the houses there are gorgeous. Did you ever go there when you lived in Morgantown?"

"I don't think so, but I recently read somewhere that it was named one of the cool small towns in America. Like Lewisburg a couple of years back. Yeah, I could do that. I'm sure there are accounting firms there, maybe not as big. But that would be okay, too. I'll check into it."

"Thank goodness. I was hoping that you'd be okay with it. I just feel like those mountains are mine, you know? They give me a sense of security. Not that you don't, but it's where my real roots are. Yours too, if you think about it." She reached over and playfully punched his arm.

"True. I did love the mountains around Morgantown when I lived there years ago. I like this plan. And, to tell the truth, I wasn't looking forward to living in Gimlet Hollow. Especially after the way you talked about some of the people there. This makes moving back more inviting."

"Oh, they're actually okay. They just don't have anything else to do but talk about each other." She laughed. "Speaking of looking into things, would you put me in touch with the land trust people? I'd like to get that started with our farm."

"Sure, I'll call my buddy tomorrow."

"Thanks, I appreciate it. Hey, what if we went home next weekend and looked for property? It would also give Annie a chance to get to know you better."

"What about your mom?"

"If she doesn't like it, she'll just have to scratch her mad place, as my granny used to say. Who knows? Maybe you'll win her over completely. Like you did me." She winked at Barry. "Besides, it's my house, too."

Barry laughed. "I'll work on perfecting my boyish charm. But maybe you'd better check to be sure she won't have the shotgun out."

"Barry," AJ said, chiding him as if he were serious.

"I'm kidding, honey. But you should warn her. Meanwhile, I'll look at houses online so we'll have something to go see."

AJ did check with her mother, but, wanting it to be a surprise, asked her not to tell Annie she was coming. Alice grumbled but promised to be on her best behavior.

◡͜

AJ and Barry arrived Friday night after Annie was asleep, so they had some time alone with Alice. They'd brought printouts of several houses they planned to see on the weekend, which they showed to Alice as the three sat at the old oilcloth-covered kitchen table.

"Mom, you could come move into town, to Fayetteville, and we'll build you what they call a tiny house on our property. Know what that is?" AJ asked.

Alice shook her head. "Ain't never heard of such a thing. What is it?"

"It's a free-standing house of roughly a thousand or less square feet," said Barry. "They're very compact. Lots of storage space is built into the walls, under the beds, even overhead. I can show you some pictures on my laptop."

"Or you can stay here, with Uncle Jimmy if he'll agree to move.

That way I wouldn't worry about you being able to take care of the farm. But if you came to town, you wouldn't have to worry about it either. No farming at all."

"Yeah, but what would I do? With Annie going with you, I ain't got no one to care for. At least if Jimmy was here, I'd have him to cook for and talk to. He's probably sick of cooking for hisself after all these years anyways. I know this here is a big house, but I'd smother in that tiny thing, whatever it is. It sounds like living in a dollhouse. No, thanks; I'll stay right here."

"Suit yourself, but if you ever change your mind, we can still build something for you." AJ rose from the table and uncharacteristically gave her mother an awkward hug around her shoulders as she passed her chair on the way to get another cup of coffee. She winked at Barry behind Alice's back as if to say, *It's all gonna be fine.*

The following morning after a pancake breakfast with an excited Annie, the three of them went to Fayetteville where they met Janet Cochran, the real estate agent Barry had contacted. She showed them the houses Barry had identified, plus three others. AJ fell in love with a log home on a bluff overlooking the New River. When they returned to Gimlet Hollow, she described it to her mother.

"Alice, it was something else. The ceiling in the living room–dining room was at least twenty feet high. With this huge stone fireplace on one end and glass windows overlooking the gorge on the other. Outside, there's a deck that wraps around the house on the river side, and inside, the walls are the other side of the outside logs. I remember Granny's log house. Of course, it was nothing like this, but I've loved the idea of living in one ever since I was a kid. You gotta see it. Annie's already picked out her bedroom. And there's a couple of guest rooms too, so you can come visit for holidays."

Barry chimed in. "The lot is big enough for your tiny house, Miss Alice, if you ever decide you want to join us. I might build one anyway, and let Miss Annie use it as a playhouse."

With that, Annie pumped the air with her fist and screamed.

"Yes! My very own house. I love it." Her tone quickly became a whine. "But Gunner. We can't take him with us."

"Honey, we can always come back here to ride. Don't worry about that," AJ said.

"Sounds like a very nice home, Audrey Jane. I *would* like to see it. Did you make an offer yet?"

"No, we wanted to tell you about it first," AJ replied. "But I think we will, don't you, Barry?"

"If it's the one you want. I must admit, it was lovely. I'll call her tomorrow. I never thought we'd find something so quickly. And the view is magnificent. You were right about that, honey." He leaned over and kissed her.

"Ewww," said Annie. She put her finger in her mouth as if she were forcing herself to puke. Barry and AJ laughed, and even Alice smiled instead of fussing at her granddaughter for being crude.

⁓

AJ and Barry spent the following two weeks looking at furniture. Their offer had been accepted, and they were just waiting on the closing, which they expected to take place in mid-May. They knew nothing was certain until all the papers were signed, but since they had only Barry's furniture, they were looking at pieces appropriate for the new house. Barry had put his home on the market as well, contingent on the closing of theirs in Fayetteville. They'd returned to West Virginia one more time for Barry to interview with the only accounting firm in town. Although it was a much smaller firm than his current one, he'd accepted their eager offer. Seems the managing partner had been hoping to expand, so he jumped at the chance to hire someone with Barry's experience and expertise.

Jack arrived at Langford Hall on May 6, just in time to surprise Isabelle for Mother's Day. Mr. Mulgrew had drawn up the sales contract, which AJ and Jack excitedly signed. Then, he and AJ spent most of the weekend as teacher and pupil. Although Jack was an accomplished business owner, he wasn't familiar with how the farm should operate. Jack was AJ's eager student. AJ asked Hank to spend one morning showing Jack around, discussing crop rotations, and harvesting. Afterward, Jack asked Hank to stay on, as AJ had hoped he would. By Sunday, there were many reasons to celebrate.

Clara cooked a big dinner, complete with lemon meringue pie for dessert. Jack, at the head of the table instead of AJ, looked very much the lord of the manor. Isabelle beamed as her son carved the ham.

"Jack, it's so nice to have you home. I never thought I'd live to see it," she said, tears welling in her eyes.

"If it weren't for AJ, you wouldn't have." He smiled at his newly found relative.

She grinned back. "And if it weren't for Barry's willingness to follow me home, I might not be leaving," She laughed. "So, there's thanks to go all around."

Jack raised his wineglass, "To Langford Hall and its many generations of Morgans."

AJ met his glass. "And to all the other Morgans, even if their names aren't Morgan."

Barry, Jack, and Isabelle echoed, "To the other Morgans."

⌒ Acknowledgments ⌒

While this is a work of fiction, it was inspired by a visit to the ancestral home of my family in Orange, Virginia. When I visited, it was owned by Mrs. Helen Marie Taylor, whose stories of long-dead relatives captivated and intrigued me. However, many of the tales in *The Other Morgans* came not from Helen Marie, but were inspired by other storytellers in my family, notably, my late cousin Lynne Frantz, and my late aunts, Elinore and Nancy Taylor. Fictionalized until they might not recognize them, they nevertheless contain gems of family lore.

Essential information regarding wills and audit procedures were provided by retired attorney John L. Hash, and by Wade Newell, CPA, of Somerville & Company, LLC. Without their patience with my many questions, I could not have written much of this book. Thanks go to my writing workshop buddies, the gangsters, Charles Lloyd, Gwenyth Hood, and Eddy Pendarvis, as well as to those who had the fortitude to read it first, and who offered the valuable advice

I much needed: Glenn Taylor, Shirley Lumpkin, and most especially, Rajia Hassib. Insightful comments from the members of Patchwork Writers kept me on my toes and on task. I'm eternally grateful to them as well. Thanks also to Joe Coccaro, whose insightful editing strengthened my story. Special thanks go to my husband, Richard Cobb, who is always my first editor and my most enthusiastic cheerleader. He deserves a crown for enduring the many hours I lived in AJ's world.